WRIGHT TOGETHER

WRIGHT TOGETHER

K.A. LINDE

ISBN-13: 978-1948427852

PART I

PEONIES

1

WHITTON

My hand flattened on the surface of my new desk. Perhaps it was egotistical to have always wanted this dream to become a reality so that I could bring a woman up here and fuck her against the glass panes. Brown hair so dark that it streamed through my fingers like an oil stain. I curled my hand into a fist, picturing the curve of her neck as I tugged the strands backward. The pant from her pert red lips as her back arched and ass pressed against me.

I exhaled and released the image.

Eve.

I'd been imagining Eve again. The enigma of a woman still confounded me, wrapping around my subconscious and burrowing down into my daydreams. I'd gone home for the summer, and those inscrutable emerald eyes still haunted me.

Now, I was back in dry, dusty Lubbock with a promotion in hand and my dream corner office. It had the massive mahogany desk, stocked bookshelves against one wall, and floor-to-ceiling windows overlooking the local university.

Who knew all I had to do to land the dream job was move to middle of nowhere, Texas?

Lubbock had never been on my radar, and somehow, it felt more like home than Seattle ever had. The only thing that misty, shadowed city had going for it was Mom still lived there. But after visiting with Harley this summer, I was glad to be back in Lubbock. The promotion sure didn't hurt.

The only thing it was missing was the girl bent over the desk.

A throat cleared behind me. "Well, what do you think?"

Jordan leaned against the doorframe. He was dressed impeccably in a black tailored suit, his hair sleek, and his command, as ever, unparalleled. Sometimes, it still made me falter when I thought about him being my brother. Half-brother technically, but my siblings and I had dropped the half part. Our father had had an affair, and we were the result—me, Weston, and Harley. We'd only found out a few years back that he had another family and two sons— Jordan and Julian. It was West's crazy scheme that had gotten us all to move here to get to know them. I'd gotten a job at Wright Construction, the company of our namesake, and now, here I was, hitting every milestone I'd set for myself before thirty.

Sometimes, life threw you on a crash course to get you to where you belonged.

"It's even better than I imagined," I confessed, straightening and buttoning the top button of my charcoal suit.

"You earned it."

"Thank you," I said with all sincerity. The last job I'd had felt like banging my head against a wall repeatedly. Every ounce that I put into it was given credit to my superior, and still, I'd wavered about whether or not to make the jump and work at Wright. Best decision of my life.

"Morgan wants to throw a promotion party," Jordan said.

I barely managed to hide my cringe. "If that's what she wants. She's the CEO."

Jordan laughed. "Good save. I can nix it."

I could schmooze with the best of them, but I'd never been one to want to draw attention to myself. I had a five- and ten-year plan. My upward trajectory was finally moving on the slope I'd always envisioned. Still, every small achievement felt just that...small. I'd celebrate when I reached the top.

"Appreciate that."

Jordan dropped some paperwork on my desk. "I know it's your first day back, but this is your new assignment."

"I never stopped working, Jor," I said, reaching for the documents. "I was remote while I was gone."

"I know. I know. But this one will be more hands on."

I flipped through the pages with a furrowed brow. "Midland?"

"It's only two hours south of here."

"I've never been."

Jordan shrugged. He'd moved here a few years before me from Vancouver. That was how our dad had been able to have two families. The cities were just close enough to fool everyone. Jordan had adapted to Texas even easier than I had. It probably helped that he'd gotten married this spring to his spitfire doctor, Annie.

"Well, read through the assignment so you can fill in the new real estate agent when she gets here. You're going to be working closely with her over the next month to get this off the ground."

I snapped the paperwork shut. "What? I have a partner?"

"We wanted someone who was familiar with the area. You did just say that you'd never been there."

He had me there.

"I see. And when will I meet this agent?"

Jordan checked the Rolex on his wrist and pursed his lips. "Hmm. She's late. Should have been here already actually."

It was my turn to be affronted. "It's fifteen past. Was she supposed to be here top of the hour?"

He nodded. "Yes. Let me check in to see if something happened."

"How unprofessional."

Jordan shot me an amused look as he pulled his phone out and started typing away.

I returned to the paperwork Jordan had given me, unable to hide my frustration. It was common knowledge that I took my work seriously. Too seriously. West frequently called me Mr. Responsibility. Harley had laughed at me all summer when I spent the days in my bedroom, staring at a computer. But West was a rockstar in the biggest band in the world right now, and Harley was about to start her sophomore year in college. She might be a genius with a full ride and every intention of becoming an attorney, but things had always come to her easy. Neither of them understood my need for control.

A need that encompassed every part of my life. Home, office, and...in the bedroom.

"No luck," Jordan said. "Let's give her a few more minutes."

"I don't need a partner. I just thumbed through this. It doesn't look all that different from what I've done in the past. I can do it alone."

At least then I could guarantee that it was being done correctly.

"This is a big contract. We're partnering with a local oil family. Do you know Dorset & King?"

The name sounded familiar. "I've heard of them. They're in Midland?"

Jordan grinned. "Yeah, and you'll need the help. The Kings are a prestigious family. They want the best. So, they came to us. We're giving this to you because we know you're good enough. Having a local to partner is a bonus."

This was my first job after the promotion. I didn't need someone getting in the way.

I opened my mouth to say that when a woman rushed off of the open elevator and hustled down the hall toward my office in sky-high patent leather heels.

"Sorry!" she gasped. "So sorry I'm late. I had car trouble."

Eve Houston stood in my doorway, her chest heaving in the white shirt she had underneath a black blazer. Her pencil skirt reached her knees with a small slit up the side. Just enough for my imagination to run wild. Her dark hair was down in waves, and she wore the red lipstick I'd just visualized on her.

My cock throbbed at the sight of her. The way her ample chest jiggled with the exertion from racing here. Those mysterious emerald eyes wide as she took in the room and finally landed on me. Her mouth formed an O, and that did things to me that were utterly inappropriate for the office.

It took everything in me not to adjust my lengthening cock.

"Eve." I drew her name out across my tongue like I was reciting a prayer.

I hadn't seen her in weeks, and somehow, she was even more striking than my filthy imagination.

"Oh, Whitt," she said uncertainly. Her eyes shot between me and Jordan, as if she wasn't sure who to address.

He wasn't oblivious to the thick layer of tension in the room. In fact, by the gleam in his eyes, he might have set this whole thing up.

It was at his wedding that Eve and I had danced the night away after all. The night I thought we'd moved past our flirtation to something more. It just turned out that we had different ideas about what *more* meant.

After her last crash-and-burn relationship, Eve wanted a hookup. And I misread the entire situation and asked for more. I was a relationship guy, and she wasn't ready for anything like that. No matter our attraction—the attraction I still very much felt—it had all crumbled.

"You were saying?" Jordan muttered in my direction.

"Never mind," I said to him with a shake of my head. "This will do."

Jordan laughed. "I thought you might say that." He extended his hand toward Eve. "Welcome, Eve. It's good to have you on board."

She breathed a sigh of relief and put her hand in his. "Thanks, Jordan. I'm glad to be here."

"Whitton was just saying how excited he was to have a partner for this new project."

"Was he?" Eve said. She took a step into my office and held her hand out. "That doesn't sound like you."

Only Eve would call my bluff like that. The girl was as fearless as she was brash. For people she didn't like, she could come off as abrasive. For her friends, she was as straightforward and loyal as they came.

"We didn't know you had car trouble."

I took her hand in mine, felt the calluses across her palm from weight lifting. A spark flared to life, and she extracted her hand quickly, as if worried she'd get burned.

"I had to take an Uber." She turned to Jordan. "Thank you for this opportunity."

"You earned it. You both did," Jordan said with a smirk in my direction. "I'll leave you to it."

Then Jordan strode out of my office, leaving me alone with the girl I'd just envisioned having in this space. I'd been all indignant and prepared to trash whoever showed up late to our first meeting. Jordan had known it, too. He'd known all of it. And now, she was here, and there was nothing to do but gesture for her to take a seat.

"Why don't we get started?"

Eve's expression was neutral, but I could still see the defiance in her irises. She wouldn't be quelled by the fact that she had to work with me.

She took the seat.

Good girl.

Maybe having a partner wouldn't be so bad after all.

2

EVE

Well, fuck.

Whitt was supposed to be gone all summer. I hadn't seen him in our mutual friend group since he'd left for Seattle, and I refused to show any signs that I was shaken by his appearance.

I couldn't be shaken by *anything*. Because unlike Mr. Wright, I *needed* this job. I needed it more than life itself. This was it. This was my break. After barely treading water, holding my head up as I inhaled the murky water of poverty, I was going to get ahead of this.

So, I couldn't leave.

Not even with Whitton Wright standing in front of me. My pulse beat a tattoo against my throat just at the sight of him. His voice was the same that it had always been—deep and throaty. Every single word causing my neurons to snap. And it was more than just his voice. It was the scent of him wrapping around me. A mix of citrus and spice that aroused ideas of him stepping straight out of a shower. It was his strong, freshly shaven jawline and too-blue eyes. The lines of his body so sharp that it might as well have been a

Renaissance sculpture. His large hands curling around the edge of the desk. His typically short, dark hair had grown out just long enough to fall forward into his eyes as he looked down at me through his dark lashes.

He was exactly as delectable as I'd last seen him. The last time things had gone completely wrong between us.

"So...when did you get back?"

"Yesterday." He leaned forward on the desk across from me.

The soft leather chair was cold against my ass as I sank into the cushion. I crossed my legs at the knee, my skirt riding up my thigh. His eyes flickered to the bare skin, a trace of the bottom of my dream catcher tattoo visible before I tugged the material over the ink.

He jerked his eyes back to mine. My throat closed at the heat that passed between us. The heat that had never evaporated in all these months.

My palms traced the arms of the chair. "Did you have a good summer?"

"It was...wet," he said.

I choked on that word out of his mouth. His eyes moved to my lips, and desire shot through those baby-blues. I definitely hadn't meant to vocalize that reaction.

I cleared my throat, hoping to salvage this conversation. "I thought you missed Seattle."

He was silent for a moment too long as he visibly collected himself before taking a seat across from me. "I thought I did, too. Turns out, I just missed my mom."

"Is she going to move down here?"

He chuckled. "No. She's lived there her entire life, and she loves her work. But she was glad to have me and Harley there."

"I bet."

I had no idea what that would be like. My family was… complicated. To say the least. They were the real reason that I couldn't seem to catch a break. It was hard to get ahead financially when half of every paycheck went home to make sure my little sister had a roof over her head and food in her stomach.

Real estate had seemed like a way to make some easy money. I'd only been doing it for eighteen months at the insistence of my now ex-boyfriend. When our relationship ended, my entire life went up in smoke. He'd fired me from his company, blacklisted my ass, and kicked me out of the apartment he had me in. No wonder I still wasn't ready for a relationship. I couldn't afford to lose everything again.

I'd finally managed to find another company that would take me in but building clientele had been a slow and painful slog. Even a year later, I had to take every new client that came my way. Steady work was hard to come by.

I wasn't about to blow it with the Wrights.

"So, this job," Whitt said. He rifled through a file on his desk. "I assume Jordan filled you in on it?"

"He hired me. We're surveying a new build in Midland."

"Yes. Working with Dorset & King."

"Ah, the Kings. Midland royalty," I mused.

"You know them?" His eyes found mine over the top of the file.

"Sure. Everyone knows them. They're a big presence in the city. Plus, I was in the same year as Nate King."

I managed to keep my face neutral when I mentioned him. Not that Nate and I had ever been together, but his girlfriends sure thought we had been. Apparently, girls couldn't be friends with guys. That had been one of my first lessons that I wasn't like other girls. And they made it blatantly clear that they didn't want to be friends with me.

I was still adjusting to the fact that the girls in Lubbock weren't like that. I'd been waiting for the shoe to drop for months with my roommates, Piper and Blaire. Kept expecting my friend Nora to wake up one day and decide I wasn't worth the trouble. After all, I had only become friends with them after they replaced Nora's cheating ex. I could be easily replaceable as well. No matter that they'd never given me that inclination, my little-girl shit circled me like a vulture after carrion.

"Well, excellent. I'll have you make introductions when we meet with them."

"Of course."

The Kings were a little out of my league. But hey, so were the Wrights, and that had never stopped me.

In fact, Mr. Out of My League was sitting directly across from me. I'd never seen him in his office before. Now, all six-plus feet of him dominated the space. He loomed over the desk, a giant in his realm.

My eyes traced the lines of his shoulders. Had he been working out? He seemed even broader than I remembered. I was a taller-than-average woman, and he made me feel dainty. Like a little pixie, like the rest of my friends. As if he could take one of those large hands and circle it around my waist with ease. Or perhaps my throat...

Could I imagine Mr. Tall, Dark, and Controlled releasing enough to choke me while he fucked me?

I dispelled that thought. I shifted my legs together, the heat rubbing up to the apex of my thighs.

Whitt had made it clear that he wanted a relationship. The night of Jordan and Annie's wedding, I was perfectly positioned to see exactly how good he was in bed. I'd basically thrown myself at him, only for him to reject me. The last thing I wanted was another relationship that could fuck up my entire life if it didn't work. No matter how broad those shoulders or how it'd feel for him to use his perfect control in the bedroom—

"Eve?"

I cleared my throat. "Hmm?"

"I asked if next weekend worked for our survey trip to Midland?"

"Whenever you're free. I can move my clients around."

He nodded and continued to discuss the details of the new build with me. I knew the basic information that Jordan had sent to me already. I was better in person than I was with the details. It was why I'd been great at real estate. Once I met my clients, things took off. It was getting that meeting that sometimes took time.

I let Whitt prattle on about the work, listening with half an ear. My eyes were on his pillowy lips. The way they moved with such assurance as he talked about what was important to him. They snapped up to his big blue eyes. Did they have gold in them? How had I never noticed that before? The irises were really a mix of colors, and blue was just the most prominent. It almost looked like he wore contacts—they were so vivid—and yet contacts could never get the exact color right.

"Unless you want to stay with your family?"

That ripped me right out of my reverie. "What?"

"Do you want to stay with your family while in town?"

Right. Drive to Midland. Where my family was. With Whitton Wright.

I'd been hired because of my knowledge of the area, but I hadn't really thought through that I'd have to go down there. The dollar signs had blinded me to the reality of what I was doing.

I was going home.

I was bringing Whitt with me.

And under no circumstances could those two worlds collide.

Fuck.

"No," I said quickly. Maybe too quickly.

His hand splayed open. An invitation to explain.

I layered on my best unbothered bravado. "I mean, no, thank you. We'll be too busy. Downtown probably makes the most sense."

"I'll make the arrangements then."

I breathed a soft sigh of relief. And then realized the other thing I hadn't considered. I was going to be staying at a hotel with Whitt.

My mind buzzed with that information. Me and Whitt, alone, in Midland for a weekend.

This beast of a man was stuffed into a charcoal suit. His pants stretched tight across his crotch. My eyes flicked down to where his cock was hidden by the expensive material. My mouth watered. Maybe not that hidden.

"How are you getting home?"

My eyes snapped back up to his. It was a testament to my temperament that I didn't blush furiously. Had he caught me staring at his cock? Christ, I needed to get it together. He was so fucking hot, and I just...had not prepared myself for him today.

"I'm going to grab an Uber."

"Don't be ridiculous. I can drive you home. You only live around the block."

"Oh, no. It's fine." I came to my feet, dragging my skirt back down my thighs. "You don't have to worry about me."

"I insist."

I opened my mouth to object and then closed it. "All right."

A flash of surprise crossed his face. He clearly hadn't thought that I'd say yes to that. Honestly, I was surprised myself. On the outside, I was the strong, resilient type who never let anything get to me. I didn't need anyone to take care of me. Let alone drive me home when I was having car troubles. I was a big girl.

And yet I couldn't say no to the offer. Not when I wanted him to take me. After all, the offer had come despite my reputation and our history.

I was known as a maneater, and it was generally well-earned.

Men were a vice. Meant to be devoured and discarded.

Whitton Wright was the only one who hadn't fallen into my Venus flytrap. Who'd refused to be chewed up and spit out. The only one I still wanted to take a bite out of.

He gestured to the door. It felt like he was asking about more than just a car ride.

"Shall we?" He strode to the door and tugged it open. The invitation palpable this time.

"I'm game."

I strode past him, swishing my hips dramatically as I stepped out into the hallway. My heels clicked noisily on the slate tiles that led to the elevator. Whitt cleared his throat behind me, and I snuck a glance back, only long enough to see him checking out my ass.

A slow smile curled my red-painted lips. "You coming?"

He straightened his suit coat and cleared his throat. "Yes. Yes, I am."

I smirked at the double meaning in his words. I liked that I managed to fluster him. The next couple of weeks working together were certainly going to be interesting.

3

WHITTON

"I'm over here," I said as soon as we were out of the overly air-conditioned lobby of Wright Construction.

Eve tugged on the lapels of her blazer. "Christ, it's a thousand degrees today."

"Texas," I said as if that explained everything.

"You chose this," she pointed out.

"It was forced upon me."

She shot me a look. "You just said you don't miss Seattle."

"That doesn't mean I'm here for Lubbock weather."

Or maybe I was.

Eve lifted her long, thick hair off of her neck and panted in the heat. Lubbock was typically a dry, dusty hundred degrees. Closer to the desert than the rest of Texas. No one was prepared for humid days like today after a freak thunderstorm.

I saw the moment that she gave up on professionalism in this weather. She bit down on the red of her bottom lip, sliding her emerald gaze in my direction. Then, she shrugged before slipping her suit coat off of her shoulders.

The first thing I noticed was the new ink across her shoulder—peonies in bloom with leaves curling toward her collarbone and down her arm.

Next was that underneath that black blazer was nothing but a thin camisole, the straps of an unlined lace bra now visible. The front revealed a touch of her impressive cleavage. Which only drew my eyes downward to where her nipples had hardened under the silky material.

Fuck.

Blood pumped to places it certainly wasn't supposed to when I was going to drive her home. I flexed my hand, trying to shake out the wave of need that pulled me under at the sight of her like this.

Because Eve was best in her element when she let her guard down. The first time I'd seen it happen, I hadn't realized how rare it was.

She played with our friends on a rec soccer league. I'd only come at my brother's insistence—I was more of a hockey guy—and then she'd caught my eye. I noticed that she was striking to look at and a force of nature on the field. But it was after the game where I first *saw* her. A random pop-up storm had everyone else running for their car, but not Eve. She stripped down to her sports bra and turned in a circle on the field with her tongue out, like she was trying to catch snowflakes.

I couldn't rip my gaze away from her. I stood in the rain and watched her enjoy it like I never could. I ruined a very expensive suit to do it. West had run back in frustration and pushed me toward the car. I'd never told him why I'd been standing there, transfixed. I'd never been able to shake that vision of Eve.

Rather than the one she showed everyone. Cautious. Always waiting for the other shoe to drop. Forever looking around, as if she expected everything to be taken away from her. She put her back up when threatened, and I still hadn't figured out how I'd threatened her.

"Whitt?" she said, her voice teasing.

I touched the handle of the car, unlocking the doors. I couldn't explain my daydream, so I made a noncommittal noise and tipped my head at the car. "Get in."

Her look was quizzical before she ducked into the passenger seat. She sank into the leather seat and crossed her legs, giving me an even bigger glimpse of her dream catcher. Fuck me. The ink on this woman did something to me.

I revved the engine to my Lexus and shifted into drive. Eve lived in Tech Terrance, just off of Texas Tech University's campus, with two of her friends. Nothing in Lubbock was more than a fifteen-minute drive away, except for the airport. An Uber wouldn't have cost her much, but I wasn't about to let her take one.

"So, what happened to your car?"

She huffed and looked out the window. "I have no clue. It wouldn't start this morning. And I couldn't jump it because Piper had to be at the winery early and Blaire was over at Campbell's place."

"I could give you a jump, if you need it."

Her brows furrowed. "Do you even know how to jump a car?"

"I'll take that as the insult it is. Of course I know how to jump a car." When she still looked skeptical, I added, "I can change a tire and my own oil, too."

Her eyes slid down my sharp suit, the perfectly knotted tie, and crisp white shirt. "Why do I find that hard to believe?"

Because she had only ever seen me as a suit. An image I

had carefully cultivated for years. West was my twin and my opposite. He was wild, rebellious, an artist, musician, and a dreamer. I was a realist and business-oriented. I was the guy with the five-plus-year plans. I had goals and ambitions, not dreams. Dreams were unactionable hopes and wants. Dreams led to disappointment.

"I can get my hands dirty."

"Oh?" she asked, leaning forward with interest. "I'd like to see that."

"Hmm," I said with an arched eyebrow.

"Who taught you to work with cars?"

"My dad." My throat was thick when I uttered the words.

Dad was...complicated. He'd been complicated before we discovered his duplicity. He was twice as frustrating now that we knew he had a whole other family. While I felt lucky to have Jordan and Julian in my life, he had uprooted all of us when it came out. He ruined everything he touched, and somehow, I still wanted him in my life.

"I see," she said softly. "I wouldn't have guessed he was a car person either."

"Not really. But I had an interest, and...he usually invested in our interests." I shrugged. "The man's flawed, but he put West in front of a piano at a young age. He wouldn't be in Cosmere otherwise."

"Maybe. I don't think either of you owe him anything for where you are," she said hotly. Her hand tightened on the door handle before loosening. "You did it in spite of him."

For a second, I wasn't sure we were talking about my father anymore. But I didn't know enough about Eve's past to know if she was projecting. We'd never gotten to the point before to discuss her family. Eve wasn't really much of a sharer. She always seemed like a creature of the present.

Anything that happened beyond the moment we were in was forgotten.

I decided to drop the whole thing. My dad was a hot topic on a good day.

"Are you coming to Jensen's thing tomorrow?"

"The mayoral announcement?" she asked with a wrinkled nose.

I laughed at her expression. "What's that about?"

"What?"

"The look."

"Politicians," she said with a little gag at the end. "What have they ever done for us before?"

"Fair, but it's Jensen."

Jensen Wright had been the CEO of Wright Construction since he had graduated college. He'd passed the helm to his sister, Morgan, a few years back to pursue his true passion—architecture. Now, he worked closely with the company he had run and was a regular fixture around the property.

Against his better judgment, someone had convinced him to run for mayor. The spot was open, and the other options were appalling. It was a clever con, and it had worked. I didn't know what his wife and kids thought about it, but Emery must have given him the green light or else he wouldn't be having an event tomorrow in which all the Wrights were planning to be in attendance.

"The girls cajoled me into going," Eve admitted. "Downtown will already be set up for the Fourth, and I can't resist a funnel cake."

"Noted," I said as I pulled into Eve's driveway behind her bright red early aughts 4Runner.

Piper's blue Jeep Wrangler was parked next to it, and she came running out, holding up her cell phone.

Eve popped the passenger door open. "Forget your phone again?"

"Having a work phone and a regular phone is ruining my life," Piper said. She winked at Eve. "What's going on here?" Her tone was light and suggestive.

I got out of the car. "Hey, Piper."

"Whitt," she said with a head nod. "Why are you driving my girl home?"

"My car wouldn't start this morning," Eve filled in.

"And you were together...why?"

"We're working together," I told her. "Eve is the agent for my new survey project in Midland."

Piper's eyes widened, and she and Eve spoke volumes without saying anything.

"Ohhh," she drawled. "Well, that sounds...fun. You told me about your new job. I didn't know you'd be working with Whitt."

"Neither did I," Eve said. She knocked her fist into Piper's shoulder. A clear sign to tell her to shut up. Piper just smirked. "Can you give me a jump?"

"Oh, I would," Piper said, her eyes flickering between us, "but I have to get back to work. Could *Whitt* do it? Sorry."

"Don't worry about it. I can do it," I told Piper. "Tell Hollin I said hi."

Piper snorted. "Tell him yourself. He's a pain in my ass."

"Literally?" Eve asked.

Piper and Hollin had been dating for a year, and sometimes, it was still hard to decipher whether they liked or hated each other. Somehow, constantly being at each other's throat worked for them.

"I'm going to forget you asked that," Piper said as she strode to her Jeep. "Thanks for taking care of my girl, Whitt."

"Anytime."

"See y'all tomorrow."

Then, she was pulling away, leaving us alone once more. Eve looked after her friend in dismay. Maybe she'd hoped to get out of my presence sooner. Too late now.

"You have cables?"

She jolted out of the reverie and nodded. She dug around in her bag and tossed me her car keys. "They're in the back. I'm just going to change."

I watched her practically hustle to get inside. Once again, I wasn't sure what to make of her. It was apparent that she was flirting with me. Just like she had the first time around. Because Eve had come on to me when we first started talking. I'd been a willing participant. But I'd dated enough back in Seattle to know that I preferred a relationship to a situationship. It was fine if that was what she wanted. It just wasn't what *I* wanted. No matter how my dick reminded me that I couldn't stop fucking thinking about getting her naked.

I ran a hand back through my hair. She'd made herself clear the first time, and I wasn't going to do this again. We were working together. That was it.

4

EVE

I leaned back against the front door and ran a hand
down my face. "Get it together, Houston."

Whitt was just a guy that it hadn't worked out with. He
was no different from the parade of exes who had masquer-
aded through my life. In fact, we hadn't even gotten far
enough for that. He'd wanted more than I could offer, and I
shouldn't still be interested just because he was hot as
fucking sin. I shouldn't make an exception for him.

Once it was over, it was over. I'd learned my lesson to
never look back. What was in the past was only ever going
to drag down my future. Or completely blow up my future,
like Arnold Sinclair had done. One moment, I'd been on a
pedestal, and the next, I'd discovered he wasn't separated
from his wife. Suddenly, I was a homewrecker and not just
trailer trash.

It had been hard to want any kind of relationship since
then. Especially from someone like Whitton. He was Wright
royalty, smart, driven, and intensely attractive. He was
everything a girl could want. But girls like me, who had
grown up in a trailer park and been crowned the town slut,

didn't end up with guys like him. And contemplating what it would be like to live through this fantasy didn't help anything.

I wasn't about to let another rich, pretty guy implode my life. Not when I was finally in a good place again.

"Right," I whispered and pushed off of the door.

With a clear mind, I headed back into my room and stripped out of my professional attire. I still wasn't used to wearing dress clothes. Not where I'd grown up. I'd always be more comfortable in my cowboy boots over my Louboutins. No matter how incredible my ass looked when I wore them.

I put my work heels in their place of honor. They gave me legitimacy for my clients, even here in West Texas. But I was over them, and I needed a different kind of armor to go deal with Whitt.

I pulled on a pair of short frayed-edge jean shorts and a baby-blue crop top. My hair went up into a sleek ponytail. Then, I slid my feet into my trusty boots. They weren't the decorative kind that the girls wore on campus with their little minidresses. I'd gotten these in the Stockyards. I'd ridden horses in them. They were sturdy leather and made to last. The last vestiges of my home.

After reapplying a slick of lipstick, I grabbed two bottles of water from the fridge. It really was a thousand degrees out there, and Whitt didn't have the convenience of changing out of his presumably wool suit and long-sleeved button-up. It was too hot for that mess. No matter how good he looked in it.

I was halfway to the door when my phone dinged in my back pocket. I fished it out and found a text from my other roommate, Blaire.

Whitt is at our house?

"Piper," I growled.

I'd been living with the girls since our friend Jennifer had moved out...and I'd been evicted from my last property. Word of advice: never move into a property your boyfriend owns without signing a lease.

But even though I'd been living with the girls for a year, I still wasn't used to the way they gossiped. I'd never had girlfriends to gossip with...only be gossiped about. And so having Piper tell Blaire I was with Whitt triggered something deep within the pit of my stomach.

Spill! I want to know what's going on. Piper wouldn't tell me anything!

I blew out a breath of relief. This wasn't gossip. This was how girlfriends spoke to each other. They wanted to know all the juicy details. Blaire and Piper were excited for me rather than talking shit about me. I needed to get used to the distinction, but it was hard to break the fear from twenty-five years of backstabbing.

He just drove me home. My car wouldn't start. He's giving me a jump.

Is that a sexual innuendo?

I snorted.

No. He's jumping the battery in my car.

Are either of you naked in this scenario?

Blaire!

Don't act prudish now!

I'm not prudish. I'm just not a horny teenager!

Please, we're all horny teenagers.

Blaire was one of those girl-power people. She'd started a successful influencing program for women to achieve their dreams and move past their insecurities. She was constantly using her therapist speak on me about embracing my inherent identity and releasing shame. But I didn't know what shame she had. She was with the hottest rockstar on the planet and picking up PR gigs all over the country. Girl practically had a fairy godmother waving a wand over her head and giving her the perfect life. I wouldn't mind one of those.

Whitt is a thirst trap.

He's probably just thirsty right now. I left him outside in the heat.

I sent her a picture of me holding the bottles of water.

You mean, he's thirsty for you. 🐶

I left her on Read and stuffed my phone back in my pocket. I couldn't justify a response. Because the way Whitt had been looking at me, he *did* look thirsty. And, fuck, so was I.

With both bottles in one hand, I opened the front door

and headed outside. Cables were connected to our two cars. Whitt sat on my driver's side and was revving the engine. It sounded like it was going to turn over, a ticking noise came from one side, but then it stopped. That didn't look like a good sign.

Whitt stepped out of my 4Runner. He'd already shed his jacket and rolled his sleeves up to his elbows, revealing powerful forearms. My eyes traveled over him as he strode to the engine. His eyes roved over the parts. I had a rudimentary understanding of how things worked. I could change a tire and jump a car. Though I knew how to change the oil, I opted for one of those fifteen-minute places instead. The only things I knew beyond that were the parts that I'd had to replace.

I'd had a radiator blow up on me at a Sonic drive-in. Smoke billowed out of the engine like a small bomb. An oil leak had come and gone for months with little patch repairs before more extensive work. I'd gone the summer before college without air-conditioning before I scrounged up enough to cover the repair. My brake pads had been burned into the ground before I had the money to make that replacement. And all that didn't include the dead battery, a few flat tires, and a Check Engine light that still flared to life every time I started the car. I'd never gotten up the courage to figure out what that was all about. I liked to live on the wild side and hope for the best.

"How's it going?" I asked as I strode toward him.

"Not great," he admitted.

He hadn't looked up yet. His fingers were currently working their way down the buttons of his shirt. My steps slowed as I watched inch after inch of toned skin appear on his chest. He slid the shirt off his shoulders and tossed it inside the car before leaning into the hood of the car and getting his hands dirty.

Literally.

My mouth went dry. Those shoulders flexed as he reached deeper into the car. His back muscles rippled as he spread his legs wider for balance. The sharp angles of his body formed a V as his torso tapered to his trim waist and into his suit pants. His impressive ass pushed backward. I tilted my head to get a better look. For a second, all I wanted to do was pour the entire bottle of water over my head.

Congratulations, sir. You have one-upped my Daisy Dukes.

"Well, it's not the battery," he said.

He brushed his hands back and forth as he straightened and faced me. Then, his jaw unhinged. His eyes slid down my long, tan legs to the boots on my feet and back up.

Then, he cleared his throat. "I think it's a timing belt."

"What?" I asked, shaken back to the moment. "No. That's bad."

"Yeah."

I passed him the bottle of water, which he downed before continuing, "I wouldn't recommend driving it even if we could get it to turn over. It'd be a more costly repair the more damage it takes. You'll probably need a tow."

I deflated. Fuck. A tow and a timing belt repair. How the hell was I going to afford that? I loved my 4Runner to pieces, but it was probably time to replace her. I just didn't have the available funds, and she was so old that no one was going to give me more than pennies for her.

"I know a guy," Whitt assured me. "I'll give him a call and see if he'll do the tow as a favor."

"What? Really? Someone would do that?"

"Sure." He already had his phone in his hand and was shooting off a text. "I collect friends like that."

"Must be nice," I said before I could think better of it.

He arched an eyebrow in my direction. "You're doing all right in the friend department."

"For sure. But no one who will tow my car for me," I said with a self-deprecating laugh.

"You do now. I can take care of you."

I smirked at him. "I'm a big girl. I can take care of myself."

"Hmm," he murmured. "Well, he said he'll be here in twenty. I told him to take you to a shop where I know the owner. He'll give you a fair price and not try to upsell you."

"You didn't have to do that."

Whitt took a step toward me. "I wanted to."

A breath lingered between us. I could lean into it. I could let him work his Wright magic and be my knight in shining armor. But this wasn't a fairy tale. I wasn't going to be swept off of my feet. Men didn't act like that in real life.

At best, a man was an accessory. He looked good on my arm, but he wasn't necessary for me to shine.

I wanted to fuck Whitton Wright, but he'd made it clear that he wanted more. So, I took my step back. Decided to keep it professional and to leave the thirsting for my daydreams.

"Well, thanks. You don't have to wait for the tow truck. I've already monopolized enough of your time."

He nodded and took another sip of water. Already, he'd responded to my distance with his own. "All right. I'll see you tomorrow?"

"Yeah, I'll be there."

His eyes snapped back to mine. "Let me know if you need a ride."

I wet my lips. Fuck, did I ever need a ride. "Sure."

He disconnected the cables, pulled his clothes back on, and then tipped his head at me before going back to the office. My heart stuttered as he drove away.

Had I made the right decision? Should I have gone for it? I didn't normally back down from a guy, especially someone that hot, but I could see all the signs that this would crash and burn. When it inevitably ended, where would that leave me?

Would all my shiny, new friends pick me over a Wright? Or would I lose everything again?

It wasn't worth the risk.

5

WHITTON

"Did you have to wear a suit?" Weston asked me.

Of course he'd shown up to Jensen's mayoral event as casual as ever. I rarely saw my brother in anything but band attire. Even today, he was in torn black jeans and a distressed Cosmere T-shirt.

"You're wearing your own merch," I pointed out.

"Thank you!" his girlfriend, Nora, said. "I said the same damn thing before we left."

He fisted his shirt and looked down at it. "I had this before I was in the band. Does it still count?"

"It counts," Nora and I said at the same time.

West pressed a kiss to her lips. "Traitor. You're not supposed to agree with my brother."

She giggled and kissed him again. I rolled my eyes and turned my attention to the rest of the Wrights in attendance. There were a lot of us. Something that I wasn't accustomed to. I was used to it being me, West, and Harley against the world. Now, Harley was in Seattle until the end of the summer, and we had two new brothers and five cousins we'd never known about.

I never would have believed we'd be welcomed with open arms until it happened. West had always been certain that they'd want to know the truth, but I certainly hadn't. Who wanted to know their family's dirty deed? But this family was a blessing I never could have seen coming.

Jensen was the highlight of the moment. To be fair, he usually took up most of the air in any room he entered. The oldest of the Wrights. He'd been there to help raise the others when their parents both passed away. He'd taken on the mantle of oldest brother and parent, all at once, at such a young age. It was no surprise that he'd agreed to run for mayor.

"You made it," Jensen said with a jovial smile.

He shook my hand and then West's. He pulled Nora in for a hug. She actually blushed. Perhaps no one was immune to his charm.

"We made it," I confirmed. "I'm glad that I was back from Seattle in time."

"But not your sister?"

"Nah, Harley wanted to get in as much mom time as possible before she comes back for her sophomore year at Tech."

Jensen nodded in understanding. "I don't blame her. If I could have a little bit of Mom time left, I'd get it."

"Fair," West said. "How's Emery?"

Jensen's eyes navigated the crowd easily to find his wife standing with their two children. Robin toddled around her feet while Logan was struggling to escape her arms. An older woman laughed and took Logan out of Emery's arms, and then Emery grabbed Robin before she could run away.

"We're lucky that her mom is helping with the kids. It's a lot for both of us, working full-time with two littles," Jensen said. "But I wouldn't trade it. I wish I'd gotten more time with Colton at that age."

Jensen had a much older son from a previous marriage. Colton lived with his mom in New York City. As far as I knew, he went to a private Upper East Side prep school, and Jensen flew his private jet up all the time to visit him. My dad had only ever been a few hours away in Vancouver. I couldn't imagine what it would have been like to grow up with him on the other side of the country.

"Are you ready for your speech?" West asked.

Jensen shrugged. "I've been making speeches most of my life. Just a bigger crowd. Can imagine that you understand that."

"No way. I hate speeches. I leave those to Campbell. Put me on keys in front of thousands, and I'll be fine, but I'm not a front man."

"I've never met a Wright who was comfortable in the background," Jensen said with a smile. "And I don't think Campbell Abbey would have brought you on if he didn't think you could fit the profile."

West beamed at the compliment. Oh, Jensen was going to be *just fine* as a politician.

"You already have our votes," I joked. "You don't have to butter us up."

Jensen laughed. "That's fair. Though I was being honest." He clapped me on the back. "Come on. Go over my speech with me. Jordan told me that you used to do public speaking in college. You were on student government?"

I groaned. "I should have never told him that."

But I tipped my head at West and headed across the backstage area with Jensen and toward his wife. The rest of my Wright cousins stopped us along the way to jab at Jensen about his announcement. They were a tight-knit family. I felt more like an intruder on their time than part of it even though I was included as if I *was* a part of it.

Jensen finally laughed off his brother Austin and pulled out the notecards he'd stuffed in his pocket. He passed them off to me and pointed to a line on the second card. "What do you think of this? Does it seem a little...conceited? I *was* asked to run by what felt like half the town, but I could cut it."

I read through the intro. It was good. He was a talented guy.

I lifted my head from the notecards to tell him what I thought when Emery rushed over. "Jensen!"

"Em? What's going on?" He immediately went into protective mode. "Is it the kids?"

"It's Vanessa." She handed over her cell phone.

Jensen reeled back, his face turning sour at the name of his ex-wife. "What does she want?"

"Something happened with Colton."

Jensen took the phone out of her hand and put it to his ear. "Vanessa?"

I met Emery's eyes. She was biting her lip and looked frightened. I sure hoped his kid was all right.

"Should I?" I gestured away from them. I was intruding on an important moment after all. I didn't need to be involved.

"No, no. It's okay."

"He *what*?" Jensen roared.

I'd never heard him raise his voice before. Emery winced. The entire backstage looked over at him in alarm. I sort of wished that I'd already backed away. But I was still holding his speech in my hand, the tips I was going to give him dying on my lips.

Jensen appeared oblivious to the spectacle he was

35

making. "The fuck, Vanessa? Are you even fucking watching him?" He waited a few seconds, apparently listening to whatever she was saying. I could hear her frantic screeching on the other side. "I don't fucking care. I don't fucking care. Stop talking. I will be on the first plane to New York, and I will deal with this."

He listened for another minute because Vanessa had never stopped yelling on the other line. I couldn't hear anything she was saying, but it didn't sound pleasant.

"I said I would deal with it," he growled. Then, he hung up the phone. He ran a hand back through his hair. His eyes closed as a tortured expression crossed his face.

I was paralyzed through all of it. I couldn't back away. I couldn't reach forward. I didn't know him well enough to offer comfort. Even Emery looked torn between interfering in his past relationship and her stepson and staying out of it. If even she couldn't decide, how could I do anything?

Finally, Jensen released a puff of air and glanced between us. "Colton was arrested."

"Oh my God," Emery whispered. "What happened?"

"I don't have all the details. Vanessa was just screaming and crying. She's going to bail him out. I have to get to New York to be there when he comes home. He clearly doesn't respect her, and he's not getting away with no consequences this time."

"Of course. Do you want me to come with you?"

He shook his head. "Stay here with the kids. I'll handle it and be back before you miss me."

"Impossible." She stepped forward into his arms and pressed a kiss to his cheek.

"Whitt," Jensen said. "Sorry about this."

"No need to apologize."

"What about the announcement?" Emery asked. "There're thousands of people out there, Jensen."

He huffed. I could see that he wanted to ditch and head straight to the city. His responsibilities were split. But I watched the moment he decided to follow through.

"I'll give the speech but skip the rest. I can't shake hands and kiss babies when I need to be with my own kid," Jensen said.

"Are you sure?" Emery asked.

He nodded. His gaze shifted back to me. "Any last notes?"

"No notes. You've got this," I assured him.

I offered the notecards back to him. He took them and tucked them back into his suit.

"I assume you're lying, but thank you anyway. Maybe we can sit down together before the next one. Jordan said you've become a valuable asset at the company."

"I'd like that," I told him and then stepped away.

Jensen's campaign manager ushered the rest of the family and friends who were backstage out of the area to fill up the VIP section they'd reserved at the outdoor auditorium in Mackenzie Park for Jensen's announcement. I caught up with West and Nora on the stairs.

West shot me a look. The weird thing about having a twin was that sometimes we didn't have to say a single thing to the other. We weren't like the twins you saw on TV, where we were the same people who wore the same clothes and said the same things. That never happened. But that didn't mean that it didn't feel like we could read each other's mind. And right now, we both felt out of place in the midst of all these *actual* Wrights.

Still, once we reached the back of the group, I explained what had happened.

West sighed. "Fuck."

"Tell me about it."

"That's terrible," Nora said. "I can't believe he's still doing all of this."

"He has to," West said. "The show must go on."

Jensen couldn't cancel. Not when the entire place was jam-packed with supporters. Not without explaining something he very publicly did not want people to know about. Not without getting in front of what had happened. Something he didn't even know about yet.

While all of that was going on, my mind was elsewhere. My eyes scanned the crowd, seeing a sea of unfamiliar faces.

Eve had said she was coming.

She'd told me she'd see me here.

Her roommates were already in attendance. Piper stood with her boyfriend and Nora's brother Hollin. Blaire stood next to them with Annie. Nora's other brother and Blaire's boyfriend, Campbell, wasn't in attendance, but that wasn't surprising. West had said that Campbell frequently got mauled in public and big crowds without security wasn't good for him. The life of a rockstar.

But no Eve.

"What are you looking for?" West asked.

I whipped back around. "Nothing."

I hadn't told him that Eve and I were working together. Or that I was still very much interested in the perky brunette. I'd given up after what happened after the wedding. Then, she'd sauntered back into my life yesterday, and a desire I couldn't ignore had reignited.

"Nothing," West said disbelievingly. "Sure."

Fuck our mind reading sometimes.

One of Jensen's staff came onstage to announce him. A roaring cheer went up from the crowd, and still, there was no Eve. She hadn't taken me up on needing a ride. I'd thought that she would get one with her roommates. Maybe her car was still messed up, and she'd tried to Uber in this mess.

I considered pulling my phone out to text her when I caught sight of her at the top of the stairs that led down to where we were sitting. She had her high heels in one hand. Her dark hair pulled up high on her head. Her blue dress formed to her curvy features. Even from a distance, she was the most arresting figure I'd ever seen. I couldn't tear my eyes from her.

"Oh," West said next to me.

And he didn't have to say anything else.

Oh was fucking right.

6

EVE

From one girl to another, I wouldn't recommend running through wet grass in thousand-dollar high heels. Louboutins were made to be admired. Preferably from behind as I bent over a fancy desk. Not ruined as they squelched into uncharacteristically soggy ground. I'd kicked them off and scooped them up on the way over. I wasn't about to turn a fucking ankle for fashion. Not when our soccer championship was right around the corner.

Now, I was not only late for the announcement I had promised everyone I would attend. I was also barefoot and perspiring.

Excellent.

I stopped before the outdoor auditorium, craning my neck for my friends. The place was *packed*. People had brought blankets and folding chairs to camp out on the surrounding grass, like they would in a few days for the Fourth of July fireworks. Only Wrights could draw crowds like this. How the hell was I going to find anyone in all of this?

My eyes scanned the crowd. Nora had texted earlier

and told me that they'd roped off an area for friends and family. I supposed that was me even if I still questioned that.

Then, in the midst of the chaos, I found him.

Whitt.

It was like two magnets snapped together by the force of their attraction. He was in a suit, taller than nearly everyone else in attendance, other than his twin at his side. And he was looking directly at me.

I considered raising my hand to wave, but I was stuck, trapped in that gaze. Even all the way across the auditorium with thousands of people between us, Whitton Wright had found me.

I shivered all over.

"No," I whispered to myself.

I'd decided not to do this. We were working together. I was going to keep it professional.

I broke the gaze and focused on getting down to my friends. This had nothing to do with Whitt. Jensen was currently being introduced by a woman that I didn't recognize. Well, at least I hadn't missed the main act.

An opening appeared on the green, and I pushed my way off the grass. I slid my heels back onto my feet with a grimace before striding purposefully down the stairs. People moved out of my way as if my high heels and work dress made me look important. Little did they know.

I shouldered past people who had clearly been there a lot longer than I had. I received some irritated looks, but I couldn't help that my friends were up at the front, and I wasn't about to stand around by myself. I hadn't really wanted to come in the first place.

Nora turned around then and waved at me. She must have seen my text that I was on my way. I waved back, not paying attention to anything but getting through the crowd and to her side.

I was nearly there when a pair of children ran under my feet. One shoved me in the back as they rushed after the other. I gasped as I careened forward, my very fancy heels giving me no resistance as I scrambled to stay upright.

It was no use. I reached blindly for anything to keep me upright. I floundered for a few precious seconds before an arm shot out, stopping my forward trajectory and cradling my body protectively.

"I got you," Whitt said.

Icicles froze up my spine at the first crash of his baby-blues against my emeralds. The rest of the world disappeared in that one look. The crowd, the boys who'd pushed me, even my friends hovering nearby. Nothing cracked through the freeze frame from being in Whitton Wright's arms again.

"Hey, Eve," Whitt said, a half-smile quirking on his perfect, lush lips.

I hastily cleared my throat and pushed myself out of his arms. "Uh, hi."

Whitt quirked an eyebrow, as if to say he'd seen exactly how I'd gone jelly in his arms. "You okay?"

"Fine."

"Hmm," he grunted.

A lie. I was not fine. Not at all. Not with him standing in front of me, looking like a whole fucking meal. Not with the lingering feel of his hands on my body. I shivered as if I could still feel every indent in my skin.

"Thanks to you," I added. "I appreciate the save."

"You're late," was his only response.

West cleared his throat, covering a laugh. "Good to see

you, Eve. Ignore my brother. Punctuality is next to godliness or whatever."

Nora snorted. "That sounds right." She pulled me in for a hug. "Glad you made it. Sorry I saw your text so late."

"That's all right. I thought I was going to miss the whole thing."

"Did you get stuck in traffic?" Nora asked.

I laughed. It was hard not to. "In Lubbock? What traffic?"

Nora breathed out heavily through her nose. "Fair. Fine. But it's a busy weekend."

"No, I got caught at a showing. It was only supposed to be one house, and the next thing I knew, we were looking at ten houses in neighborhoods all over town."

"Real estate agent problems."

"Tell me about it."

I put up with a lot of shit, but I actually liked these clients. It was why I'd put in the extra effort. I wanted them to find their dream home. That moment when they walked through the house in a daze and just *knew*. Their eyes meeting across a kitchen island as they pictured filling the space with their things and making memories. It was the best.

"How's the car?" Whitt asked.

West and Nora jerked their heads to him simultaneously. Whitt didn't deign to meet their interested expressions.

"Still at the dealership. They gave me a loaner. Thanks for the assist."

"Sure," he said, his gaze intense.

"What assist?" Nora asked, interjecting herself into our conversation.

West was looking at his brother, but Whitt purposely glanced away.

"I had some car trouble, and Whitt helped me out," I said as if it were no big deal.

And honestly, from anyone else, it wouldn't be. Nora would have done it in a heartbeat. But of course, I didn't want to bang Nora.

"Really?" West said. "Whitt is good with cars."

"Found that out," I admitted.

A vision of him shirtless with his hands under the hood flashed through my mind. A flush rushed through my chest and centered on my core. Yeah, I couldn't stop thinking about that muscled torso and biceps and shoulders and...

Fuck, brain! Shut the fuck up!

"What did Brian say?" Whitt asked.

"He agreed with you. Timing belt."

And it was going to be at least five hundred dollars. I'd winced at the amount when I'd first heard it. He'd even said it was a deal because he was friends with Whitt. I didn't know how he knew everyone in town when I'd lived here longer, but I was thankful for the discount. Even if the amount quoted was going to bankrupt me until I got that Wright money coming in.

Nora sidled up next to me. I could see that she had questions in her eyes. Nora, after all, was the person who had first tried to get me and Whitt together. I'd admitted my attraction to him, and she'd laid the groundwork for us. She'd never understood when I told her it hadn't worked out. I bet I was going to get an earful once we were alone.

Thankfully, she didn't dive in at that moment because the crowd roared its approval as Jensen Wright strode out onto the stage. I winked at her and faced forward. Whitt's attention was still on me though. I might have been able to fool Nora if he wasn't still intently staring at my face. Watching me as if I had a secret that he was trying to decipher.

West hit him on the shoulder, and he broke my gaze to look at his brother. Then cleared his throat and faced Jensen as he began his announcement speech.

I didn't give two shits about politics. The politicians and policies certainly hadn't been designed for people like me. But it was hard not to get swept up into Jensen's enthusiasm. He had a charisma onstage that couldn't be faked. Either you had it or you didn't. And Jensen had it in spades. No wonder he'd been an incredible CEO for the company. With the Wright good looks, a sharp wit, and an even wider smile, he won the crowd over instantly. By the end of the speech, the audience was in a fit, screaming his name.

"That was so good," Nora said. "Especially considering what happened."

"What happened?"

Nora sighed. "His son was arrested."

My eyes widened. A *Wright* had been arrested. "Here in town?"

"No," Whitt said. "He has an older son from his first marriage. He's in high school in New York."

"Oh yeah. I've seen him around before." But still, I was shocked that a Wright would do anything to get arrested. "What did he do?"

"We don't know," Whitt said.

"And it's none of our business," Nora added. She nudged me.

"I bet the news is going to report on it once they find out since Jensen is running for office," Whitt said.

"Why do you have to be a Debbie Downer?" Nora joked. "West, make him be nice. This is just going to blow over."

West chuckled. "Have you met my brother? He's probably formulating a new five-year plan for Jensen to take this stain off of his immaculate reputation."

"I'm doing no such thing."

"He's a Wright. He'll be fine," I said immediately.

"Can we go to the carnival and forget about this?" Nora asked.

I'd promised another client that I'd see them in a few hours when they got off work. Which meant I had a few hours to kill...

"All right. I have clients later though."

"Boo!" Nora said. "Get out of it! Think about it—you, me, Ferris wheel!"

"Funnel cakes," Whitt added.

My eyes snapped back to his. So, he really had been listening. "I suppose I can't resist a funnel cake."

"That's the word on the street," he teased.

I licked my lips and averted my gaze. My phone buzzed in my pocket, and I pulled it out to see that my sister was calling.

"I have to take this. Y'all go ahead, and I'll catch up."

"I can wait," Whitt offered.

I stepped aside, my stomach sinking. There were few reasons why Bailey would be calling me. And every single one of them was a bomb waiting to go off. I didn't want to take this call. But I couldn't *not* take this call.

"Bailey?"

She immediately launched into conversation about what was the newest problem in Midland. My heart sank as I listened and watched the crowd of people migrate from the auditorium toward the carnival grounds. It was like watching from outside of my body. So easy for everyone else to live in the moment. To forget the world around them and head to the carnival, where they could spend money without worrying about where every dollar had come from and laugh without wondering if someone was going to tear them apart for just existing.

The longer I was on the phone with Bailey, the more I remembered why that wasn't my reality. Why I couldn't be that carefree. Not when a tether held me under the water. Not when my responsibilities back home were still drowning me.

Whitt hesitated nearby, as if he was going to wait for me. The promised funnel cake inviting me to get off the phone quickly. To forget what my sister was saying on the other line. To get lost in him.

But I couldn't be the girl who ignored the call. I had to deal with this. If I didn't, then no one else would. It had to be me. Even if I wanted one day when I didn't have to deal with anything.

Instead, I waved him off.

His brow furrowed. I thought he might disagree with me. That he might wait. But eventually, he nodded and left with the rest of the group.

I sighed. "Okay, okay. Slow down, Bails. I'll handle it."

Like I always did.

PART II

DREAM CATCHER

7

WHITTON

"Knock, knock."

I glanced behind me to find Jordan striding into my office with a roguish smile on his face. I'd been working with Jordan long enough to know that wasn't a good thing.

"What happened?"

"Why does something have to have happened?" Jordan asked.

"Because I know you."

He laughed and took the seat across from me, crossing his ankle at his knee. Oh boy.

I closed out of the memo I'd been writing on the survey Eve and I were going to look at in Midland this afternoon. She'd done every scrap of work sent her way almost immediately. Her lateness only seemed to be in relation to meeting in person. Which hadn't happened since I'd seen her at the mayoral announcement.

She'd claimed that she was going to come to the carnival, and then she'd bailed without a word. Even Nora seemed concerned. I spent the rest of the afternoon wishing

I could bail, too. Between being in Nora and West's lovey-dovey gravity and fending off West's attempts to get me to explain what was going on with Eve, I'd been exhausted by the time I did get home.

West didn't really know how to take no for an answer from me. I'd say it was a twin thing, but I was pretty sure he was just an annoying younger brother. I'd get the same treatment from Harley if she were here.

Not that there was anything to say. Eve and I were working together. We'd flirted while I helped her with her car. That was all it was.

"I'm giving you an intern for the summer."

I blinked at Jordan. "An intern? Why?"

"Special circumstances."

"There's only eight weeks left before the end of summer."

"I know."

There was something he wasn't saying. I hadn't ever asked for an intern. Really, I hadn't ever wanted one. As nice as it was to have someone to file my paperwork and run for my coffee, I didn't have the time to train anyone. Not with this massive project on my plate. What was Jordan thinking?

"Let's call it a personal favor," Jordan said with a grin.

"Since when are we doing personal favors at work?"

"Since Jensen's kid is coming in from New York City and needs someone who won't coddle his ass."

I nearly choked. "Colton is coming to Lubbock?"

"Yep."

"Because he was arrested?"

"Yep."

"And you want him to work for me? The boss's kid?"

"I want someone who won't treat him like the boss's kid.

He can't work for anyone who has grown up with him. And he can't work for anyone who will treat him with kid gloves. He's not glass; he won't shatter under pressure."

"You think I'm that person?"

"I know you are," Jordan said with a laugh. "If you're half as hard on him as you are on yourself, then it'll be fine."

"Dare I ask what the kid did?"

"Breaking and entering and vandalism," Jordan said. He scrolled his phone and passed it to me. I looked down at a black-and-white photo of Colton Wright. I'd seen him once before. He looked just like a teenage version of his father. "He and a few of his friends broke into the rival prep school and spray-painted dicks all over the gym."

I snorted. "Sounds right."

"Yeah. It was stupid, and they might have gotten away with it, but they'd bragged about it before it happened. So, some of the kids from the other school showed, and there was a fight. Administration found out and refused to let them all go."

"Both sides were arrested?"

"Yes. Jensen got them to back down by saying he was taking Colton back to Texas."

"And money, I'm sure."

"I'm sure." Jordan stood and took his phone back. "So, are you up for it?"

"It doesn't sound like I have a choice."

"That's the spirit," Jordan said. "He'll start Monday."

I couldn't hold back my laugh. It was a ridiculous notion. What was I going to do with a fifteen-year-old New York City brat? I already had an assistant, but from what it sounded like, I couldn't foist Colton off to him. Jensen Wright's son would steamroll my assistant. I'd need to come up with a game plan to try to deprogram the little shit.

"Fine. Monday it is."

"Knew I could count on you." Jordan leaned against the doorframe. "Everything set for Midland?"

"Yeah. Eve should be here any minute."

"She's late, isn't she?" Jordan asked with a smirk.

"Fifteen minutes and counting."

Jordan grinned. "It's good to see you flustered. Wasn't sure anything did that."

"My brother would say everything does."

"He'd be wrong." He tapped the door twice. "Good luck this weekend. Text if you need anything."

"Will do."

Jordan was leaving just as my phone beeped.

In the lobby with my suitcase. Ready when you are.

I blew out a breath. Thank fuck. At least when we were together this weekend, she couldn't be late to our meetings with the Kings. Not when I had the car.

I shrugged my suit coat back on and headed downstairs. She was standing amid the black-and-white lobby in black skinny dress pants and a silky teal blouse. She was in those same black heels that I couldn't stop fantasizing about. Eve in those heels, only those heels. The red-lacquered backs visible from her on all fours. Christ, sometimes, I wondered what it would be like to ignore my relationship needs and give in to my baser desires.

Eve turned as she heard my approach. A slow smile spread across her red-painted lips. "Hey, you."

"Hey. Ready?" I asked.

"Sure thing."

"Is this all you packed?"

"We're only staying one night," she said with a laugh. "How much does a girl need?"

"From my experience? A lot." I took the white suitcase out of her hand and wheeled it toward the door.

"I can carry my own stuff," she argued, reaching for the suitcase.

I moved it away from her. "No."

"No?" she asked, rearing back. "I lift weights. I could probably squat you, sir."

"Sir?" It was my turn to shoot her an amused look.

"Oh, do you like that?" she teased.

Wouldn't mind her saying it in the bedroom. Not that I could say that out loud.

"Just a reminder of who is in charge here."

She rolled her eyes. "We're partners. No one is in charge."

She was very wrong about that.

"We'll see."

I unlocked my Lexus and added her suitcase next to mine in the trunk. She leaned her hip onto the side of the car and held her hand out. I stared down at it in confusion as I closed the trunk.

"What?"

"Keys," she said with a wicked grin.

"Keys to what?"

"The car, of course. I know where all the cop traps are on the drive. I can get us there in an hour and a half."

"If you're going the speed limit, it doesn't matter where the cops are."

She rolled her eyes. "It also takes an extra half hour to get there."

"Are we in a rush?"

"Come on, Whitt," she said, making a gimme gesture with her hand. "Live a little."

"No one drives my car." I wrenched open the driver's door. "You're just going to have to suffer."

"Can I at least choose the music?" she asked as she took her seat next to me.

"No."

She laughed. "You're a real control freak, you know that?"

Our eyes met across the leather interior. She'd said it as a joke, but she was completely right. Control was ingrained in my being, and it wasn't just about who drove my car or chose the music. It was about so much more than that.

My hands flexed on the steering wheel. "I'm well aware."

She licked her lips, crossing her legs tight together. "Ever let your hair down, sir?"

"No, but I'd let yours down."

I wrapped her thick ponytail around my palm and gave it a playful tug.

A soft exhale was the only sound in the electrified space between us. Part of me wanted to tug her forward by her thick hair and fit her lips to mine. It'd be so easy to claim her lips for my own.

But not only were we on a work trip where it would be incredibly unprofessional, but I also remembered the sting of rejection when I'd told her the truth—that I wanted more. I could fuck her. I could fuck her day and night for ages and never be tired of it. I knew that for certainty. My cock throbbed at the thought. I also knew that was all she'd give mend I wasn't sure that was enough.

I released her hair.

"So," I said, clearing my throat and starting the engine, "where exactly are these cops located?"

Two hours and several disagreements about my music choices later, we arrived at the downtown hotel in Midland. To say the place was slammed was an understatement. I had to park in the very back of the lot and only snagged a spot after an enormous black truck pulled out.

"The fuck?" I murmured. "I didn't think Midland was this busy."

Eve pushed the door open and stepped out. "It's usually not. Unless it's Friday Night Lights, and then all bets are off."

"Think we're safe from high school football." I popped the trunk and extracted both of our suitcases.

"I can take mine," she said, holding out her hand.

I ignored her and continued forward with both suitcases. She huffed, falling into step beside me.

One thing became immediately apparent; there were an exorbitant number of cowboys in the lobby. Men in boots, enormous belt buckles, and cowboy hats were standing around in groups of three or four. They all seemed to know each other. The noise as they caught up and laughed and chatted was...a lot.

I glanced at Eve. "What the fuck is going on?"

"If I had to guess?" Her eyes slid over the men with a smirk. "Rodeo weekend."

"Oh. That's a real thing."

She laughed. "You live in Texas now, cowboy," she teased playfully.

"You're making me regret it."

"Come on. I could take you this weekend. We could get you some chaps."

My eyes widened. "Excuse me?"

"Assless chaps are definitely your look."

"Has anyone ever told you that you're ridiculous?"

She laughed. "What? You don't think you can pull off assless chaps?"

"This feels like a trap."

"I can pull them off," she said with a wink.

The image that flashed through my mind made everything else in the room go fuzzy. Suddenly, the fantasy of fucking her over my desk in high heels was replaced by her in assless chaps. That perfectly pert ass jiggling under the slap of my hand.

Fuuuck. I screeched that image to a halt. She was saying something else. I needed to be in the moment.

"What?"

She arched an eyebrow. "At least let me get you some quality boots. Not the stupid fake leather ones they sell all over the place."

"Where am I wearing cowboy boots?"

She blinked like she'd never considered this question. "Everywhere?"

"I'm not wearing cowboy boots in Lubbock."

"We have rodeos in Lubbock, too."

I slid my gaze to her. "I'm not going to a rodeo in Lubbock either."

"Fine. They're better in Midland anyway."

"I'll have to take your word for it."

I stepped up to the counter, passing over my ID and company credit card. "Two rooms under Whitton Wright."

"Yes, sir," the man said as he typed away on his computer. "You here for the rodeo?"

"Does he look like he's here for the rodeo?" Eve asked with a laugh.

The man glanced up and then joined in with her. "No, I

suppose not." He passed back my ID. "Okay. Here we are. Whitton Wright, one room, checking out tomorrow."

"Wait, I have two rooms," I said.

"Sorry. It does look like we only have one room under that name. Could it be under another name?"

Eve bit her lip. "You did make the reservation, right?"

"My assistant made the reservation," I told her in dismay.

Had he screwed it up and only gotten *me* a room? I was sure that I'd told him that Eve would need her own room. Fuck, this was why I handled everything myself.

We tried Eve's name, but nothing came up.

I sighed heavily. "Fine. I'll take another room then. Whatever you have."

The man winced. "Sorry. With the rodeo in town, we're all booked up."

"The whole town will be booked," Eve said.

He nodded. "I'm surprised y'all were able to get one reservation as it is," he admitted. "We're usually booked up months in advance."

I clenched my hand into a fist. What the fuck were we going to do? We couldn't reschedule. Our meeting was in an hour. It would be a shitty thing to do at this point. I couldn't do anything to jeopardize this deal.

"Is it at least a room with two beds?" I growled in frustration.

"Well, no. There's only one bed." At my irritated expression, he added quickly, "But the room does have a couch in it. It's not a pullout, but it would be comfortable for one night."

"That's fine." Eve spoke up. "I can sleep on a couch."

"No, this is unacceptable."

She elbowed me. "We need this job. Just take the room, Whitt. What's the worst that could happen?"

I would be trapped in a room, alone with Eve Houston all night.

"It's one night," she said with a gleam of challenge in her eyes. "I'm game if you are."

I'd never been able to back down from a challenge. Was it insane to be alone with her when I could barely control myself in her presence? I'd wanted *more* distance between her and my needy cock. Not less.

And yet I found myself nodding. I could do this. What was one night in the grand scheme of things?

"Fine," I said with a nod. "We'll take it."

8

EVE

The hotel situation was fresh in my mind through our meeting with the Kings. We hadn't reconciled what to do about the one king bed in the room. We'd had enough time to throw our stuff upstairs, change, and head over to meet Malcolm King. Neither of us had even glanced at the bed. And now, I couldn't stop thinking about it.

It didn't help that Whitt had barely looked at me since. What was he thinking about all of it? Not that we'd had time to talk about it while we were surveying the different locations. I gave my opinion on the different acreage based on my experience in real estate as well as living in Midland. We drove behind Malcolm King's pickup truck to the different sites. I wasn't sure if he had noticed anything strange between me and Whitt, but everything I knew about him said that he was observant, brilliant, and intimidating. I'd been friends with his younger brother, Nate, who was more on the brash, jokester, and wild spectrum. I was glad that Malcolm didn't remember me. It was easier this way.

"Thanks for your time," Whitt said, shaking Malcolm's hand.

"No, thank you. Coming down on a Friday afternoon on a rodeo weekend is a lot," he said with a grin. "I appreciate your expertise. Think this will be a great step forward."

He shook my hand next. "Thank you, Eve."

"Our pleasure. Let us know if there's anything else you need from us."

"I will do that." He furrowed his brow as he released my hand. "You look familiar. You said you were from here?"

So much for not remembering me.

"Uh, yeah. I went to school with Nate."

Malcolm's eyebrows shot up. "Oh."

"Not like that!" I said quickly.

"Not like what?" Whitt asked. His jaw clenched.

Malcolm and I exchanged a look and then laughed.

"My brother has...dated a lot."

"That's putting it mildly. He's a total womanizer," I told Whitt. "He even dated Blaire for a bit before she and Campbell got together."

"Really?" Whitt asked. "That must have been before my time."

"It was."

"And you and Nate were just friends?" Malcolm asked dubiously.

"I was not one of his conquests," I assured him. "Ask him about Eve Houston. He'll tell you."

"Good to hear that some women have some sense," Malcolm said.

"Taste," I corrected with a wink.

Malcolm laughed harder at that. I could see why all the girls had gone wild for him in school. He was several years older than us and the starting quarterback that took our high school to state. He had been every girl's Friday Night Lights dream.

My eyes slid to Whitt, who had stuffed his hands into the pockets of his suit pants. He was watching our interaction very closely. Almost like he was interested in what was going on. Or even...jealous?

We'd flirted since he'd gotten back from Seattle, but besides the one tug of my hair—holy fuck me sideways— he'd been stiff ever since. Maybe I was misinterpreting his intentions all over again. Mr. Long-Term Relationship probably didn't care if Malcolm and I had a little banter. Right?

"If y'all are free, my family is having a summer barbecue tomorrow night. We'd love for you to join us," Malcolm said.

"Appreciate the offer," Whitt said, "but we'll be back in Lubbock by then."

"If the hotels weren't all booked, I'd say we should stay another night," I said apologetically.

"Completely understand. The rodeo eats up the entire town. Next time."

"Sounds good."

"I'll send over the final paperwork when I get back into the office on Monday," Whitt said, shaking hands with Malcolm one more time.

Then, we were striding away from the empty, old oil land and back to his Lexus. It stood out in the dusty, desolate fields. We probably would have been better off with my 4Runner, but after the timing belt issue, I wasn't sure it would make many more Midland trips. I needed to reserve them for Bailey.

"Where to now?"

"It's late. We should probably go eat at the hotel and crash. We'll have to leave early in the morning."

I rolled my eyes as we slid into the car. "Absolutely not. The hotel will be swamped with rodeo guys, and we need actual food."

"You have a suggestion, Houston?"

"Yes, sir," I teased. It was the first time since we'd checked in that he turned his full attention to me. His lips were slightly parted. Those big blue eyes roamed my face. I wondered what he was thinking in that moment. "I know just the place."

He turned the car on. "Lead the way."

Fifteen minutes later, we were striding inside a hole-in-the-wall barbecue joint, attached to a ratty, old gas station. In Texas, the best barbecue was always one step away from a dump. It had a tin roof and leaned slightly to the left. The tables were old picnic benches, and dry air blew in from the screened-in windows. Out back was a bar the length of the place, where regulars came and got drunk on pulled pork and ribs slathered in their signature spicy sauce.

Whitton parked his rather conspicuous Lexus in between a set of Harley-Davidson motorcycles and an old junker pickup with more rust damage than body left.

"Where the hell have you taken me?"

"Only the best barbecue in the state."

Whitton looked skeptically at the building. "It looks one step away from a health violation."

I put my hand to my chest. "How dare you! Lee's is an institution."

"If you say so."

I strode around the car and grabbed his arm, tugging

him toward the restaurant. "I swear, Whitton, we're going to have to find your sense of adventure."

"I know precisely where my sense of adventure is."

"Oh, yeah?" I asked, linking our arms together.

"Yeah. Locked up tight in a vault with everything else I don't have time for."

I leaned my head against his enormous bicep and looked up at him through thick lashes. "Well, hand over the key to your vault, Wright. I'm here to get you out of your comfort zone."

"But comfort zones are comfortable."

"Here's the deal," I said, dragging him to a stop before the door. "We're off the clock. No one here knows who you are. No one here even cares. Just trust me and have some fun at least until we get home."

His eyes searched mine for a second, as if waiting for the rug pull. I didn't have one. This was my hometown. As complicated as my relationship was with it, we could have a good time here. A chance that we never really gave ourselves back home. Not with the entire town watching our every move and me still too fucked up by what had happened with Arnold. Why couldn't we have some fun?

"Fine," he said with a sigh. "You win."

"Oh, I usually do."

Then, I pulled him inside before he could argue.

I ordered heaps of food and cold Mexican Cokes. Whitton insisted on paying, and I didn't even argue since it was going on the company per diem.

"To fun," I said, holding up my glass bottle of Coke.

He clinked his glass against mine. "To fun."

The food arrived ten minutes later with meat, potato salad, and macaroni and cheese piled high on oversize Styrofoam plates. We dug in, and it was just as incredible as

I remembered. I hadn't been here in years. My throat closed up at the thought.

"Well, you were right. It's incredible," Whitt said. He licked the sticky sauce off of his fingers.

"I know."

"How'd you hear about this place?"

"Gram used to bring me here all the time. She knew the owner before he passed and his son took over."

"Are you close with your grandma?"

"I was," I said, emphasizing the past tense.

His face fell. "Sorry. I didn't know."

"Yeah. She passed last year." I swallowed back the lump in my throat. "It was a lot. I still miss her."

I nearly choked on those words. I hadn't spoken about my grandma to anyone. She'd practically raised me, been my safe harbor, and when she got dementia, the world turned upside down. Her loss had made everything exponentially harder.

"I'm sorry, Eve."

His hand reached across the picnic table and covered mine. Electricity shot through me at the touch. The pads of his fingers sent shock waves through my system. It would have been easy to lean into that, but I didn't want sympathy. Sympathy made me uncomfortable in the same way that adventure made him uncomfortable. I didn't need to be vulnerable with anyone. I could handle it.

I pulled my hand back with a laugh. "Yeah. It's fine. She was in her eighties. What can you do?" I jumped to my feet. "You done?"

He nodded, and I snatched up his plate to toss it. But not before I saw the look on his face that said I was a mystery he was trying to solve. I dumped our plates in the trash can and felt Whitt follow me. I really didn't want to make a big deal out of this. Not when I'd just gotten him to relax some. I was about to put on some heavy bravado when I heard the worst thing in the entire world.

"Evie Jo? Is that really you?"

I groaned. "No, no, no," I muttered under my breath.

But I turned around anyway to see Rusty Cook eating up the short distance with his long legs. I straightened at the sight of him, my back going up to protect myself. He was a man in his fifties in tattered overalls and a flannel underneath with oil-rig-tanned skin and greasy hair, pulled back into a ponytail. And unfortunately, I'd known him most of my life.

"Evie Jo, that *is* you."

"Hello, Rusty."

Whitt looked between us, adjusting his posture so that he appeared even taller than he was. As if he could be a physical shield between me and this man. I didn't know how he'd read me that quickly, but I hadn't wanted to see anyone that I knew from home. Not with Whitt at my side. Not when I was dressed like I didn't belong here anymore.

"Shoot. I almost didn't recognize ya," he said with a head tip in my direction. "Look at that fancy outfit. Ya look like a classy lady."

"Thank you."

"Who's ya friend?" Rusty asked.

His expression wasn't exactly kind as he looked at Whitt. No one around here liked outsiders. And Whitton, with his fancy suit and shiny shoes, definitely didn't belong.

"Rusty, this is Whitton. We work together. Just here today for business. We actually have to get going."

"Well, I don't wanna keep ya, but I had to come say howdy." Then, he continued on as if I hadn't said we needed to leave. Typical. "Saw your pa round church last week. He misses ya, ya know? Good man, your pa."

I jerked slightly backward at that phrase. A good man. A *good* man. "I'm so glad, Rusty, but really, we have to go."

"Course, course. I'm gonna tell him that I saw ya. Ya been down to see him yet?"

"No," I bit out. "No, I haven't."

Whitton didn't miss my inflection that time. He took the step between me and Rusty, who was still running his mouth off, and cleared his throat. "We're going to be going. Have a nice day."

Rusty finally shut up. He looked up, up, up at Whitton's intimidating frame before nodding. "Oh, sure. Good seeing you, Evie Jo."

I waved good-bye and let Whitt hustle me out of there. By the time I was back out in the fresh air, I'd let the anger pass, and I was tired all over again. I should have thought about who I'd see at Lee's, but I'd been so excited to take Whitt out of his comfort zone that I hadn't considered what stepping into mine would mean.

To Whitt's credit, he didn't ask me any questions. He must have seen that I didn't want to talk about it. Bless him.

"So..." he finally said once we were back on the road. I braced for the worst. "You know the closest liquor store?"

I whipped my head to him. "What?"

"Is there a liquor store nearby?"

"We're in Texas. There are liquor stores on every block."

"Good."

"You want a drink?" I asked in surprise.

I'd heard West joke that drunk Whitt was the best Whitt, but I'd never seen it before. He'd always been buttoned-up Whitt in my presence.

"You said we were off the clock, right?"

"Yes..."

"We should celebrate our success today."

Just like that, he'd walked away from the complication that I didn't have any interest in addressing and pulled us right back into the game we'd been playing since he'd gotten back from Seattle.

I grinned devilishly. I could use a drink. "Turn left."

9

WHITTON

"Still can't believe they had Wright wine in the liquor store," Eve said as we carried our purchases upstairs. She hefted the bottle of red for me to see. "It has your *name* on it."

"Yeah. It's weird."

Wright Vineyard had been started by Jordan, Julian, and Hollin as a joint venture. Between Jordan's business acumen, Julian's charisma, and Hollin's vineyard work, it had taken off beyond their wildest dreams. They'd won state wine awards, and they were now distributing into most of Texas, New Mexico, Oklahoma, and Colorado.

"Is it weird, working at a company of your namesake?"

"I've gotten used to it." I swiped the key card against the door and gestured for her to go in before me.

To be honest, working at Wright was both as weird as she'd made it out to be and more incredible than I'd imagined.

Eve stepped inside, glanced at the bed, and then quickly away.

My eyes landed on it, too.

One bed.

Fuck me. How had my assistant gotten this so wrong?

Not that I didn't want to hoist Eve over my shoulder, throw her down on the single bed in the room, and bury my cock in her. But there was more than one complication with that scenario. Starting with colleagues and ending with what had happened after the wedding. And everything in between was the way I wanted to wrap my hand around her throat and hold her down as I fucked her...and how that would probably scare her off forever.

I set the bottles of wine down on the desk and shifted my dick while she had her back turned. God, I was going to have blue balls for days if I didn't take care of this.

"I have an idea!" Eve whipped around a second later.

I quickly moved my hand. "An idea?"

She rummaged through her bag and held up two very small articles of clothing. That was *not* helping.

"What's that?"

"Hot tub," she said with a smile. "Still want to have some fun, sir?"

Yes. Fuck yes, I did.

"I didn't bring trunks," was what came out of my mouth.

"I'm sure you brought something to lounge in. You do lounge, right?"

I arched an eyebrow. "I do."

"Then, let's go."

"I don't think that's a good idea."

Unless she wanted me to fuck her.

"Well, you're wrong."

She waggled her eyebrows at me and darted into the bathroom. The door shut with a click, and I pushed my palm hard against my cock. I could not have a boner right now. I couldn't change out of my suit or else she'd definitely fucking notice. My lounge shorts in a hot tub...it was a recipe for disaster.

A few minutes later, Eve opened the door again, and this time, she was in the tiny scrap of clothing she called a bikini. It was a hibiscus floral pattern in a square neck across her impressive rack with bottoms that came up high on her hips. Every ounce of ink was visible on her voluptuous body. She did a little twirl to reveal the full thong back of the bottoms.

I wanted to bite my fist to keep myself from reaching for her. Because, fuck, I wanted to reach for her. Wanted it something desperately. Her *entire* ass was on display. This was ten times worse than assless chaps. Fuck, fuck, fuck.

"Well, Wright, you game? We're still off the clock."

I forced down every vulgar thought I had at the sight of her. "Fine. I'll meet you down there."

She grinned, swinging a towel over her shoulder. "Sounds good. Bring the drinks!"

Then, she scampered off for the hotel hot tub. Lord help me if there were a ton of rodeo cowboys in the pool. I might have to evacuate the premises.

As soon as the door shut behind her, I stripped out of my suit and turned the shower to its coldest setting. The shock of the change in temperature jolted me to reality. I shivered in the freezing cold and only stepped out when I felt like I could put my shorts on without being at full mast for the entire hotel.

Once I toweled off, I changed into my shorts and a T-shirt and grabbed the alcohol on the way down. This was likely going to be a disaster, but how could I deny her when I'd seen her in that bikini? If she'd been wearing that after the wedding, I might have done whatever she wanted then, too.

I took the elevator to the main floor and swiped my key card to allow access to the pool. Blessedly, the hotel pool and hot tub were empty, save for Eve, who was already lounging in the bubbling water. Her head was tipped back, and I could see the full column of her throat. So much for the cold shower.

The door snapped shut noisily, and she lifted her head. "Took you long enough."

I shrugged without giving an explanation. It wasn't like I was about to tell her about the cold shower.

I dropped my towel on a table next to hers and set to opening the bottle of wine. I'd snagged the plastic cups from our room. It wasn't fancy, but it would do.

I took both cups into the heated water. "Here you go."

She took the cup. "Thanks."

I sank into the stone seat across from her and took a sip of the wine. "It's pretty good."

"Surely, you've had Wright wine before."

"Of course. They had it at the wedding."

Her eyes sparkled in the dim light. "Oh, I remember. I think I imbibed half the vineyard."

"You weren't that bad."

"Oh?" She arched an eyebrow. "That's not how I remember it."

"How do you remember it?"

She shrugged. "The same way you do."

"That I very much doubt," I told her.

I downed the contents of my first glass and set it down on the side of the hot tub. I waited for her to talk more about the wedding. Were we finally going to have this conversation? After all this time, she'd refused to discuss it.

She met my gaze. Her eyes were pensive. "Why didn't you ask about the guy at Lee's?"

I blinked at the change of subject. "Did you want me to?"

"No," she said at once.

"Well then...good."

"It was good. But I don't understand why you let it go."

"The guy was a jerk," I growled. "He either didn't realize or didn't care that you were uncomfortable. I don't care who he was or why he made you feel that way. All that mattered was that he left you alone."

She tilted her head. "You know you're not a real knight in shining armor, right? I can take care of myself."

"I know you can," I told her. "But you weren't."

"I wasn't what?"

"Taking care of yourself." I rested my arms back against the lip of the pool. "So, I did it myself."

Her mouth opened into a small O before quickly returning to neutral. She took a long gulp of her wine and then hopped out of the tub. I watched her toned ass as she strode toward the table and lifted the bottle of wine.

"Refill?"

I cleared my throat. "Sure."

She brought the bottle to the pool and poured wine into my cup. She set the bottle down next to the hot tub, then slipped back into the water. She brought the red liquid to her already-red lips and sipped as she watched me intently. I didn't know what was behind those emerald eyes, but I was transfixed. I couldn't have looked away if I wanted to.

"You really don't want to know why he made me uncomfortable?"

Was I interested? Of course. The situation had seemed screwed up. There must be a reason that she wasn't talking about her family. From that one small interaction, I had a pretty good reason why. But I wasn't going to force her to talk about it if she didn't want to.

"Honestly, it was enough to see that he did. If you want to tell me, I am all ears."

She shook her head. "No, just trying to figure out who you are."

"I'm an open book."

She stepped forward until she was between my spread legs. We weren't quite touching, but the hot tub wasn't the only thing heating up. I lifted my chin to catch her gaze. It took every ounce of my self-control to not lunge for her when she was this close.

"I don't think you are," Eve finally said.

"This is who I am."

"I don't think so." She reached forward with a wet hand and coiled the front of my hair around her finger.

"Careful," I growled.

She shivered at the word. "Or what?"

And she certainly didn't stop. Her hand pushed back into my hair, brushing it back off of my face. I reached up on reflex and grasped her wrist in my hand. She froze at the force of the movement. Our gazes locked on one another.

"I said, careful."

"I heard you," she said in a breathy voice. I'd never heard it from her before, and it made my balls tighten with need.

"You don't listen very well."

"No," she agreed.

I still had her wrist in my hand. Fuck, I wanted to pull her forward and claim those cherry-red lips. Take her right here in the hot tub. My blood pumped harder in my veins as the time stretched between us.

Then, I released her hastily and shifted in my seat. "What are you doing?"

"I told you, I'm trying to figure out who you are. You've been flirting with me since we started working together."

I scoffed, "You've been flirting with me."

"Well, yes," she said with a soft laugh. "But you've been flirting back." I opened my mouth, and she covered it with her hand. "Don't deny it."

I pulled her hand away from my mouth. "I wasn't going to deny it."

"Really?" she asked, surprised. "Then, what do you want?"

"The same thing I wanted last time."

This woman drove me entirely mad. I knew if I had her even once, I'd never want to let her go. Sex would be fun, but would it be enough?

"What if I can't give you that?"

She took the final step into me. Our chests nearly touching. Her other hand worked its way down my bare chest. My Adam's apple bobbed as she moved lower and lower.

"You're going to be the death of me."

Her grin was devilish. "You can't deny you want this."

I grasped her harshly by her hips and jerked her forward into my lap. Her legs slid onto either side of mine. She settled down harshly against my lounge shorts, which, as expected, hid *nothing*. My cock was hard and ready for her. And she realized it as well. Her eyes widened in shock and then to satisfaction. A slow Cheshire cat smile painted on her lips as she sank her weight fully onto my lap.

"Fuck," she gasped.

She shifted her hips side to side, as if to get comfortable. The friction only made me lengthen against the surface of her very tiny bikini bottoms. I gripped her hips harder.

"I'm a relationship guy, Eve."

"And I'm over relationships. Guess we're at a stalemate."

She was saying one thing, but she meant something else entirely. She meant, *Come over to my side. Come to the dark side. Give up relationships and get lost in me instead.* I could see it all over her tempting mouth and in the shine of her diamond eyes.

This was what had happened after the wedding. I said that I wanted more. She'd said this was all she had to give. Someone had fucked her up so bad that she refused to consider any other option. And I knew all too well that outside of a relationship, my sexual preferences weren't desired.

One of us had to break.

It might as well be me.

10

EVE

There was no sweet seduction. Whitt slid his wet hands up into my hair and crushed our lips together.

The tang of red wine coated his tongue as he delved into my mouth. We'd kissed...once. A soft thing on my doorstep after the wedding. More a good-bye than a start to anything. It had been an opening gambit to a long game.

This was the closing. An endgame move.

He was claiming the queen and dragging the piece to his side by force. Nothing could have stopped me from hanging on for dear life under the force of his kiss. There might as well not have been another kiss. Nothing compared to this. To him ravaging my mouth with a quick, controlled precision that said he had been thinking of exactly how to take me apart piece by piece.

And I was keen on letting him.

"Oh," I gasped against his mouth.

He smirked, pulling back slightly with my bottom lip between his teeth. He slowly released it, and I had to shift to keep from combusting at the look of satisfied possession on his face.

I hadn't been lying when I said that I was trying to figure out who he was. Every time I felt like I understood exactly who Whitt was, I was surprised all over again. On the outside, he looked like the uptight businessman. Rigid with his commitments and unyielding in his principles. There was no room for someone as flexible as I was in a life like that. I'd only just started to put myself back together after the last time I tried to mold myself to another's idea of me. I didn't want that again.

And here was Whitton Wright, bending to my whim. A man I'd never thought would crack under the pressure of my seduction. Let alone throw out his entire rule book to get his hands on me.

"This is what you want?" he asked. His powerful hands slid their way over my wet skin. He traced the line of my peony shoulder tattoo, across my ribs, under my breasts, and along my navel, heading south.

I arched into his touch. "Yes. God, yes."

His hands went under the water, still tracing the outline of my body. The pads of his fingers ran along the line of my bikini bottom. Not dipping any lower, even when I adjusted myself to try to get him to go exactly where I wanted him. One strong hand landed on my thigh. He was running his fingers over my dream catcher.

His mouth went to my throat, and he worked his tongue up until he sucked gently on my earlobe. "I like your ink," he growled into my ear. "I want to trace every inch of it with my tongue."

I gasped, pushing my hands up into his thick hair. "By all means."

His fingers dug into my thigh, holding me tighter against him. His cock jutting upward. Only two strips of thin material kept me from impaling myself on him. And,

Christ, was he enormous. I'd silently hoped that the size of his hands and his over-six-feet height meant what I thought it meant. But now, there was no question in my mind, except how I was going to fit the entire thing inside of me.

"We should go upstairs," he said. "And I'll do just that."

"I don't think you're fit to leave this hot tub."

"Hmm," he said. "I guess you'll have to fix that."

I pulled back and looked into his eyes in surprise. I hadn't expected public anything would pique Whitt's interest.

"That so?"

He held my gaze as his fingers moved upward, tugging the material on my bikini aside and slipping one finger down the seam of my pussy. I gasped both in pleasure and shock. Where had my good guy gone, and when had he become this daring? And why was I twice as turned on by the thought of doing this in public with him?

"Like this?" he asked and thrust a finger inside of me.

My head dropped back, and a strangled, "Yes," escaped me.

He withdrew his finger and inserted two the next time. My entire body shuddered. His thumb found my clit and circled it as he worked up a slow, controlled rhythm.

"I...I was thinking your...cock," I gasped as I rode his hand.

"You'll get my cock," he assured me. "You'll get it when I'm good and ready to give it to you."

"Yes, sir," I said, only half-teasing with the nickname.

His free hand tightened on my hip, almost to the point of pain. It only intensified everything all at once.

"I want you to come for me first. Get you good and ready to take me."

"I..."

Whatever I'd been about to say flitted from my mind as his mouth descended on my breast. He nipped at my nipple, dragging it between his teeth through the fabric. It pebbled at his insistence. All while his fingers thrust in and out of me.

"Fuck, I've dreamed about your tits."

I inhaled sharply. "You have?"

His gaze found mine briefly before he pushed one strap of my top off of my shoulder, baring me before him. There, he could see my erect nipple and full breast. We were in a public place, and I should have cared, but somehow, I didn't.

His head descended again. His tongue trailed along my breast before he took my nipple in his mouth, sending shock waves down my body. Everything came to a head at once. His mouth against my nipple. His fingers and hard cock grinding against my exposed pussy. The water lapped against my clit as his thumb applied the perfect amount of pressure. I stood no chance.

"Whitt," I gasped.

"Come for me. Come now," he ordered.

And there was no holding back. My back arched, pressing my breasts against his chest, and I came hard in the water. An incoherent whimper left my mouth as I came down off the high.

"Fuck, that was beautiful. I need to fuck you now."

"Yes," I gasped.

He shucked his lounge shorts to the bottom of the hot tub, and I got my first distorted view of his cock. My mouth salivated at the sight of him. He was every inch as glorious as I'd suspected he was. A slight flicker of fear ran through me. I was turned on. I'd just come. And still...he was massive.

"You can take it," he told me, as if reading my expression.

"You'll be gentle?" I asked with a smirk on my lips.

"No. No, I won't."

My pussy pulsed at the words and the firm grasp of his hips as he guided me down onto his cock. I groaned in unrestrained desire and agony at the first feel of him. He was going to tear me apart. Every single part of me wanted him to do his worst.

For the first time, I was starting to wonder if I had misjudged my good guy. He might be good, but he was pure *bad* in bed.

I was halfway saddled on him when he got impatient and thrust upward. My hands clamped down on his big, broad shoulders, and his landed on my ass, dragging me down as he jerked upward. A muffled moan of pleasure came out of his mouth, and it might have been the hottest thing I'd ever heard.

"Eve," he groaned. "You feel...fucking incredible."

"You're...you're pretty incredible yourself," I managed to get out as I was fully seated on his impressive cock.

"This is going to be quick," he said when our eyes met. "I'm going to fuck you hard and fast because I cannot hold out any longer. I need to come inside your pussy."

"Yes," I pleaded.

Whitt took that as all the permission he needed. Even though I was on top, he was in complete control. His hands on my ass were the leverage he needed to lift me up and slam me back down on top of him. The water made me practically weightless. I met each of his precise thrusts with a push down until we were a tidal wave in the hot, bubbling water.

I didn't think he'd be able to heat me up again so fast.

But watching him work my body sent me into a frenzy. The feel of his cock pounding inside of me over and over again. The part of his lips as he got closer to the edge. The smack of skin on skin.

Any minute, someone could burst into the pool. The hotel was, after all, full of cowboys. A fact that I thought Whitt would care about. But if he didn't, then I certainly wasn't going to say anything about it. Not with his cock inside of me. My breasts exposed to the entire place. An orgasm already rocketing through me.

"Fuck," he snarled. "Eve..."

"Yes," I gasped.

His nails dug into my hips. "Goddamn it, I'm going to come. Are you going to come?"

It was a statement, worded as a question. There was only one answer.

And I responded by leaning back and crying out into the echo chamber of the indoor pool. He grunted as my orgasm triggered his that he'd been holding on to by a hair trigger.

Then, his mouth was on mine again, needy and demanding. Our lips colliding as we both came down from a powerful climax that left my legs shaking. Finally, finally, he released me.

A small sigh puffed out of his lips. His eyes half-lidded. It was the filthiest look I'd ever seen in my life. And as inconceivable as it was, I was turned on again.

His thumb reached up and brushed across my bottom lip. I stuck my tongue out and grazed the digit. His eyes heated again.

Just then the door to the pool opened, and a host of rowdy cowboys barreled inside, carrying a few pizza boxes and a case of Miller Lite. I hastily pulled my top back into place so they couldn't see my bare breasts. For a second, I thought that he might revert to the regular Whitt. That their interruption would remind him we were in a public place.

But he just lifted me off of him and said, "Get your ass upstairs so I can fuck you again the way I want to."

The growl in his voice sent a shiver straight back to my pussy. It didn't matter that I'd come twice in quick succession. I was more than ready to do it again.

"Hot tub time!" the first cowboy cried.

"All yours." And then I scampered out of the hot tub.

Whitt discreetly pulled his shorts back on and followed me out as it was commandeered by the rodeo guys. I wrapped a towel around my chest while Whitt grabbed the bottle of wine, tossed our glasses, and then took my hand, all but dragging me toward the exit.

We were both still dripping wet when we stumbled into the empty elevator. I fumbled for our floor number as he slammed me backward into the wall. Our mouths fit together as he kissed me. My body molded to his. Two pieces coming together to become one.

His hand slid low, pushing aside my towel and cupping my pussy. I gasped against him, and he just grinned.

"Going to own this tonight, baby."

I purred against his chest, "Yes, sir."

The elevator dinged open. Whitt grabbed my hand again, and together, we hurried down the hall to the only room available in the entire establishment. Even if we'd had two rooms, we only would have used one. He tapped the key card against the entrance, and we fell inside.

Towels dropped on the floor. I pulled the strings of my bikini top, letting it follow. My bottoms went next and then his shorts. My jaw dropped open at the sight of his cock in all its glory. The water had not done it justice, and my pussy clenched in shock that I'd been able to handle all of that. Let alone on top of him.

"Come here," he growled.

His hand snaked out to grasp the back of my neck and tug me into him. Our lips collided once more as we fell backward onto the bed. His hips settled between my spread legs. His cock poised to take what he'd already claimed.

"So much for deciding who gets the bed," I teased as I nipped at his bottom lip.

"If I had it my way, you'd be on my cock all night."

"Have it your way."

He smirked. "Think you can handle me all night, baby?"

He punctuated his question by rubbing his hard cock against the folds of my pussy. I shuddered at the friction. The feel of my own wetness coating him. The rough brush against my already-sensitive clit.

"Only one way to find out," I challenged.

He grinned, a wicked thing like I'd never seen on his features. It made me want to get on my knees and beg. I'd crawl for him. I'd do anything he wanted if only he would give me all that his solid body and dirty mouth were offering.

He pulled back then. I made a sound of protest, but he just grabbed my hips and flipped me over. I scrambled onto all fours.

"Ass up," he commanded as he pushed my head down into the mattress.

His hands moved over the bottom of my ass. I knew it was a sight to behold. I did enough squats and dead lifts and hip thrusts to make it as round and juicy as it was. All those days of sweating in the gym had really paid off for this moment. I was going to have to tell my personal trainer that I had a new ambition. Not just having the greatest ass possible, but an ass that would make Whitt Wright want to spank it. A girl had to have goals.

I saw God the first time he thrust into me. My body could barely contain him at this angle. It was as deep as it would go. I could practically feel his cock in my stomach.

My hands clenched into the hotel comforter. "Fuck."

Maybe he was right. He'd called my bluff. I wasn't sure I *could* handle him all night. Not if I had to walk tomorrow. Or drive back to Lubbock. Oh fuck.

"That's right," he said, thrusting in and out again. "Let your filthy pussy take it. Take it all. Every"—he slammed into me harder—"single"—again—"inch."

I rocked forward with the force of his last thrust. I was incoherent with need as he railed into me. His hands tugging my hips backward, the wet smacking of his balls against my clit. y vision went in and out, and it took all of my strength to not let my arms give out.

Before our time in the hot tub, I would have said there was no way he could bring me to climax twice. Let alone three times. Now, I was bent forward at the waist—my face in the mattress, his hands on my ass, his cock buried in my pussy—and I was pretty sure he could make me come until I saw heavenly bodies.

"Oh—oh God," I gasped. "Please. Please."

My murmurs turned incomprehensible. He just chuckled and sped up. Then, it all hit a crescendo at the same time.

He roared behind me, emptying deep inside of my pussy. I screamed his name into the hotel, hoping that every cowboy in the place heard me do it. Then, I collapsed forward against the bed. Sweaty, panting, and exhausted, I crawled to put my head against a pillow and promptly passed out.

11

WHITTON

The next morning should have been awkward.

Instead, I'd rolled Eve over, fucked her senseless for a third time in so many hours, and then we packed up and drove home. We didn't even mention it on the drive. I let her pick the music, but not drive the car. There was only so much bending a man could take.

Once we got into Lubbock, she kissed me long and hard and drove herself home in her beat-up 4Runner that continued to cause her problems. And I'd sat in the parking lot, wondering what in the fuck I had just done.

I was still trying to figure it out on Monday morning as I worked on the paperwork for the Midland survey. Instead, my mind could only replay in *vivid* detail exactly what had happened after we completed the survey. The taste of her skin and the round of her ass and the feel of her dripping wet pussy.

"Fuck," I growled, low and irritable.

If I didn't get my thoughts under control, I was going to get hard at my desk. And there was nothing I could fucking do about it here. My hand certainly wouldn't sate what Eve had awakened when she offered me a taste of her sweet sin.

"Knock, knock," a voice said.

I cleared my throat, erasing the memories from my conscious mind, and turned to find Jensen and Jordan standing outside of my office. You'd guess they were siblings rather than cousins at first glance. It still surprised me that we all looked so much alike. If I'd had any real doubts about whether we were all related, it'd died with our appearance.

"Hey. How can I help you?" I came to my feet, buttoning my suit coat closed.

"You already are," Jensen said. "Whitton, meet my son, Colton."

He gestured behind him where a little mini me stood broodily. He was already almost as tall as his dad at only fifteen. His dark hair was long and moppish in what must be the current fashion. He was in a suit, and he wore it like he'd been born into it. A slouchy, disinterested posture painted across his figure.

To his credit, he met my eye straight on when he was introduced and held his hand out. "Nice to meet you."

So, maybe he wasn't a total shit. Just an entitled one who had grown up incredibly privileged. A fallen prince.

I shook his hand—hard. "So, you're my new intern?"

"So they tell me."

Jensen cleared his throat, and Colton shot his father an irritated look.

"I mean, yes." His eyes snapped back to me. "Sir. Yes, sir. Happy to be here."

The words were there, but the sincerity was lacking. What had I thought would happen anyway? He'd been sent here, likely against his will, for the shit he'd pulled back in

New York. So, I wasn't just saddled with the boss's kid, but a surly, unrepentant one. Well, I could work with that.

"Great. I like my coffee with one cream and two sugars. It's down the hall, to the left."

"Coffee," Colton repeated.

"At least he's not sending you to Monomyth for the good stuff," Jordan said with a smirk.

"They have good coffee in this town?" Colton asked with a quirk of his lips. "Doubtful."

"Unfortunately, no coffee runs. He won't have his license until February," Jensen said.

Colton mumbled under his breath, "I won't need a license in the city."

"If you go back," Jensen said through his teeth. He reached his hand out again. "Thanks again."

"No problem. I can handle this."

Jordan clapped Jensen on the shoulder and gestured for him to leave. The worried father looked back once at his troubled son and then disappeared from my office with Jordan. Colton waited for him to get on the elevator before sinking into a chair and kicking his feet up.

"Glad that's over. Can you tell them I'm doing a good job and, like, let me out of prison?"

I brushed his feet off of my desk. "Listen here. I don't give two shits who you were in New York City, but here, you're nobody. A nobody who is now my responsibility. You can drop the poor little rich-boy act. It isn't going to work on me." I watched his cool expression morph into dismay. "I have a lot of work to do, and I'm not babysitting. You're here to work."

"But—"

"Coffee, one cream, two sugars."

Colton slowly came to his feet again. His jaw was

clenched, and he looked ready to argue. Thankfully, he was smarter than that. "Fine."

"My assistant can get you up to speed while I finish this, and then we can sit down later and figure out what exactly I'm going to use you for in this office. Understood?"

"Sure," he said and then sulked from the office.

I watched him leave with a sigh. That was going to be a work in progress. And probably not a fun one.

———

The rest of the week was much the same with Colton. I shouldn't have been surprised that he wasn't going to suddenly and miraculously turn into a good worker. He was a *hard* worker at least. He did everything that was asked of him, but not a single thing beyond the scope. Half the time, I found him dicking around on his phone. I'd realized quickly that Jensen had put some kind of block on it and he was trying to circumnavigate it. So, he could be clever when he wanted to be. Maybe, one day, I'd figure out how to get him to use that for something other than moping about his circumstances.

By the time Friday afternoon rolled around, I was exhausted from him. I'd said I wasn't babysitting, but fuck if it hadn't slowed me down considerably. Especially since it turned out that he terrified my assistant. No wonder he'd been given to me. A fifteen-year-old shouldn't be this much work.

"Is your dad coming to pick you up?" I asked as we headed downstairs.

"Emery," he said, typing on his phone.

"Do they know you hacked your phone?"

Colton jerked the phone to his chest. His eyes narrowed. "Who said I hacked my phone?"

"I did."

He assessed me. "Are you going to tell them?"

"Do I look like your parent?"

"No?" he asked cautiously.

"Correct."

He looked suspicious. His brow furrowing as if he were waiting for the punch line. When none came, he said, "Thanks."

"Yeah. Just don't be stupid. What are your plans this weekend?"

"As if there's anything to do in this bumfuck town."

I laughed. "Fair. I grew up in Seattle. It does feel small. But doesn't your dad have a lake house?"

"He won't let me go," he grumbled.

"Probably earned that."

Colton shot me a dirty look.

"Well, there's an indoor soccer game tonight. I don't know if a city boy like you would be interested in something like that."

He frowned. "What's in it for you?"

"Believe it or not, people do things that have no benefit for them at all."

A car pulled up at that moment, stopping directly in front of us. The window rolled down, and Emery smiled at us both. "Hey, Colt. Let's get going."

"Can I go to a soccer game with Whitt tonight?"

Emery bit her lip and looked up at me. "Uh, we'll have to ask your dad. You want him to go?"

"Sounds like he needs to get out of the house," I said with a shrug.

"Yeah," she said, and her eyes told the story of what it

must be like, living with a disgruntled teenager right now. "We'll ask Jensen, okay?"

"He's going to say no," he muttered and then got into the passenger seat and stared out the window.

"Good luck," I said with a laugh.

She sighed again. "Yeah. Thanks, Whitt."

I had serious doubts that Colton would be there tonight. And since it would be the first time I'd see Eve since last weekend, maybe it would be for the better.

***

"Go out there and kick ass," West said as he planted a kiss on Nora's lips.

She laughed. "Uh, I think I kind of suck, but thanks."

"You'll do great."

I rolled my eyes as West drew his girlfriend in closer. They were saccharine sweet. I was happy for my brother, but the public displays were sometimes too much. And I wasn't the only one.

"Get your hands off my sister," Campbell said, punching West in the shoulder.

"Campbell, shut the fuck up," Nora said with an eye roll. "You're always all over Blaire."

"Yeah, well, Blaire isn't anyone's little sister."

"That's a ridiculous double standard."

I tuned out my friends as my eyes roved the indoor soccer center for the woman who occupied my thoughts and dreams. With the way she operated, she'd probably be running in after the game already started. The only time I'd known her to be on time was when someone else was driving her.

I checked my phone to see if she'd texted and found a message from an unknown number. I clicked on it.

Dad said no

Its Colt btw

Obvs

I shook my head. This kid. I hadn't given him my personal cell. Had he hacked my phone, too?

It was worth asking, I suppose. Dare I ask, how exactly did you get my number?

Bruh

Do u always rite in complete sentences

I do, in fact. Do you always have shit grammar?

I do IN FACT bruv

You're exhausting.

Facts

Live stream that shit 4 me

Ur girl playing?

He really *had* hacked my phone. What a shit.

I don't know what you're talking about.

The girl.

U txt her all day

I'm ending this conversation now. Be there on Monday morning.

Bffr bruh tell me who wins

I closed my phone and shook my head at Colton Wright, adding him as a contact. It was interesting to learn multiple things from that conversation. He was super bright when he applied himself to his interests. He *had* interests. He'd probably played soccer back in New York. And he was too goddamn observant.

Also, he wasn't wrong.

Where exactly was the beautiful woman that I couldn't stop texting?

"Hey, you," a voice said behind me.

I whipped around to find Eve dressed in her Tacos uniform. The red T-shirt, sponsored by Wright Vineyard, and Adidas soccer shorts with a bag slung over her shoulder and her indoor shoes in her hand.

"You're on time."

She snorted. "I'm never late for soccer."

"I see where your priorities are."

"Some of us enjoy our hobbies more than our job," she teased. Her hand came to the front of my black polo and traced the buttons. "Look at you. No tie."

"I can dress down," I told her with an arched eyebrow. "I have lounge shorts."

Pink tinted her cheeks, and I relished even the slightest blush on her tan skin.

"Fair."

"Come on, bish," Blaire said, slinging her arm across Eve's shoulders. "We have a tournament to dominate."

"Hell yes," Eve said. She winked at me. "See you after."

My eyes followed her the entire way onto the field, where she'd get ready and warm up. My cock wondering exactly what we were going to be doing later. How quickly could I get her naked after this?

"What the fuck was that?" West asked.

Nora had followed the girls onto the field to play the game, leaving us all alone.

"What was what?"

"You and Eve. I thought that was over months ago."

I shrugged. I didn't have to say anything for my brother to know exactly what was happening. And I wasn't ready to discuss it with him anyway. I wasn't sure what we even were at this point. All I knew was that I'd bent until I broke, and I'd do it over and over again for this girl.

12

EVE

We won the first game five–nil and the second game two–nil, which put us in the championship match on Sunday afternoon. My legs felt like they'd been run over. After nearly a hundred eighty minutes of continuous play, I was surprised that I could still stand.

"I need a shower," Julian said.

Hollin cackled, shaking out his long hair, raining sweat down on the rest of the players.

"Gross, Hollin!" Annie said, smacking him on his sweaty chest. "I do not understand how Piper puts up with you."

"She doesn't," Julian said. "She puts him in his place."

"Fucker," Hollin said. He grabbed Julian by the neck and mussed his hair, which had somehow stayed perfectly in place the entire two games.

"Hey!" Julian roared.

And then the two were on the ground, wrestling. Like idiots.

I looked up at Annie, Nora, and Blaire. We all shook our heads and promptly left the guys to their stupid behavior. I stripped out of my T-shirt, dropping it into my bag and stretching my arms overhead.

"Pizza?" Annie asked.

"I could go for a very large cold beer," Blaire said.

"You're such a pick-me," Annie teased.

Blaire stuck her tongue out at her as she slid on her signature baseball cap. "You're lucky I love you."

"Should I even ask what the fuck Hollin is doing?" Piper asked when she reached us.

"Wrestling," Nora offered. "They're guys. I still don't know what to make of him, and he's my brother."

"Bless you," Blaire said with a laugh, patting Piper's shoulder.

"I'm going to kill him," Piper muttered under her breath.

"What about you, Eve?" Blaire asked. "Pizza?"

"Definitely."

Even though I'd never been the silent type a day in my life, I still sometimes couldn't believe that I fit in here with these girls. That I could just settle in here and it all made sense. I didn't even have to join in the conversation as it flowed seamlessly around me. I wasn't a speed bump. It was the best feeling.

"Turn the Jeep on; it's a thousand degrees out there," Piper said, tossing Blaire the key to the car we'd all driven over in.

"Take more than ten minutes, and I'm driving."

Piper's eyes rounded. "You wouldn't dare."

Blaire cackled and dashed for the entrance. I shook my head at the theatrics, but I wasn't upset about it. Every second like this was a win in my book.

I came upon the rest of our friends. Nora was already making arrangements for everyone to meet at our chosen spot, Capital Pizza. Whitt's hand landed on the small of my back, and a shiver coursed through me. I'd been playing it cool all week. Too busy to see him. I could have run over for a booty call, but I wasn't sure exactly where we stood on that. He'd given in one night. Would he do it again?

"Hey," I said, turning into him. "You coming for pizza?"

"I could be persuaded." His eyes were on my lips.

"And how much persuading would you need?"

He dipped low until his mouth was level with my ear. "I wouldn't mind hearing you beg again."

My core tightened at the words. Oh fuck.

"I..." I began.

"You coming?" Nora asked with a twinkle in her eye.

"Yep," I said hastily, taking a much-needed step away from Whitt. I'd thought I was hot at the game. Now, I was on fire.

"Y'all go ahead," Whitt told her. "I'll drive Eve."

Nora and West exchanged a pointed look.

"Sure," Nora said. "See y'all there."

The rest of the team filed out of the indoor facility. Whitt grabbed my bag and slung it over his shoulder.

"Hey!"

He shot me a look that said he wasn't going to budge, and I gave up. If he wouldn't let me carry my own luggage, it seemed he wouldn't let me carry my soccer bag.

"It isn't even heavy," I muttered.

He laughed. "That's not the point."

We trailed the stragglers into the parking lot. Whitt's shiny Lexus stood out like a sore thumb against the backdrop of pickups. He slung my bag into the backseat. I reached for the handle of my door, but he was already there. His hands on my hips, pressing me backward into the car.

"Oh," I gasped softly before his lips descended on mine.

Then, there was no talking involved at all. His tongue split delved in between my lips, massaging against my own. My hands fisted in his polo as I arched against his chest. Our bodies fit together, thighs to hips to stomach. I moaned at the taste of his sweet kisses and the feel of his body against mine.

His hands buried into my thick ponytail. He grasped it and tugged it backward to reveal the column of my throat. His mouth roved over the skin, heating me from head to toe.

"Fuck," he growled. "You taste good."

"Sweaty," I said with a strangled laugh.

"Want to taste you all over," he said as he ran kisses across my collarbone. "Didn't have enough time before."

"We don't have enough time now."

He adjusted my sports bra strap off of my shoulder to continue to kiss me. "We don't have anywhere to be."

"Pizza," I reminded him.

"So, we'll be late."

I nearly choked. "Whitton Wright? Late? Have you been abducted by aliens?"

He pulled back long enough to give me a lascivious look. "What did you say to me? Oh, right. Some of us enjoy our hobbies more than our job."

I gaped at him. "And your hobby is?"

"Eating your pussy."

He jerked open the back door, and we fell into the interior of his Lexus. I could have probably argued the point, but why would I want to? He didn't seem to care that I'd just played two games. Not as he all but ripped my shorts off of my hips and slung them somewhere in the front seat. My panties came off next, and for a second, there was panic.

"Whitt, are you sure?"

He didn't dignify that with an answer. He just buried his

face in between my legs. The first lick of his tongue up the seam of my pussy drove me wild.

"Oh God," I cried. I twined my fingers into his hair and pushed my hips upward.

His hand clamped down on my hip while spreading my legs apart. "Fuck," he groaned. "So fucking sweet, baby."

I gasped at the words. The torture as his tongue swirled around my clit. His hot breath on my core. His fingers bruising my thigh. The feel of abandon as we hooked up in the back of his car like we were in high school.

"Please," I pleaded.

"Please what?"

He sucked my clit into his mouth, and I saw stars. I wasn't going to last much longer. Normally, it took an age for me to come like this, but the anticipation from waiting to see him and the public location and just...him, it made it all so heightened. So desperate. I was going to unleash any second. I couldn't hold out even if I wanted to.

"Please don't stop."

His fingers snaked their way up my inner thigh, leaving a trail of goose bumps in their wake. He split my lips with two fingers. My slick wetness coated his fingers as he pushed them inside of me.

"Oh, baby," he said, "I have no plans to stop until you've come all over my fingers."

My head tipped backward, crashing into the door. He worked up a rhythm until I was panting so hard that I was worried I'd fog up the windows. My orgasm sat on a precipice. I hung suspended in time and space. Everything narrowed to this one celestial moment. The stars overhead singing to the heavenly bodies.

A series of *yes, please, yes, God, please* escaped me and then he shifted, curling his fingers inward. I shattered into a million little pieces. My chorus of passion dissolving into incoherence.

Whitt raised his head to watch, a fascinated expression crossing his hungry face. I threw my hand over my eyes and felt my entire body collapse into nothing.

What sort of spell had this boy cast over me?

"Wow," I whispered. My voice was raw and raspy. I coughed, trying to clear it, and he just grinned wider. "Amazing."

"Good."

I lazily reached out for him. I had zero energy to perform, but I understood reciprocation. And from my vantage point, he was hard as a rock and more than ready.

He chuckled and took my hand in his, pressing a kiss to the top of it. "You look like you could pass out."

"I feel like I could. You reduced me to ashes." I bit my lip and glanced down. "But I could..."

"That's not why I did that."

"Oh," I whispered.

Had I ever been with a guy who didn't expect something in return? Especially after something so mind-blowing? I waffled for a second. He seemed sincere. Whitt wasn't the kind of guy I expected to bullshit. If he wanted something more from me, his pants would be on the floor with mine. I wouldn't have even minded. And yet he just tossed me my panties and went looking for my elusive shorts.

I heaved myself to sitting. "Thanks."

He found my shorts and handed those off to me, too. "Still want to get pizza?"

"Our friends are going to freak the fuck out."

"So?"

Right. I was the one who wanted to keep this casual. No one would be surprised that we were hooking up. It didn't have to mean anything. Because it meant nothing that this man could get me off in a matter of minutes or that I was now anticipating the next time we could do exactly this. Or so much more.

No, I didn't have space or energy for a relationship. I'd gotten Whitt to agree to this. I didn't need to complicate things.

He stepped out of the backseat and offered me a hand. I gulped at the sight of it. That felt like more of an invitation than I'd prepared myself for.

Casual. I could do casual. Casual was my middle name.

I didn't take his offered hand. Instead, I crawled over the center console and into the passenger seat.

He laughed and walked around to the driver's side. "Ready when you are."

I nodded resolutely. "You're right. Let's go."

13

EVE

"Holy shit, Eve," Blaire said when I strode out of my bedroom.

"What?"

She gestured up and down. "You look totally bangable."

"Is that even a word?"

"It is now," Piper said. She slung her boots onto the floor and rose from the ottoman she'd been lounging in. She had on fitted bootcut jeans and a little crop top. "Are you trying to get fucked tonight?"

I ran my hands down the green dress I'd picked out. Honestly, I'd thought it was tame. I had much slinkier pieces. Sure, it had a V-cut and showed off my rack, but wasn't that the point?

"I don't think she'd mind one bit," Blaire said with a smirk on her lips.

She was in a miniskirt-and-crop combo that was mostly athletic-inspired. But at least we'd gotten her out of leggings, an oversize T-shirt, and a baseball cap.

"Not after last weekend," Piper agreed.

"I don't know what y'all are talking about. Are we going?"

"Ahh, come on." Blaire jumped up and grabbed my arm. "Give us the details!"

"There are no details," I said with a laugh, shaking her off. "Honestly."

"There is nothing honest about the way Whitt looked at you last weekend," Piper said. "Hollin is more surreptitious."

"Hollin couldn't keep a secret if his life depended on it."

Which wasn't precisely true since he'd kept mine when I needed him to. But Hollin was loud, bold, and generally just...a lot. Whitt had hardly been *that* obvious.

"Oh, she's got it bad," Blaire said.

"Is the dress for him then?" Piper asked.

"The dress is for the party, obviously."

"Did you buy it so he could take it off?" Blaire winked at me.

"I will not deign any of this with a response."

"She's a steel trap." Piper sighed. "We're never going to get anything out of you."

Blaire pouted. "You're no fun."

"Y'all are being ridiculous."

"Of course we are," Blaire said, throwing an arm over my shoulders. "And you do look hot."

"Super hot," Piper agreed.

"Bangable even," Blaire added.

I just shook my head. "You're not going to give up, are you?"

"Can you just tell us if you're dating?" Blaire's eyes were wide as we all grabbed our purses and headed out to Piper's Jeep.

She was legitimately interested. Even Piper looked like she wanted the answer.

"No," I told them as I got into the backseat, "we're not dating."

"Why not?" Piper asked.

I shrugged. "I haven't really dated since last year."

Piper pursed her lips, looking at me in the rearview mirror. "You're still upset about Daddy Sinclair?"

I couldn't help but smile at their nickname for Arnold. It wasn't *wrong*, but it was *so* wrong. "I'm not still upset about him. I wasn't even upset when it went down." I brushed my hair off of my shoulders. "I should have known separated wasn't divorced, but, oh, he was a good liar."

"Bastard," Blaire growled.

"But he did fuck up my entire life, and I'm not interested in a man doing that again."

"But Whitt isn't like that," Blaire said earnestly.

Piper nodded. "He seems like a real stand-up guy."

I almost opened my mouth to say the part that I was actually afraid of. When it inevitably went south, where would I be? Wouldn't these wonderful girls, who I was just starting to call friends, choose a Wright over me? Didn't everyone in this town?

Instead, I just laughed. "You're telling me. He's definitely too good to be true."

"You say that like it's a bad thing," Blaire said.

I shrugged. Things that seemed too good to be true... usually were.

When I didn't say anything, Piper forced a change in topic. The girls chatted about Blaire's wellness speaking tour happening this fall while I sat back and got lost in their conversation.

Why did everyone have to complicate things? Whitt and

I were whatever we were, and that was good enough. Safe enough.

Twenty minutes later, we pulled into the parking lot of Wright Vineyard. The lights were on inside, and I could hear music filtering through the speakers. Wright Construction had rented the place for Whitt's promotion party. I was honestly surprised that he had let anyone throw him a party. It didn't seem like him, but I'd agreed to come when he texted to ask. I was, after all, currently under contract with Wright Construction. I belonged, even without my friends.

Piper parked up front, and we piled out of the Jeep.

Wright Vineyard was a sprawling expanse of land on the south side of Lubbock. A large barn sat in the middle of the grape fields with an office and cellars nearby. The barn was now used for parties, weddings, and occasionally Campbell and Weston's band, Cosmere. When Cosmere showed up though, there were thousands of girls trying their hardest to get inside the place. They'd needed security a few times just to keep people off the property. I didn't know how Blaire and Nora dealt with having boyfriends that famous. If I were in a committed relationship, I wasn't sure I'd be that okay with sharing.

We traipsed down the stone walkway and to the double doors. The bouncer, Max, stood guard with his beefy, tatted arms crossed in front of him. We'd hooked up briefly a few years ago. He'd been a fun fling at the time, but we were friends now. His buddy did all my tattoo work.

"Hey, Max," I said with a grin.

He eyed me up and down. "Eve. Stunning, as always."

I winked at him. "Thanks."

"Can I see it?"

Blaire and Piper exchanged a look.

"See what?" Piper asked.

"My latest ink," I reassured them. I flipped my hair to the side and drew my strap off of my shoulder so he could see the full peony work.

Max whistled. "Damn, Joseph does some good-ass work."

"He really does."

"May I?" he asked, gesturing to the tattoo.

"Yep."

He gently lifted my arm and examined Joseph's work. Max was working on full sleeves. I'd considered it, but right now, I was so enamored with my peonies that I wasn't sure I wanted anything to take away from the beauty of it.

"Damn," he said.

A throat cleared behind him. I glanced up and into the piercing eyes of Whitton Wright. His jaw was set, and he had a hard, possessive look across his features. Blaire's and Piper's eyebrows shot up. Max dropped my arm. I slowly dragged my sleeve back up to my shoulder.

"Hey," I said with a smile. "Congratulations."

Blaire and Piper jumped in immediately.

"Oh, yes, congrats!"

"The man of the evening!"

"Thank you," Whitt said, his voice as smooth as glass.

"We'll talk later," I told Max. I patted his arm twice and then stepped across the threshold to the very tall, aggressive alpha male who looked like he was ready to eat me for dinner. "Hey," I repeated.

"Hey," he said.

"You look nice." I ran my hand down the front of his green tie.

Somehow, we matched, and it was a complete accident.

"I like your dress," he said, his voice tight.

"Well, that's good. Blaire and Piper think I wore it so you could take it off."

"Did you?"

"Maybe," I teased.

He arched an eyebrow. "Why don't I believe you?"

"Because I'm a modern woman and I wear my clothes for myself. I don't need to do anything for a man."

A grin cracked through his veneer. "Ah, there's the Eve that I know."

I looped my arm through his and moved us toward the bar. "And you? Did you wear that suit so I could take it off?"

"Obviously."

"Is that why you were all alphahole when you saw me with Max?" I raised an eyebrow questioningly.

"Alphahole? Is that a real thing?"

"Oh, definitely a real thing."

Whitt cleared his throat when we reached the bar and ordered us drinks. I took my wine, glad it was an open bar, thanks to the Wrights' generosity.

"You and Max used to date, right?"

"Sure. A couple of years ago."

I waited for him to say something more, but he didn't. He let that simmer between us.

I took a sip of my wine. "Was there another question in there?"

"He was touching your tattoo."

I laughed. "Yeah. Jealous?"

"Curious," he said instead.

"Max's buddy Joseph does both of our ink. He's a genius. Max hadn't seen my new peonies."

"Oh."

I smacked his arm with a laugh. "Yeah. Oh."

He looked like he wanted to say more. I could see Mr.

Relationship all over him. The need to know whether Max and I were well over. The possessive glint I'd seen in his eye that said he didn't like anyone else touching me. I'd be a liar if I said it didn't turn me on. I could see that he was half-tempted to throw me over his shoulder and walk out of the room with me. And even though I'd said that I didn't belong to anyone, I wouldn't complain. Not a bit.

"So, how did they get you to have this whole party?" I asked him.

The place was *packed*. Not just with Wright employees, but all of the Wright friends and family were in attendance, too. Couples were dancing in the center, people drinking near the bars and congregating around food displayed on long white-clothed tables. A *Congratulations, Whitt!* banner was strung up across the top of the stage. A balloon arch was against one wall with a *WC* logo backdrop for pictures. All of this must have been courtesy of Nora, who was the vineyard event planner. I didn't know how she had the time since she was planning celebrity weddings now as well.

"I tried to get out of it," Whitt admitted. "Jordan told me we weren't having a promotion party."

"And yet..."

"Yeah, you try saying no to Morgan."

Morgan Wright was a fierce and wildly independent go-getter. That was how she'd made CEO of her family company before she turned thirty. She was a force. I didn't blame him one bit.

"Fair."

"It's not so bad," Whitt said. He held his glass up. "Free drinks."

I quirked my lips. "If you think you're selling this, you've failed."

"Yeah." He took a long sip of his wine. "I'm incredibly

competitive, but only with myself. I want to succeed to meet my own wickedly high expectations. I don't need the acknowledgment from anyone else to know I've hit my goals. It sounds strange to other people, but…"

"It doesn't sound strange," I told him. "It sounds like you."

He nodded. "Yeah, I suppose you're right." Then, he took my hand in his and placed a kiss on it. "I'll admit that having you here in that dress sure makes this all worth it."

I flushed at the compliment. Much better than when he'd been jealous about Max. "If you keep talking like that, I might actually let you take the thing off."

His eyes heated. "Is that a challenge? Because we just acknowledged that I am very motivated to win."

I bit my lip. "I suppose we'll see tonight, won't we?"

"Challenge accepted then, Miss Houston."

14

WHITTON

Eve's pink cheeks made me want to forget the whole party. Anything that made her blush made me hard as a rock. If the party wasn't in my honor, I would have already left with her.

Unfortunately, I couldn't leave. She'd already monopolized too much of my time. I was sure that there were others who wanted to shake hands and schmooze. It was all so exhausting. Part of the job in its own way, but my least favorite part.

"Hey, don't look so glum about it," Eve teased. She flipped her dark hair off her shoulder. "The party won't last *all* night."

"It feels like it might," I said.

I glanced around the room. All the Wrights and my coworkers and so many people from the company that I didn't know. The networking part was half the reason I hadn't advanced in my last job. I couldn't kiss ass well enough. I did the work, but I hated brownnosing. At least here, that counted for something.

Then, I caught something over Eve's head. Colton

Wright was here. Huh. I was shocked that Jensen had brought him. Maybe he didn't trust him alone at home, and what kind of babysitter would watch a fifteen-year-old who could run circles around them?

He was leaned back against the wall in the shadows of the barn, typing on his phone and sneaking sips of wine from a glass he not-so-sneakily hid behind his back.

My face went white, "Fuck."

"What's going on?"

"Give me a second."

My gaze swept the room with a more discerning eye. Jensen was standing near the stage with Jordan. Emery was at the center, dancing with her friends Heidi and Julia. Morgan was in a conversation with Austin, Landon, and her husband, Patrick. Julian was ordering drinks with Hollin, West, and Nora. Anyone who would be looking into Colton's activity was currently occupied. I didn't know if someone was supposed to be watching him or if they thought he'd be fine at this party. Clearly, they were wrong. And if anyone saw him drinking, I had a feeling shit would hit the fan.

"Whitt?" Eve asked, concern in her voice. "What's wrong?"

"Come with me and act natural."

She shot me a curious look but did as I'd suggested. I could have stormed over there myself, but there was no way I would make it across the entire barn alone without someone stopping me. Plus, if someone realized exactly what I was doing, it might alert the remaining Wrights that I wanted to keep them ignorant of what was going on.

Eve stayed on my arm the entire walk over. She smiled and waved at people, but we didn't stop to make conversation. With her at my side, I had more immunity to the party.

She must have realized what I had a second before we reached Colton.

"Oh," she whispered.

Colton caught sight of us approaching him and shoved the wine behind his back. He took a step away, as if he were going to head for the exit.

I stepped in front of him before he could bolt. "Either you want to get caught or you're stupid. Which is it?"

Colton pursed his lips and set the wineglass down on a nearby table. "Don't know what you're talking about."

"I don't think you're stupid," I continued. "But if you get caught, that would be really stupid."

He looked ready to argue with me. I didn't know what good it would do. Trying to get his dad's attention by drinking at the only event he'd been allowed out of the house to go to, other than work, was pretty stupid. He'd probably known it and done it anyway. That rebellious streak was familiar. I'd done stupid things like that to get my dad's attention, only to realize that nothing worked. I didn't think Jensen was that way at all, but Colton was desperate and mad after what happened in the city. None of those things made for good decision-making.

"I drank all the time in New York, you know," Colton finally said.

I laughed. "I believe you."

"I was drinking at fifteen, too," Eve said. "Doesn't mean that I should have."

Colton did a double take at the sight of her. "Who's this?"

"Colton, this is Eve. Eve, Colton."

"This is the girl you're texting all the time?"

I wanted to put my head in my palm. "Yes, this is Eve."

"Damn, boss. You did good," Colton said with a nod of his head.

Eve chuckled. "Uh, thank you?"

"You know the boss is super into you?"

"That so?" she asked with an amused look.

"Sure. Can't blame him." Colton grinned deviously. A look that probably broke the hearts of many high school girls.

Eve looked like she was trying not to laugh.

"Stop hitting on her," I said, smacking the back of his head affectionately.

Colton laughed. "Worth a shot." He met my gaze again. "Are you going to tell my dad?"

"Would I have come over here if I was going to do that?"

"Guess not."

"Go be a kid or whatever," I told him. "Try not to get in trouble for an entire night."

"Lame, bruh," Colton said. he just winked at Eve and then disappeared into the crowd.

I wasn't sure it would keep him from drinking. He wanted attention, and we'd given him some. Hopefully, that would slake his thirst for the spotlight. One that was surely going to get him arrested again if he didn't get his shit together.

"What an...interesting kid," Eve said.

"He's a little shit."

"Yeah. Weren't we all at that age?"

"I wasn't."

She snorted. "Of course not. Whitt Wright has never done anything wrong."

"Well, I was a shit at a younger age than him. Then, I realized it wasn't getting me anywhere and turned it around. I hope he does, too."

Eve nodded, a small frown touching her features. "Yeah, I wish we all learned that lesson."

Before I could ask her what she meant by that, Jordan was at a microphone, and my name was being called. "Whitt! Come on up here."

"Oh fuck," I grumbled.

Eve pushed me forward. "Go on. Get your recognition."

"You're supposed to save me."

"Later," she promised with a discreet ass grab as I walked away.

I jerked around to find her straight-faced, somehow smothering the laugh still evident in her eyes. I shook my head at her and then strode to the stage. The crowd cheered me as I stepped onto the stage. Jordan shook my hand. Morgan was there a second later, congratulating me for my new position. I smiled in the hot lighting as they went on about my achievements at the company. I hadn't even been there that long, and already, I was such an asset.

It was overwhelming. And as much as I hated the spotlight, it was everything I'd ever wanted.

A round of congratulations. The entire company applauding me. The CEO personally throwing a party for me. I'd thought the corner office was the epitome of the top of my goals, but I needed to have bigger goals.

Once everything quieted down, I stepped into the backstage. I'd been here a few times with West when he was playing the venue, but this time, it was empty. I breathed out a sigh of relief.

Okay, I took it all back. That had been too much. I did *not* recharge with large crowds. I was way better one-on-one. I could fake it for the crowds, but being alone was definitely better.

The door to the backstage opened behind me, and I prepared to put my peopling face back on.

Then, I heard, "Hey there, handsome."

"Eve," I said with relief.

"The man of the hour, hiding out backstage, away from his adoring fans."

I shrugged. "I didn't ask for any of that."

"But you did so well with it."

"Hmm," I said with a shrug as she stepped up to me. "But now that you're here..."

I reached out for her, and she sidestepped with a giggle.

"I actually have a present for you."

"Oh?" I asked, intrigued.

"Yeah."

"Is it that dress on the floor?" I teased as I reached for her again.

She backed up again. "Not quite."

"Hmm," I said. "Because that's what I'd like."

She beckoned me toward her as she backed to the exit. I was mesmerized by this woman and would go wherever she wanted in that moment. I couldn't deny that I'd rather be doing this than schmoozing, even at my own party.

Her back hit the exit, and she pushed it open. "Well?"

I strode after her as she left the building. I let the door click shut behind me and found her eating up the gravel pathway in her high heels. I caught up to her in a matter of steps, and she smiled up at me with pure abandon.

What must it be like to be Eve Houston? Wild and carefree.

She took my hand when I reached her and picked up her pace. A few minutes later, we came upon the cellar doors, and she pushed them open.

"This way."

I followed her through the darkened interior. My name was on the building, and I'd never been in here. I could just make out the barrels that held the aging wine. It smelled sweet and rich. The whole place felt more like a dream than reality for someone who worked inside a cinder-block palace.

"What..." I began.

Then, her mouth was against mine, and words left me. Her body pressed me against one of the barrels. My hands came down to her waist, grasping the silky material of her dress. I forgot the intensity of the party for the rush of Eve. Just her in my arms, her red lips tight against mine, her tongue brushing into my mouth.

"Do you want your present?" she rasped in the darkened interior.

"Yes," I growled.

I would take anything and everything this girl wanted to give me.

Her hands went for my belt buckle. It was undone in a second. She popped the button on my pants, tugged my zipper down, and ripped my shirt out from my waistband. Her nails raked against the exposed skin of my abdomen. I exhaled sharply. My cock responded instantly to her movements. Her hand dived into my boxer briefs and skimmed across the length of my cock. I groaned deep in the back of my throat. My head tipped backward. I'd thought of nothing but this woman for days, and here she was, giving me exactly what I wanted. And yet...

"I thought the dress was going on the floor."

She withdrew my cock from my boxers. "That's not my present."

"What is then?" I asked.

She grinned wickedly as she dragged my pants over my ass. "My mouth."

Then, she lowered herself to her knees, took my cock in her hand, and brought it to her hot, wet mouth. I swore I saw the stars at the first sweep of her tongue against the head. She drew nearly the entire length of it into her mouth.

I gasped, my hands going into the dark strands of her hair. I fought for control as she pulled back and began to bob on my cock. I watched it disappear into her mouth. The way she worked her lips around the head before lapping back down on the shaft. Her hum of approval as she took it deeper.

I had to hold back. I couldn't let loose. She wasn't mine, all mine, yet. She would be if I had my way. But I couldn't do all that I wanted when she was still on the edge. If she knew exactly how I wanted to fuck her, would she stay? She hadn't complained when I stuffed her face into the mattress or when I ate her sweet cunt in the backseat. What else would she approve?

My hands moved of their own accord, taking control of her. She'd been taking her time. A thing that I very much enjoyed, but I needed more. I needed everything.

"So good, baby. You're doing so good," I said. "But I need you to take this dick like a good girl."

She gasped at the first thrust into her mouth. A soft, breathy thing that made me just want to force it out of her again. I was careful though. I didn't push all the way to the back of her throat. I didn't wait for her to swallow down the head, like I wanted. I just took a faster pace. Fucked her mouth while she slid one hand back and forth along the shaft and used the other to massage my balls.

"Fuck. Fuck yes," I groaned.

Everything went white as my climax hit me like a tidal wave. I grunted into the darkened interior of the cellar and emptied into her mouth. My cum hit the back of her throat, and—bless this woman—she didn't even choke, just swallowed.

I removed my cock from her mouth when she was done. She sat back heavily on her heels and tilted her head up at with a glazed look in her eyes.

I bent down to press a kiss to her lips. "That was perfect."

"I..." she said shakily. "I...that..."

I grinned. "Yeah. Best present I've ever received."

She laughed and then wiped at the edges of her mouth before slowly coming to her feet again. "I'm a good gift giver."

"And here I thought, I was going to have to work to get that dress off."

"It's still on," she teased.

I grasped her waist and tugged her against me, swinging us around so her back was against the barrel. "Fine. I'll just take that wet cunt instead."

"Oh!"

Then, I hiked her up by her thighs and set her ass down on the barrel behind her. I pushed her panties aside and was inside of her again with one quick thrust.

"Fuck," she cried out.

She was so fucking wet and tight. I'd thought she'd been ready the first time. Somehow, she was even wetter. She was practically dripping down her thighs with it.

"Did me fucking your mouth get you this hot, baby?"

"Ye-yes."

I grinned. Maybe she wasn't going to be so afraid of

what else I could give her if that got her this wet. Maybe she'd want more. Maybe she'd want everything, too.

"And are you going to come for me?"

She nodded, her pussy tightening around my cock as I bottomed out deep inside of her. She tilted her head back and came hard and fast. I watched her uninhibited expression as she let go. It was pure ecstasy. I wanted nothing more than to find a way to do it over and over again.

I was hit with the same feeling that I'd had all those months earlier. If I got close to this girl, there was no way that I could survive her. I wanted more than just sex with her. I wanted a relationship. I wanted a future.

I just needed to figure out how to convince her of that.

PART III

BE HERE NOW

15

EVE

Days later and I still couldn't stop thinking about Whitt and me in the cellar. Something had clicked together down there. I didn't know if it was the darkness or the location or just *us*, but it was beyond mind-blowing. We'd been texting nonstop since then. The messages progressively filthier and more intimate.

The way he'd taken control of my mouth. Jesus fucking Christ, I was a goner. How long had I been looking for someone who knew how to handle me? And somehow, Mr. Responsibility was the one who'd unleashed in that cellar. It was almost unbelievable.

Another text came in from him.

Or you could come over to my place after you finish your showing.

I glanced up at the couple wandering the half-a-million-dollar ranch house in Lakeridge Country Club. They'd been disinterested in the dozen other houses I'd shown them. It was the wrong time to buy, but they'd just moved here from

Colorado, and they had a teenage daughter, so they needed to be in the house before school started. Maybe they'd like this one. I certainly did.

I texted Whitt back.

Maybe.

Despite our flirtation, neither of us had been at each other's place. We hadn't gone on a date. In fact, I'd purposely made it so we weren't doing anything that resembled dating. If we were in the same place, that was one thing, but if I went out of my way to see him, that was completely different. That meant more. Right?

Tease.

God, I was.

A tease who was avoiding relationships like the plague. I didn't want to complicate this thing that had been working so well. Or take a chance to see if it would work. Ugh.

I went to put my phone away when it started ringing. I panicked, thinking it was Whitt. We only texted. Phone calls were more intimate. Phone calls became phone sex, which became us ending up at his house, having real sex.

But it wasn't Whitt. It wasn't a client either. It was my sister.

My heart dropped.

"What now?" I muttered under my breath.

I answered the phone. "Hey, Bails."

"Evie, hope I'm not bothering you."

I glanced at my clients, still discussing the merits of an open floor plan. I waved the phone at them. The wife shot me a thumbs-up.

"I'm showing a house. What's up?"

"I just have news. I got a job."

My brain paused at those words. "You...got a job?"

"Yeah. It's part-time, nights and weekends."

"But school is starting in a few weeks."

"I know, but I'll be able to do this and school."

I exhaled slowly through my nose and stepped farther away from my clients. "Bails, we talked about this. You don't need to get a job. You need to focus on school and getting into college this year."

"I am. I mean...I will," she stuttered.

"Did Dad put you up to this?"

She hesitated for a fraction of a second too long, and a fiery pit of anger erupted in my stomach. I tried to force it down. There was only so much that I could do from Lubbock. I felt guilty enough, not being in Midland for Bailey, but this was another line that man was crossing.

"He did, didn't he?" I asked furiously. "He needs to back off. I am working so that you don't have to."

"I want to help. I already owe you so much."

She sounded so much like the small girl I'd helped raise after our mom ditched us. She might be seven years younger than me, but we'd always been so much closer than other siblings I knew. Gram had done what she could to keep us together after Mom left, and I did what I could for Bailey. Dad certainly wasn't helpful. The only thing he'd done was keep Gram from getting custody of us both.

Things I couldn't change or do anything about. It made me want to burn the entire world down.

"You don't owe me anything. Dad and I have an agreement, Bails."

"Yeah, but—"

"Is he around? Put him on the phone."

"He's not here," she said with a sigh.

"Then, I'll call him. You know you have to bring your GPA up if you want to get into college. That's your entire focus."

"I know. I know. Okay. Don't call Dad. I don't want to have to hear it from him, too."

"Bails—"

"It's fine, Evie. I'll go do my summer reading."

"Bails," I repeated with a sigh.

My anger dissipated as soon as it had come. I was left with an exhaustion that I couldn't escape for the life of me. Running my own life was impossible. Being two hours away and trying to help run Bailey's was so much worse.

"It's *fine*," she repeated. "I get it. I know what the stakes are."

"I'm sorry," I told her earnestly. "I really am. Just stop listening to everything Dad says. You know I'd have you here with me if I could."

"I know. Love you."

"Love you, too."

I hung up the phone and breathed out heavily. Well, that couldn't have gone worse. I was too young to be an overbearing parent to my seventeen-year-old sister. Fuck. It had been a while since I'd let this feeling settle over me. I wanted to cry, but I just wasn't there yet. I needed to process this.

"Eve?" my client called from the other room.

I swallowed back my feelings and strode back into the living room. "Sorry about that. What do you think?"

"We love it," she said. "We're going to need to bring our daughter to see it before we put in an offer. Are you free again tomorrow?"

"Sure. Luckily, the sellers have already moved. So, the place is open whenever you're free."

"Perfect. We'll be in touch."

I shook hands with them both and then walked them to the front. They got into their shiny Audi SUV and drove away while I locked up the house. It was a nice place. Nothing I could afford. Not with everything saddled on my shoulders.

I slid my arms out of my blazer. It was too damn hot out here. I tossed it into the passenger seat of my 4Runner and cranked the air conditioner.

My head tipped back on the headrest, and I fought back tears. God, I hated this. I hated every bit of this. The feeling of helplessness. Like no move I made was forward. It was always a sidestep in an endless game that I was one step away from losing completely.

I didn't know what to do about Bailey. I didn't know what to do about Dad. I didn't know how I could keep going without Gram. I ran my finger across the inside of my bicep, where the words *Be here now* were written in her familiar scrawl. That had been her motto. The words she'd always used for me when I was struggling. I had to stay here in the moment. I had to keep moving even if it was sideways instead of forward.

My hands shook on the steering wheel. I clenched it harder to try to get them to stop. Usually, Gram's words helped, but right now, I felt unglued.

"Fuck!" I yelled into the empty vehicle.

I dug my phone back out and opened the last text from Whitt. He'd responded to me a few times while I was inside. Flirty things. I scrolled up and again read the message where he'd invited me over. Maybe...maybe I should do that. Maybe it'd be good to be held by someone right now.

Is that invitation to come over still available?

The response was almost immediate.

Always.

I swallowed and then put the car in drive. Here goes nothing.

I'd never been to Whitt's place before, but he'd given me the address while we'd been texting as an invitation to come over whenever I wanted. The thought of doing that had crossed my mind many times, but I'd never given in to that urge. Our situationship was good the way it was. Why was I suddenly complicating it? All because Bailey had called? I'd been dealing with that for so long it shouldn't have bothered me. And still it had.

His house was a new build on the south side of town. Not that far from where I'd been showing houses. It had immaculately cut green grass, even in the blazing August heat. Trees in the front provided some shade. Comfy porch furniture sat in front of the brick house. I passed through the open stone archway and knocked on the black iron door.

Whitt appeared a minute later in very familiar lounge shorts and a gray T-shirt. "Hey, this is a surprise."

"Hey."

He opened the door all the way for me. I hesitated on the threshold.

Was I making the right decision here? I didn't feel like I could come back from this. All those walls that I'd built up between us. I'd spent months denying myself, just to wind up here anyway.

I didn't have to walk inside. I could stand on this

doorstep in the evening heat and talk. I could...turn around and get back in my car and ruin everything. Except I couldn't do that. Not with his big blue eyes all lit up at the sight of me. That smile, unusually bright. I'd done that. I made him happy. A thing that I found myself enjoying and wanting to continue to do.

Maybe there was an inkling of selfishness in there, too. I wanted to step inside. I wanted to *want* to step inside. I hadn't felt that in so long.

"Do you want to come in?" he asked almost hesitantly.

"Sure. Yeah," I said, realizing that I'd been standing there awkwardly. "Thanks."

I stepped into the house, and Whitt closed the door behind me. It was everything I'd expected. Hardwood floor, giant open floor plan, carefully selected furniture, and a massive television over the fireplace. The whole place screamed Whitt. Minimalist, clean, everything in its place.

"I wasn't sure you'd come by."

"I was nearby."

Which wasn't the reason I'd stopped by at all. Work had nothing to do with this.

"How did your showing go? Did they like the house?"

"Yeah. They're bringing their daughter to look at it tomorrow."

"That'll be good for you. Another sale."

I brushed my hair off of my face. "I don't really want to talk about work." The words fell abruptly out of my mouth, but I just couldn't bullshit. My barometer for small talk was nonexistent on a good day. And today wasn't a good day.

"Okay," he said slowly. "Something on your mind?"

I sighed. "It's been a long day."

Whitt leaned back against the kitchen island and waited

for me to explain further. I didn't know how he knew that I needed the space, but he clearly did.

After a minute, he finally asked, "Did something happen?"

I blew out a harsh breath and ran a hand down my face. "Just a lot on my mind."

"Do you want to talk about it?"

"No," I said with a stilted laugh.

"Hey," he said, taking my hand and drawing me closer. "You can talk to me if you need to talk. You look like someone kicked your puppy."

"I don't have a puppy."

He tilted his head to the side. "You know what I mean."

God, I wasn't ready for this. I couldn't spew all of my family drama to him. Yeah, he didn't have the perfect family or anything, but it was too much. I didn't want to do this. I wanted things to be light and easy between us. Flirty and fun and...uncomplicated.

"Maybe this is just a booty call." I tried for levity.

Whitt pursed his lips. "As much as I want you, I don't think that's why you're here. You could have come over at any point for that, and you never have. What's going on?"

What could I say? My life was a disaster, and the minutes when I could pretend it wasn't with him made it better. I was barely coasting, and I didn't know how to fix the hole I'd dug myself into. Sometimes, it felt like my entire world was falling apart, and I was clinging to the surface to keep afloat.

I stared up into his earnest face and knew I couldn't say any of that. I turned my back on him. This was hard enough for me without looking into his pretty face. What if I saw pity there? What if he thought less of me? God, I wasn't the type of girl to care what anyone thought. I was fearless. I was strong. I was fiercely independent. And I hated myself for every one of those adjectives right now.

"It's just...do you ever feel like no matter how hard you try at something, it isn't good enough?"

Whitt clucked his tongue, as if he were really contemplating the question. "Well, I did. All the time growing up."

I turned slowly. "Really? Mr. Responsibility?"

"You don't know what it was like growing up with my dad. West and I, we were always trying to be the family he wanted to come home to. There was nothing we could have done differently to make him choose us. And we didn't even know he had a whole other life."

I hugged my arms around my waist. "Yeah, that sounds terrible."

"Eve, what's going on?"

I opened my mouth to tell him, but the words wouldn't come out. Whitt could talk about everything so easily. Could discuss being the other family like it was some minor thing that had happened to him. I couldn't even bring myself to utter my dad's name. I hated talking about him. I hated him. I swore under my breath as the shaking took over my limbs.

"Hey, hey, hey," he said, taking my hands. "It's okay. Breathe."

But I couldn't breathe. Tears were threatening to fall again. I had to hold it together. I had to be strong. If I let go, even for a second, I didn't know if I'd ever be able to get myself back together.

"Baby," he crooned softly.

He tipped my chin up to look into his bottomless ocean eyes. Tears lined my bottom lids. I blinked rapidly to clear them, but it did no good, as they collected in my lashes.

"You don't have to shoulder everything alone."

"Don't I?"

"Not anymore."

"We're not even..." I trailed off. "We're not..."

"It doesn't matter," he told me. "Whatever we are isn't what's important right now. I'm here for you regardless."

At those words, the tears finally did spill down my cheeks. I leapt forward, throwing my arms around his shoulders. He wrapped his tight around my waist. I couldn't remember the last time I'd cried. I hadn't even done it at Gram's funeral. I'd held it all in and let it simmer on low. For so long, the world had gotten the hardened version of my vulnerable heart. I hated showing it to anyone, and yet here I was, unleashing on Whitt.

When I tried to pull back, he scooped me up in his arms and carried me in a cradle to the couch.

"I don't...you don't have to..."

"I know. I want to." He brushed my tears aside with his thumb. "Let me take care of you. You're safe."

I was safe.

I was safe here with him.

That was why I had come in the first place. Despite the distance I'd put between us, there was something more here. A new fear arose at that thought, but I smothered it. I needed this tonight. I needed it more than I'd even known. I could feel that fear another time.

For now, I leaned back against his broad chest and let him hold me. We could figure the rest out some other time.

16

WHITTON

"Remind me again why I missed you."

Harley cackled as we strode into Thai Pepper for lunch. "Because I'm awesome, obviously."

"Obviously," I grumbled.

Harley waved frantically at West, seated at the back corner table. West saluted her with a bemused smirk on his lips. A few girls were not-so-surreptitiously snapping pictures of him from nearby tables. Consequences of celebrity.

"God, you're obnoxious now," Harley said as she plunked into the seat next to West. She crossed her long legs, dangling a Doc Marten boot.

West laughed. "Uh, thanks? Missed you, too."

"Of course you did. Both of you did."

"We did," I agreed with a shake of my head.

We were quite a trio. West in his unshakable rockstar garb—ripped jeans, band black T-shirt, and Vans. Harley dressed like she was on her way to Coachella in cutoff jean shorts, some kind of bra top, and a sleeveless crocheted jacket that I had no name for, but I'd guess she'd made

K.A. LINDE

herself. And then there was me, in a suit. No one would fit us together, and yet we'd always been inseparable. So much so that I hadn't even moved to Lubbock when West did because I wanted to wait until Harley graduated and could come with me.

Harley ordered for all three of us when the waiter appeared, insisting we try this dish she'd eaten daily while interning at a law office in Seattle.

"So, still law school–bound?" I asked.

"Can you leave the five-year plan for a whole minute?" West asked with a smirk.

"He really can't," Harley said. She pursed her lips and shrugged. "I think so. I sort of hate lawyers. They're scum. But I could change the world."

"You don't have to go into law to change the world," West said.

"Don't discourage her."

West rolled his eyes. "Then, don't encourage her to do something she doesn't love."

Ah, the tried-and-true argument.

"Y'all both shut up," Harley said with a laugh.

West and I both put our hands up in surrender. We could bicker as good as any siblings, but somehow, our little sister was the mediator.

"Did everyone in Seattle make fun of you for using *y'all*?" I asked.

Harley grinned. "More or less. But I like it."

Our food came, and we all reached for chopsticks at the center of the table.

Harley rolled hers together before digging in. "Tell me what I missed while I was gone. How was the promotion party?"

134

West smirked up at me before dropping his gaze to his food when I glared back.

"What?" she asked. "What happened? Did you humiliate yourself in front of everyone?"

"Of course not," I said with a shake of my head. "It was fine. I just don't love the attention."

"For someone so driven, you should really get over that. If you're going to rise to be CEO or whatever, you're going to need to get used to giving speeches and the spotlight and shit."

"Eloquent, Harley."

West snorted. "He did fine. It was the disappearance afterward that he's not talking about."

"I didn't disappear."

Even though I had. My mind returned to that darkened cellar. The feel of Eve's mouth around my cock. Her dazed look as I had come into her mouth. The wet drip of her pussy as I had driven into her. I cleared my throat and returned to my pad thai.

"Oh my God, is there a girl?" Harley asked, excitement in every syllable. "Are you dating someone?"

"Eve Houston," West supplied.

"Thanks for that," I grumbled.

"Oh, Eve is way out of your league." Harley laughed. "How'd you land someone like that?"

"One, I take offense to that. And two, we're not dating."

West snorted. "You disappeared with the girl at the promotion party for, like, forty-five minutes. You couldn't stop staring at her at that mayoral announcement thing. Not to mention, you showed up late to the soccer celebration at the pizza place."

"Late?" Harley choked out. "You're joking."

"I'm not." West shot her a look. "And they're working together."

Harley glanced at me with wide eyes. "Care to explain yourself, dear brother?"

"Nothing to explain," I grunted.

"Bullshit," West said.

Harley sat back and held her chopsticks out. "You don't get like this unless there's a girl."

"I'm not like anything. We're not dating."

"So, just fucking?"

It was my turn to nearly choke. "You're too young for that word."

Harley rolled her eyes. "I'm almost twenty. I've had sex. Jesus."

"Don't need to know that," West said, firmly in agreement with me.

"I know you're your own woman and all that," I told her, "but if I ever met the guy, I'd definitely beat the shit out of him."

"Seconded," West said.

"Y'all are gross. Your misogyny is showing," she said, brushing at my suit coat. "Now, rein in the patriarchy for one goddamn minute and tell me how this happened with Eve."

I let my chopsticks clatter. "I already said, we're not dating."

"Right, but we've established that neither of us believes you."

West nodded. "Basically. Look, we know that you subscribe to the hot-and-crazy model of a perfect girlfriend. Eve acts like she fits that mold, but she actually seems really down-to-earth and chill."

"Wait," Harley said, holding her hand up. "Why exactly does she seem that way?"

"Yeah, West, why does she seem that way?" I asked, crossing my arms.

"I...I," he stammered, as if realizing he'd put his foot in it. "Look, she has a rep, all right?"

"Explain," Harley insisted.

"She was seeing Santi from the band for a little while," West said with a sigh. "He mentioned she'd dated a dude that could have been her dad. You remember Chase Sinclair?"

Harley swallowed hard. "Uh-huh. We met at the wedding."

I arched an eyebrow at her, and she purposely didn't look at me. What exactly had happened that night?

"She dated his dad, and then rebounded with Santi. He just...said she was wild." West cleared his throat and looked down. "In bed."

"Wow," Harley said. "Men are *disgusting*. He had *no* right telling you that. And then you bring it up in conversation when Whitt is interested in this girl."

West held his hands up. "Hold the feminism. I'm just repeating what was said."

"News flash: she's allowed to sleep with whoever she wants," Harley argued vehemently, as if it was a personal offense. "Just because she hooked up with these men doesn't mean anything. God, when did y'all start slut-shaming?"

"I didn't say anything," I reminded her.

"Right!" Harley said, pointing at West. "You need to get your act together. LA is ruining you."

West stammered out an apology, but I couldn't stop

smiling. Leave it to my sister to defend Eve to her last breath.

I'd heard the same rumors that West had stated. Eve had bad reputation written on her forehead. Maneater. Homewrecker. Starfucker. All that bullshit that centered around a woman for seeing multiple men. If I'd done the same, no one would have even blinked. Hell, I'd guess rockstars slept with more people than that in a weekend. I knew about her reputation and didn't give a fuck. She was just Eve with me.

"When do I get to *meet her*, meet her?" Harley said. She put her chin on her fist and looked at me with wide, excited eyes.

"Uh, she'll be at the fundraiser for Jensen this weekend."

"Oh, yeah. Jordan sent me an invite," she said. "And she's your date?"

"Not...exactly."

"You keep saying you're not dating, and I'm starting to wonder if you've asked her," Harley said. "Because if I find out you're fucking around with her emotions, we will have words, Whitton Wright. Situationships suck, bro."

"Hold up. She was the one who wanted it to be casual."

"So, something *is* happening," Harley said with satisfaction.

I blew out a breath. "Damn, you're going to make a good lawyer."

"I know." She made a face that said *obviously*. "So, you're asking her out then?"

"I'm not going to be bullied into this."

Even though I wanted nothing more than for Eve to go to this thing with me. I'd wanted it all from the start.

And spending time with her like we had the other night

made me want a relationship. I'd never seen Eve vulnerable. Never seen her cry. I could have held her all night if she had let me. We didn't even have to kiss. I loved the other stuff, but holding her and comforting her were on the same level. I just needed to convince her of that.

"Tell me more about Seattle," I said instead.

Harley huffed and then dived back in.

Harley's words burrowed into my brain and stuck there. Eve and I were in a situationship. It didn't suck as much as she'd claimed it did. I wanted the hot cellar sex and the cuddling on the couch as I rubbed her back. Was that too much to ask for?

I'd said that I didn't want to be bullied into it, but now, it was all I could think about. I wouldn't have an answer unless I asked. I'd bent for her. We were as casual as it got. Maybe she'd see that something more was worth it and change her mind, too.

I pulled my Lexus to the curb in front of Eve's place and strode up the front walk. I knocked twice, nerves settling in my stomach. I didn't want to ruin what was happening, but I needed to know.

"Whitt!" Blaire said when I answered the door. "Hey, Eve is out."

"Oh. She said that she was on her way back from the gym. I must have beat her here."

"No problem. You can come in," Blaire said with a knowing glint in her eye.

I stepped over the threshold and found Campbell Abbey lounging on the couch with his signature guitar in his hand. He was humming some tune that I didn't know.

He and West were best friends, and so I rarely saw Campbell without him. It was strange to be in his presence without my twin.

"Hey, man," I said with a short wave.

Campbell glanced up from his guitar and grinned. "Hey, Whitt. Here for Eve?"

"Yeah."

"Smart."

Blaire took the seat next to him and plopped her feet into his lap. She reached for her laptop, typing away as he went back to strumming. They looked so comfortable together. My heart ached. Just seeing that made me realize more than ever that I wanted that with Eve.

The jiggle of the doorknob had me turning away from the display. Eve stepped inside, and I froze. She was dressed in high-waisted sky-blue shorts, a matching sports bra, and platform Converse. Her long hair was up in a high-braided ponytail. She wore barely a drop of makeup, and she was stunning.

"Hey," she said. Her smile lit up her face. "You got here fast."

"I did."

I took several steps closer. I wanted to kiss her. Screw the conversation I'd been planning. I wanted to lift her over my shoulder, carry her to her bedroom, and forget the rest of the world.

"I really need a shower," she said by way of what appeared to be an apology. "All sweaty."

"I never minded before."

She flushed. "That's true." She nodded her head to the side. "Come see my room?"

"Lead the way."

Blaire and Campbell said hi to Eve as we passed. Blaire's

knowing look was almost too much. As if she expected us to be stripping out of our clothes before we got to her room. Not that I'd mind...

Eve's room was bare bones. A bed in a corner, a small dresser, and a full closet. Nothing on the walls or floor, except a few unpacked boxes and her half-full suitcase. As if she was waiting to be kicked out of the place and needed a fast getaway.

"Really moved in," I joked.

She shrugged. "Oh, yeah, I'm sort of the worst at unpacking. It's such a hassle." She dropped her gym bag next to the suitcase and stretched her arms overhead.

"How was the gym?"

"I feel like I was run over. My trainer had me do everything to failure today. He's a masochist." She rolled her neck out. "You're in a suit. I thought you were meeting Harley."

"I met her for lunch with West. I took a half-day."

"Look at you, taking time off," she said with a laugh. "Didn't think you had it in you."

"Well, Jordan sent me home early. He's sending us back to Midland and told me I should take some time because we'll be there on a Saturday."

"Oh yeah, I got that email," she said with a smile. "Should be fun. Maybe two rooms this time."

I shook my head. "I don't think so."

She grinned, running my tie through her fingers. "You think I'll share a bed with you again?"

"We don't have to share the bed," I said, dragging her fingers up to my lips. I pressed a kiss into each knuckle. "We could share the couch and the shower and the desk." I kissed up to her wrist. "The floor." Another kiss up her arm. "The wall."

"Okay, okay," she gasped breathlessly. "I get the picture."

"I could draw it for you." I pressed our lips together.

She leaned into me with a sigh. "Fine. One room. You convinced me."

"Can I convince you of something else?"

"What's that?" she asked, rising on her tiptoes to try to get to my lips again.

"Go to the fundraiser dinner with me."

She dropped heavily onto her heels. "What?"

"The dinner this weekend."

"Right. I mean, I'm going. We're both going. Nora hired a limo for the group."

"I know. I want you to go with me."

"What's the difference?" she asked warily.

"You'd be my date."

She opened her mouth and then closed it. I waited patiently for her to think it over. I could see the cogs working through her mind, but she didn't pull away from me. Part of me wanted to push. Maybe at the start of all of this, I would have, but I'd seen her come to me of her own accord now. I'd held her as she cried. We were more than casual. Somewhere between that and dating, and I was ready to take the next step. I wanted her to be ready, too.

"Okay," she finally said. "Okay, I'll be your date."

I sealed her promise with a kiss.

17

EVE

"So, a *date* date," Nora said.

I held the cocktail dress up to my figure. Nora had insisted on going dress shopping for the event tonight. We were currently in Chrome, a local designer clothing store, handing off potential dresses to the hovering salesclerk. I wasn't sure I could afford anything in this place, but here we were.

Now, I was pretty sure she'd only asked me because West had told her about my date with Whitt tonight.

"A *date* date."

Nora squealed. "Oh my God, I'm so excited for y'all."

"It's *one* date, Nor," I reminded her, replacing the dress on the rack.

"You've been dating for weeks!"

"No, we've been hooking up for weeks."

She huffed and picked up a green dress. "Try this one on."

I took it out of her hands and held it up to me. Yeah, this could work. I passed it to the salesclerk.

"That's probably enough. I don't even know if any of this

is going to fit." Part of me hoped they didn't fit so I could wear something I already owned.

"Something will fit."

"You don't have boobs," I pointed out. "Clothes aren't made for people with giant boobs. Material isn't supposed to stretch the way it does around these things."

"Girl, I am so jealous of your boobs."

"Don't be. They're a hassle."

"Whitt doesn't think so."

"Good Lord!"

Nora laughed. "I'm just saying!"

"I know what you're saying."

I strode into my dressing room and tried on the first dress—a pink number that I immediately knew didn't work. Nora stepped out in the cutest little blue minidress. The little pixie looked good in everything.

"But you like him, right?" Nora asked.

I gestured to my dress. "I don't like *this*."

I strode back into the dressing room and tried on more dresses, hating all of them.

Nora sighed. "You know you can talk to me about this. I'm excited."

"It's still too early to be excited about anything."

"It's never too early to be excited."

"Not when all my previous relationships have crashed and burned."

"You haven't even dated anyone in the last year. And honestly, should we even count Daddy Sinclair?"

I snorted. "Stop calling him that."

"It's a perfect name, and I will not stop."

"Okay. Fine. And no, I haven't dated since him, just hooked up. It's not that I'm still upset about him or whatever. I just needed to live in my single era."

"And now, you've found a great guy," she pointed out. "So, maybe that era is coming to a close."

I bit my lip. "Maybe it is."

Nora cheered as I went back into the dressing room for the final dress.

When I stepped out, both of us were speechless.

"That's the one," Nora said in awe.

"It so is."

I didn't even complain about the price tag. This was *the* dress.

"Are you nervous?" Blaire asked.

"Excited?" Piper piped in.

"Hyped!" Nora added.

"Y'all need to calm down. It's a date for an event we both were already planning to attend." I lounged back in the overstuffed chair and crossed one Louboutin-clad foot over the other. Tried-and-true heels for tonight.

"But it's your *first* date," Blaire said. "You must be feeling something."

"What did you feel on your first date with Campbell?"

Blaire laughed. "Well, we were in high school. He was the coolest fucking person in the entire school, and he noticed me skating at Sonic. I basically fell over myself about him every chance I got."

"So...nothing's changed," I joked.

"Pretty much."

"And you?" I asked Piper.

She sighed heavily. "I mostly could not believe I was sinking this low."

We all laughed. Their enemies-turned-lovers relationship was legendary. We all turned to Nora to get her perspective.

"Oh." She blushed as bright as a tomato. "Well, we kind of accidentally hooked up a few times while he was teaching me to date."

"Teaching you to date!" Blaire gasped. "Nora Abbey, do not let your brothers hear that."

"Oh my God, don't tell them!" she said to both girls.

Piper laughed. "I was just glad to see you move on from August."

"Tell me about it," Nora said. "But once we started *dating* dating, it was just..." She sighed, going all starry-eyed. "And I want that for you!"

"All right," I said with a laugh. "I'll work on sighing heavily like I'm in a cartoon."

Nora smacked my arm. "One day you're going to be so head over heels for someone that you'll understand. I hope it's Whitton Wright so I can look back on this conversation and make fun of you."

I shrugged. "If wishes grew on trees."

The doorbell rang, and all the girls jumped up at once. Even I stumbled to my feet. As much as my bravado showed before the girls, I couldn't deny that I had butterflies in my stomach. This was my first official date in more than a year. I was glad it was him, but it didn't make me any less jittery. The last thing I wanted to do was fuck this up. I was becoming more certain that the girls wouldn't turn their backs on me if it didn't work, but it wasn't etched in stone.

Plus...I liked Whitt. A fact I found I could no longer deny. That maybe this date could be the first of many. After all, he kept surprising me. He hadn't asked about Evie Jo when we were in Midland, and he'd held me the other night after my conversation with Bailey. He didn't push me to divulge more, and it was nice to feel safe for once.

The door swung open, and in walked our gentlemen. Hollin, Campbell, and West strode through the door. And then behind them, to my surprise, was Harley in a black mesh dress that clung to her every curve. She waved at me with a wide grin on her face. I waved back cautiously.

Then, Whitt entered, and everything else went hazy. I'd been making fun of Nora for her sighing over West. Now, I was here, unable to even form coherent thoughts. He was dressed in a black suit with a crisp white shirt and black tie. He'd gelled his hair back and shaved his sharp jaw clean. I wanted to drag my nails down that perfectly smooth skin to feel it for myself. He stood like a statue as he caught sight of me.

The green dress hugged my figure like a glove. As brilliant green as my eyes with boning running across it to give it structure and put my ample boobs on display. The straps were skinny black leather that only accentuated my cleavage. I opted for a bare throat and shiny teardrop diamonds in my ears.

"Wow," he said as he approached me. "This dress..."

"A winner?"

"You could say that."

I grinned like a Cheshire cat. "Thank you. I thought it was the one."

"It *is*," he nearly groaned.

"Hi, I'm Harley!" she interrupted. "You look hot as fuck."

I laughed. "Thanks. I like your dress, too."

"Thanks. I told my brother you were out of his league, but he decided to ask you out anyway," she said with a grin. "Good choice on his part." She leaned in with a wink. "You can do better."

I snorted and glanced at Whitt to see him rolling his eyes.

"Harley," he ground out.

"All right. I did my due diligence. We should get out of here."

I slipped my hand into the crook of his elbow, and we filed out of the house behind everyone else.

Whitt leaned down. "I'm sorry about her. She's a menace."

"She seems sweet."

"She's like a sour candy really. Sweet on the inside, but you have to get past the sour exterior."

"Harley and I have that in common," I said, deadpan.

He laughed in surprise. "I'm not sure I like comparing you to my sister."

I bit my lip. "That's fair."

We hopped into the back of the limo with the rest of our friends, fitting snug in a corner, Whitt's arm draped casually across my shoulders. Champagne flutes were passed around even though we were only driving the ten minutes to Wright Construction to use their penthouse restaurant for Jensen's mayoral fundraiser.

I'd been in a limo once with Arnold when he took me to Vegas for the weekend. I could rate that experience as a one on a scale from one to ten compared to this. I'd never known precisely what I was missing by not having friends like this. And here, in the back of the limo, drinking champagne and enjoying the gentle ribbing about Whitt and me, I could see how my entire life could have changed had someone accepted me.

I finished a glass of champagne and passed it back to a giggling Nora as we drove up to the front door. It was strange to step out onto the familiar pavement. Wright

Construction was a staple of the community, and until I'd started working here, I'd never been inside. Now, I was here as a guest for a fancy dinner. All of it felt surreal.

"You ready?" Whitt asked, holding his arm out.

I took a deep breath and then nodded, agreeing to so much more than he could know. "Let's do it."

The group piled into the elevator and took us up to the restaurant that Wright was famous for. It took up the entirety of the top floor of the building with windows around the entire perimeter for a spectacular view of the sunset as it fell over the Texas Tech campus.

Nora sighed in delight next to me. "The campaign event planner is spot-on."

The place had transformed from the business locale it typically was used as to an elaborate and elegant dinner party, complete with a dozen circular tables decorated with fresh flowers. Waiters, dressed in black suits, carried trays of champagne and hors d'oeuvres. Hollin snagged a little finger sandwich and held his hand up to stop another waiter carrying champagne. Piper rolled her eyes at him, but she took the proffered glass.

The rest of our group took drinks, too, and then headed across the glossy hardwood floor to the table with our names written in calligraphy on small white cards. I swayed lightly to the soft classical music coming from a string quartet. My stomach flipped as I looked around the room—the fancy party, the abundance of florals, and all the important people in town. I couldn't believe *I* was here.

"This is incredible," I told Whitt.

"Jensen knows how to throw a party. That's for sure."

"I need to go talk to the planner," Nora said with wide-eyed wonder.

West laughed. "I'll go with you." He grinned at his brother before disappearing after her.

"He's smitten," I said.

"No shit."

I laughed. "Why do you sound disappointed?"

"I'm happy for him. He's like a lost puppy when he's in love."

"It's cute."

"I think so, too," Harley said. She smacked Whitt's arm. "You could use a little more lost puppy in your life."

He grinned at his sister. "So could you."

She rolled her eyes. "I'm nineteen. I don't need to fall in love."

"College guys suck anyway," I told her.

Her eyes roamed the already-busy dinner party. "Tell me about it."

"Whitt!" a voice called over the increasing chatter.

Whitt turned to find Jordan and Julian standing in a group with other people from Wright Construction. They waved him over. He glanced down at me in concern.

"I'm a big girl. I'll be fine. Harley and I will get to know each other."

Whitt paled. "That's what I'm worried about."

Harley and I laughed at the same time. But Whitt shook his head and walked over to his brothers.

"Well, I like you already," Harley said. "Though you're waaay too good for him."

It was my turn to give her a skeptical look. But Harley barreled on, like she hadn't said something entirely unbelievable.

"I mean, look at you. You're hot as fuck."

"Thank you."

"Drink?" Harley asked, snagging champagne for the

both of us.

"Aren't you underage?"

"I won't tell if you won't." Harley winked at me.

I laughed. "Just don't let your brothers see you."

"Trust me, my entire life is getting around my brothers seeing anything I'm doing."

We chuckled at that. I wasn't going to parent her. I had done worse at her age. If a few glasses of champagne were the worst she could do here, then I thought she'd be fine.

We were chatting about her trip back to Seattle for the summer when a tall figure appeared before us. He was all tall, blond, and undeniably handsome. He looked so much like a younger version of his father. Charming and relentlessly good-looking. My heart beat in my throat at the sight of him—Chase Sinclair.

This was a problem that I hadn't foreseen. Of course the Sinclairs were going to be in attendance. Did Chase's appearance mean that Arnold would be here as well?

"Hello, Eve," Chase said. His voice was only slightly strained at the edges when he said my name.

He knew that I'd been with his dad. Everyone knew. Great.

But his gaze slipped from mine to land on Harley, and something shifted in them. From discomfort to desire, like a light switch. An almost-hypnotic, restrained look to him. With one hand clenched at his side, as if he needed to physically hold himself back.

My eyes snapped to Harley and saw a coquettish expression on her face. This was not the first time they'd met. The memory of them dancing close at Jordan and Annie's wedding came back to me. Whitt and I had left before the night ended. Had something happened between Chase and Harley in our absence?

"Harley," he said with a tip of his head. His voice rough, like a shackle around his throat.

"Chase," Harley said, all unbothered cool girl in her voice. All flirtation in her look.

"It's good to see you both."

"You, too," I said as I sized up what was going on. "Is it just...you representing your family tonight?"

"Indeed. Just me."

I relaxed despite the awkwardness. What a relief.

"Maybe you can save me a dance later," Harley said.

Chase swallowed. "Perhaps."

And then he excused himself and disappeared back into the crowd.

I whipped around. "He is *ten* years older than you."

Harley arched an eyebrow. "And? Didn't you date his dad?"

"Obviously," I said, waving away the fact. "But I don't have two older brothers who would probably kill him if they saw what I just saw."

"And what did you see?" Harley asked with an interested glint in her eye.

"That he was barely holding himself back from attacking you."

Her smile vanished, and her gaze slipped from mine. "That's not true. He's not interested."

I raised my eyebrows. "That's not what it looked like."

"Trust me, Chase Sinclair has no interest in me," she said with a sigh that made it sound like a tragedy.

Jesus, what the hell had gone down with them?

I didn't have a chance to ask before Whitt returned, snaking an arm around my waist, and Jensen stepped up with a microphone in hand to welcome everyone to the fundraising dinner for his campaign.

18

WHITTON

Eve was in my arms as we twirled on the dance floor. My fingers holding her narrow waist. Her arms draped across my shoulders. The night was beyond perfection, starting with the delicious dinner—steak braised in some indescribable sauce with whipped potatoes and an array of colorful vegetables, the rolls fresh and slathered in butter, the wine perfectly complementing every bite, and we'd shared our desserts: mine a decadent chocolate explosion, complete with raspberries and a dollop of whipped cream, and hers a perfectly fired crème brûleé with a swirl of rosewater caramel—and ending with us dancing in the middle of the room with our friends.

If only my sister wasn't still drinking.

"Should I say something to her?" I asked Eve.

"You're hovering. She's fine. She's had two glasses of champagne all night, and she ate a full meal. We have the limo, so she's not driving home. And you know she's in college, right? Because I'm pretty sure we all drank in college."

"Yeah, but..."

"Maybe hold that thought and consider kissing me instead."

I laughed, taken off guard by her boldness. "I could do that."

"Oh yeah? I haven't gotten a single kiss all night."

I drew her closer against my body. My hand slipped to her lower back, pushing our hips together. She made a noise of pleasure. My head dipped down to her shoulder, where I pressed a faint kiss into the bare skin. She shivered at the touch, and I worked upward, kissing a soft trail up to just behind her earlobe.

"Like that?" I breathed.

"Not...not exactly what I had in mind," she said, her words slurred with desire.

My mind flared with all the possibilities for tonight. Taking her back in the limo, driving her to my place, spending all night in my house, having sex on every available surface. I wanted that so fucking bad.

But then another thought crossed my mind. We were in Wright Construction. My office was only two floors below us. My office with my enormous new desk and floor-to-ceiling windows. The desk I'd dreamed of fucking her on since the moment I'd gotten the upgrade.

"I have an idea."

She pulled back to meet my gaze. "Why do I hear mischief in your voice?"

I grinned. "You wanted me to have some fun, right?"

"We've been having a lot of fun."

"Ready for some more?"

I could see she was before she nodded. I tucked her hand into the crook of my arm and then escorted her off of the dance floor. I left our friends to their good time and was out of the hall and halfway to the elevator when I saw a face that I hadn't expected. All the excitement from a moment ago fled my body.

"Colton, what are you doing here?"

He was with three older boys. One surreptitiously hid a bottle of tequila, which I would bet money they hadn't paid for. I didn't recognize the other boys. Only that they were all on the verge of wasted.

Colton enough so that he laughed when he saw me. "Boss man!"

There should have been fear there. Instead, it was only idiocy. Fuck.

Eve squeezed my arm and did a perimeter sweep. As if she knew before I had to say it that no one else could see this.

"Are you supposed to be here tonight?" I reached for his sleeve.

Colton brushed me off, gesturing to his friend. "Monk thought it'd be fun to come see my dad's big party."

Monk was the one with the tequila. The ringleader then. I didn't know how Colton didn't see that he was bad news. He was dressed nice in khakis and a polo with boat shoes, but Colton had more sense than to be fooled by private school flunkies. Where was all of his New York City smarts?

"Hey, man," Monk said, offering his hand.

I just glared at him.

Monk slowly lowered his hand. "Lame party anyway. Come on, Colt. Let's get out of here."

Colton shrugged. "Whatever."

My hand came down hard on Colton's shoulder. That wasn't happening. "Who drove?"

Colton pointed at another kid. "Chet has his license."

Chet was a tall, scrawny kid who looked high as fuck. He

had a joint tucked behind his ear. The third guy was smiling like an idiot, as if he found all of this to be a huge joke.

"I don't think that's a good idea."

Colton tried to free himself from my grip with no luck. "We're just having a good time."

"You're smarter than this."

He seethed at those words. "I don't *need* your help."

"Colton Wright!" A voice cracked across the divide.

Colton and I winced at the same time. We both recognized Jensen's voice from a mile off. The other guys should have known what was coming, too. They all should have gotten out of there while they could. This wasn't going to be pleasant. I'd done what I could to try to save Colton, but there wasn't going to be any saving once his dad took one look at him.

"Dad," Colton said, finally jerking out of my grip.

"What are you doing?" he asked, striding toward us with all the power of a man who always got his way.

He was dressed like the mayoral candidate in a black suit and tie. None of the familiar good ole boy who wore jeans and drove a pickup truck tonight. Colton wasn't just getting the enmity of his dad; he was getting it from the man who would own the city.

"Just heading out," Colton said.

"Out. You are supposed to be at home."

He shrugged. "I was bored."

"Bored," Jensen said softly, dangerously. His eyes flicked from his son to the three losers he was standing with. He took in the scene in an instant.

Eve put her hand on mine, as if to say we should leave. Jensen should handle this. But, fuck, I felt sorry for the kid.

"I can take him home," I offered.

Jensen turned back to me, as if processing that I was

there. "That won't be necessary."

"Sir, I think—"

"I said, that won't be necessary," he all but snarled.

He was barely clinging on to control. My presence was only making it worse because, now, I was a witness.

I glanced at Colton, but he wouldn't even meet my gaze.

"Just go," he ground out.

It felt wrong. I should say more. Colton Wright was fifteen and drunk and making every wrong decision. He deserved whatever was coming to him. He'd deserved being sent to Lubbock as punishment for getting arrested. And yet I felt for the kid. Growing up with no rules, with a father so far away, I could empathize.

Jensen's dad had died when he was in college. He'd had to come home and help raise his younger siblings, take over the company. He might have gone through it, but I was sure he was judging his own son on a different scale.

Jensen pushed open a door and pointed at it. "The four of you, inside."

"We were just..." Monk pointed back to the elevators.

"Now!"

All four boys snapped to attention like they were in the military and grumbled as they strode into the open conference room. The door swung behind them, and Jensen sighed heavily. The frustration vanished, and in its place was a concerned father who had no idea what to do with his little troublemaker.

He held his hand out to me. "Thank you. For looking after him."

"Of course."

He smiled at Eve and offered her his hand as well. She shook without a word. "Glad you two were here."

Then, he nodded at us and wrenched the door back

open. We watched his back disappear.

I'd done my best. I couldn't save a lost cause. Colton would have to learn this lesson the hard way.

"Come on," I said, reaching for her hand.

But she was still frozen, staring at the closed door. Her eyes were distant. Somewhere very, very far off. Like I'd have to cross a desert to reach her in that moment.

"Eve?"

She blinked and came back to herself. "Sorry."

"You okay?"

"I'm glad he has you to look out for him."

I scoffed. "Little good it's doing."

"More good than you know."

"Doesn't feel like that." I ran a hand down my face. "He deserves better. I know his parents care about him and they're doing the best they can. But he needs...a friend. I don't think any of the shits he knew in New York fit that bill. And those idiots he's with certainly don't."

"I get it." Her gaze slid up to me, and there was that haunted look again. The one she'd worn before collapsing into my arms last week. "My dad...well, he didn't really want us."

"Us?"

She swallowed. "Me and my sister, Bailey."

I masked my surprise that she was opening up to me. I wanted this. I wanted to know everything about her. I wanted to know what her tears had been about, and how to make them stop.

"I didn't know you had a sister."

"Yeah," she whispered. Then, she laughed softly. "I don't know when I got like this. Everyone in my life used to know about her. We were inseparable."

"Is she back in Midland?"

"Yeah. She lives with our dad. She's about to start her senior year in high school." Her eyes were empty.

"Why didn't you live with your mom?"

She sighed. "Mom left when we were little. Bailey was only three. I haven't seen her since then. No card or email or anything."

My jaw clenched. "What a coward."

"Yeah. My dad mostly dumped us on his mom. Gram did most of the raising." She shrugged, as if she wasn't relaying a tragedy. "But Gram died last year."

"I'm so sorry."

"Yeah," she said, hollow inside and out. "And now, it's just Dad."

"Your sister is with him?"

"Yes. Last year was hard for her. Between Gram and then living with Dad." She wrapped her arms around her center. "I see so much of Colton in her. The anger. The pain. The recklessness. Dad makes it all worse. And I can't move to Midland to be with her. Dad won't let her move here to live with me. There's so little that I can do."

Her eyes finally met mine. Unshed tears gathered in her dark lashes. My heart felt near to bursting. This miraculous woman, who never seemed to let anything bother her. The girl that I'd seen dance in the rain after a soccer game. The one who had wrapped a fist around my heart and held it hostage. She was full of all this pain and longing for a life that she was never afforded. One that she wanted for her sister, as if Bailey were her own.

If I'd thought I was falling for her before, this tipped me completely over the edge.

I gathered her into my arms. Her narrow shoulders were heavy with the weight of problems she never let anyone else see. I wanted to be the one she could rely on rather than one adding more stress. She'd come apart in my arms the other day, and she was finally showing more vulnerability. I wanted to be there to help put her back together.

"I'm glad you told me."

She sniffled. "I feel ridiculous. I hate crying. Seeing Colton shouldn't have triggered this so bad."

"You're not ridiculous." I pulled back and rubbed a thumb under her eye, careful not to smudge her makeup. "And you're beautiful when you cry."

She laughed hoarsely. "That's a new one. I don't think any guy has ever seen me cry."

"I'm glad you feel comfortable enough to do it in front of me."

"Twice." She shook her head. "I'm losing my touch."

I pressed a soft kiss to her lips. "Nah, you just can't resist me."

"Oh, is that so? You make a lot of girls cry?"

"Well, when you put it that way."

She chuckled. "Thank you. You know, for being there for me the other day and for this."

"You don't have to thank me. I want to be there for you."

"Yeah, but we were going to have fun, and now, I'm crying."

I kissed her hand as we slowly headed back toward the party. "There'll be time for that later."

"I'm going to take you up on that."

"You'd better," I said, squeezing her ass just before we got back inside.

Maybe I hadn't gotten to live out my desk fantasy, but I'd gotten something better. As much as I loved our sex life, I wanted to know every single thing about her. Now more than ever, I wanted to be a part of her life. Because with one tear-streaked look, she had claimed me completely.

19

WHITTON

"Colton, get in here," I called from my desk on Monday morning.

He toed the door open and shuffled across the floor as if he were walking to his death sentence. "What?"

Oh, poor surly teenager.

"Where's my coffee?"

"Probably still in the pot."

My eyes caught his. Defiance was in his irises.

My assistant had messaged me privately to say that Colton was in a "mood" today. I knew exactly why he was acting like this. Consequences to his actions from this weekend. But it wasn't fair to take it out on my assistant or me because he'd fucked up.

"Do you think this is going to make anything better?"

He shrugged and slumped into the chair in front of my desk. "I don't know."

"What happened after I left?"

He crossed his arms over his chest and stared out the windows. "Got yelled at. Then, Dad drove me and my friends home and spoke to everyone's parents."

Yeah, that sounded right. "How'd that go over?"

"Everyone's grounded."

"You were all drunk and going to drive. I don't know what you expected."

"Dad told me if I fucked up again, then I wasn't going back home."

I winced. Ah, there it was.

So, if he got in trouble again, then he wasn't going to get to return to the city. I hadn't known the details of the arrangement he had with Jensen. I'd assumed that he was in Lubbock for good after getting arrested. But if he was only here for the summer, the threat of not going back to New York at all would explain how pissed off he was.

"Have you considered not fucking up again?"

Colton rolled his eyes at me. "What else is there to do in this town?"

"The soccer league is starting back up."

Colton's head popped up. "The Tacos? The team your girl is on?"

"The one."

"Dad wouldn't let me go," he grumbled. "He doesn't trust me to be unsupervised."

"What if you were playing?"

He eyed me like I'd grown a second head. "That's for *adults*." He said the word like a slur.

"It'd be fine. You'd play a few games until you go back to the city. No one will care. We're Wrights, remember?" I told him. "We run this town."

Colton straightened. As if he'd probably heard it before, but not in the context that I'd given him. Honestly, it was a realization that I was still reckoning with.

"I'll even ask your dad," I offered.

I didn't know why I was helping the him so much, but I

couldn't leave him like this. One mistake could cascade into a row of dominoes that he might never come back from. Sure, most fifteen-year-olds were moody, hormonal monsters, but I liked this one. So...

"You'd do that?"

"If you get me my coffee, then yes."

Colton laughed as he came to his feet. Some of the morose behavior falling off his shoulders. "Deal, boss."

I watched him head out of my office with his chip back on his shoulder. Little shit. My coffee had better be hot because I was about to go to bat with Jensen Wright for him.

Eve blinked at me from the passenger seat of my Lexus on the way to the game later that week. "You did what?"

"I got Colton on The Tacos."

"But...what? How?"

I cleared my throat. "A good deal of cajoling."

"Explain."

"Well, I called his dad."

"You called Jensen."

"Sure did," I said with a grimace. "It was super fun. In the end, he agreed to let him play. He and Emery are coming to the game tonight, too."

"But is he even any good?" Eve asked with a hint of desperation.

I laughed when I realized that was what she was really worried about. "I have no idea."

"Well, he'd better be. Isaac is going to kill us if we bring on a fifteen-year-old kid *and* he sucks. Maybe we can bench him."

"Eve."

"I mean, he can't be worse than Nora. Love her to death, but ball-handling skills aren't her strong suit."

I snorted.

"Don't make that sexual."

"Oh no, never," I said with a smirk. "Maybe later, we can practice your ball-handling skills."

"Shut up," she said with a laugh, smacking my chest.

"It's going to be fine. He went to a private school in New York. The only thing I've heard him talk about other than drinking and girls is soccer. I'd guess he doesn't completely suck."

"He'd better not. Or you're in for it, Whitton Wright."

"I accept that."

"Wait, you did run this by Isaac, right? I am not going to be the one to tell him..."

"I spoke to Isaac."

Isaac had put the team together and was the unofficial manager. He was married to Piper's sister and had played soccer in college. The Tacos team was his baby.

"Phew," she said, breathing out heavily. "Good."

I parked my Lexus in the parking lot for the outdoor fields. Already, a dozen teams were out on the pitch, getting ready for the start of the season.

I stopped Eve before she could get out. "And another thing. I heard from Jordan today that he wants us to head back to Midland next weekend. You free?"

She grinned devilishly. "Two rooms or one?"

"One."

"Good answer."

She leaned forward and captured my lips for a brief kiss before getting out and grabbing her soccer bag. I joined her on the walk to the open field. Our friends were already in attendance, warming up or chatting. I shook hands with

Hollin and West, fielded good-natured ribbing from Isaac, and accepted Julian's rundown of the season even though I still wasn't a huge soccer guy. Blaire grabbed Eve as soon as she saw her, and they disappeared onto the field to run drills. Nora kissed West and then joined them in their warm-up.

But no Colton.

I checked my phone to see if I had some shit text from him, but there was nothing. Had Jensen changed his mind? He'd been adamant about Colton not joining the team when I first suggested it. Something about rewarding back behavior. But I'd insisted it'd be good for Colton to direct his feelings of resentment into physical activity. It was like getting the wiggles out of toddlers. Necessary and effective.

Then, I saw Jensen's truck pull into a spot at the front. Colton hopped out first with Jensen and Emery coming behind him. They must have left the kids at home with a sitter to be here for him. That was the right call.

"You made it," I said, holding my hand out to Colton.

"Yeah, boss," he said, slapping my hand instead of shaking. "Can't believe I'm here."

"Eve wants me to ask if you've played before. As if that didn't cross my mind in all of this."

Colton shot me a look that said I was an idiot. "Of course I can play. Watch me run circles around everyone out there."

"Ah, so the competitive streak runs straight through our family."

"I take offense to that," Jensen said, holding his hand out to me.

Emery just laughed. "Uh, there is no offense there. You're all competitive. It's ridiculous."

Jensen's gaze on her was like the moon turning toward

the sun and feeling its warmth for the first time. "You're lucky that I love you."

"Ha!" she said, elbowing his side. "You're the lucky one."

"Obviously."

He kissed her, and Colton gagged. "Can you two not?"

I shoved him toward Isaac. "Go meet your team captain and get a jersey."

"Sure, boss."

All three of us watched him run toward Isaac to introduce himself.

"Thank you," Emery said. She touched my arm. "I really appreciate you looking out for him. Jensen said you found him the other night at the party."

"Yeah, I'm glad that you agreed to have him play."

Jensen shrugged, defeated. "I love him. I want him to be happy. If this helps the behavioral problems, then he can play as much soccer as he wants."

"Okay, but real question," I said, glancing back at Colton. "Can he actually play? Because otherwise, Eve might kill me."

Jensen laughed. "He can play. It's not just ego."

"You mean, *all* ego," Emery said. "Because the boy has *your* ego."

"Can't help it if we're naturally good at everything, love."

Emery rolled her eyes. "Oh, good at *everything*, huh?"

"Obviously."

"Now, whose ego is showing?"

"You married me."

She snorted. "As you keep reminding me."

I left them to lovingly bicker and took my seat in the stands with West. He shot me a look that I read as, *What the hell have you gotten us into?*

I just shrugged. We were about to find out.

Isaac didn't start Colton since he was the newest member. So, he stood on the sidelines, bouncing on the balls of his cleats and shouting encouragement to his teammates. He was a completely and entirely different kid in a uniform. Gone were the attitude and defiance. All that was left was camaraderie, excitement, and a drive to get out there.

Isaac pulled himself out first to let Colton on the field. The kid full-on sprinted to the center midfield position, and as soon as the whistle was blown, he was off like a bullet. He had boundless energy, dribbling up to Blaire and Eve to assist for shots, pulling back to defense to hand the ball off to Annie and Hollin, and moving seamlessly through the center field with Julian and Nora. He played selflessly. None of the ball hogging I would expect from someone with his self-esteem. And damn him, he *was* good.

Good enough that Isaac didn't pull him out when he came back in. He rotated the rest of the team to keep Colton on the field. Isaac had a daughter. He must have seen, the same way I had, that the kid needed to be out there. Or maybe he just wanted to win, and Colton was assisting Blaire and Eve to multiple goals, where girl goals counted for two points.

By the whistle blow, the Tacos were up by an outrageous amount to an opponent that West insisted they'd barely beaten the year before. With Eve and Colton on the pitch, they were unstoppable.

Eve ripped off her Tacos uniform top, revealing the sports bra, toned body, and tattoos underneath. She vaulted the bleachers and plopped into my lap.

"Okay, I forgive you," she said.

West laughed next to us. "This should be good."

Eve kicked West's shin. He yelped.

"I accept your forgiveness?" I said more as a question.

"The kid's good. We'll keep him," Eve said.

"Excellent."

"Pizza?"

"I'm down."

Eve leaned back and waved at Jensen and Emery. "Hey, we do pizza after every game. Can the kid come with us?"

Jensen exchanged a look with Emery, who shrugged. "We have to get home. Her mom is watching the kids."

"We can drive him home," I said automatically.

"I don't know," Jensen said.

"Maybe you should let him," Emery said. "He played really well."

"We'll be with him the entire time," I insisted.

Jensen breathed out heavily. "Fine. Keep me up-to-date, all right?"

"Of course." I turned back to the pitch and called to Colton, "Hey, kid. You want some pizza?"

A fifteen-year-old boy never ever, ever said no to pizza.

"Fuck yes."

"Colton!" Jensen growled.

But Colton was on a high from the game. "Can I go?"

"Whitt said he'd drive you home, but if you step out of line with him, then we'll have to reevaluate you playing with the team."

"Is that a yes?" Colton asked defiantly. A smile still stretched his face.

"Yes," Jensen said with a smile and a shake of his head. "Kids," he grumbled under his breath.

I nodded my head at Colton. "You're with us."

"Let me grab my stuff," Colton said excitedly.

Eve hopped off my lap, and we followed the rest of the team off the bleachers. I wrapped an arm around her waist and leaned in, "Guess we won't get to have fun in the car."

"Maybe we can have fun after then," she teased.

"You've convinced me."

"You did a good thing. You know, letting him play."

I shrugged. "I'm glad it worked out."

"Me too."

"So this weekend, I heard a rumor."

"Oh?" she asked, throwing me a look.

"That it's your birthday."

She groaned. "Nooo. How did you find out?"

"What matters is, you're going to let me take you out on a date."

"Am I?"

"You are. You're going to dress in one of your hot fucking dresses and those heels you always wear. I'm going to pick you up with flowers and take you to a fancy dinner."

"And after?"

"And after, I'll fuck your brains out."

"Happy birthday to me," she said, leaning in to me. Her pupils were dilated, and I was pretty sure she would let me fuck her right then and there if I wanted.

"I'll pick you up around seven."

She bit her lip and then nodded. "Seven it is."

Colton jogged up to us then. "All right, boss man. Gimme those keys. I want to drive."

I shoved him in the back of his head, and he cackled. "Get in the backseat. No one drives my car."

"You're no fun."

But I knew he didn't mean it.

Eve laughed at our antics. I loved seeing her like this. Both of them like this. It felt like things were finally coming together.

20

EVE

Even though it was my birthday, I spent all day showing houses to my clients. No rest for the wicked.

My last showing was around six, and I dashed home to spend adequate time getting ready for my date tonight. I preened in the mirror. Date. I was going on a date...for my birthday. Something I actually wanted to do. I hadn't known that I could feel like this again. That Whitt, of all people, could make me feel like this again.

I spent extra care on my hair and makeup, pulled out the fancy lingerie for tonight, and slid on a little black dress and heels. I grabbed a teeny clutch just as the doorbell rang, and I darted into the living room. My roommates were out with their boyfriends or working. I hated to admit that I was disappointed that no one else knew it was my birthday. Not that I'd told anyone. Which meant that I had no right to be disappointed. Still, I was...

Whitt hadn't told me how he'd found out.

I was going to get it out of him one way or another.

I yanked the door open and found him in a sharp charcoal suit that had tailored lines and barely contained his height and bulk. I lived for him in a suit.

"Happy birthday," he said as he held up a bouquet of peonies.

My favorite flower. Gah.

"You went all out."

"I promised flowers."

He grinned as he passed them to me. I brought them to my nose and drew in the floral scent.

"You delivered." We strode into the kitchen, and I found one of Blaire's many vases to put them in. "Shall we?"

But Whitt's eyes were still set on me in my little black dress. "Trying to get my fill."

I bit my lip. "Well, I wore something special for you, but you can't see it until after dinner."

His eyes blazed at that news. "Oh?"

"Yes, sir," I teased.

He walked me into the kitchen counter. "What exactly is so special?" His hands fell to my bare thighs and began to work their way up under my dress.

I smacked his hand. "After dinner."

"Oh, but now I'm interested."

The man dropped to one knee in front of me. My mouth watered at the sight. How could I deny him anything when he supplicated before me as if I were a goddess?

His nose ran along my inner thigh. "Anyone else home?"

"No," I gasped.

"Oh good."

He found the edge of my black garter belt and groaned deep in the back of his throat. He rucked the dress up to my hips, revealing my black garter and thong set. His eyes were wide with desire.

"Well, well, well," he drawled, "this is a surprise."

"It was *supposed* to be. You're ruining the surprise."

He teased the line of the belt with his tongue, and I shivered all over. "It's still a surprise."

"Don't...don't we have a reservation?"

"We have somewhere to be, yes."

His hand slid under the lace of my thong. He trailed a finger down the seam of my pussy, feeling the slick wetness for him. He looked up at me, grinning like a devil.

"Someone is ready for me."

"So ready," I panted.

His eyes were on fire when he asked, "Do you want to come on my hand or my dick?"

"Yes," was the only correct answer.

He laughed, slipping two fingers inside of me and pressing the heel of his palm against my clit. I shuddered at the intense pressure. I was shameless enough to ride his hand, wanting the release that only he could provide. I might as well toss my vibrator for all the use it had been getting since I'd started seeing Whitt.

"Oh God," I groaned.

His fingers curled inward, hitting a spot so perfectly that I cried out from shock. Every nerve in my body went into overdrive. Heightened awareness suddenly sharp as glass. And then I unleashed.

My body released like I'd been waiting for that orgasm all day. It had taken a matter of minutes with his dirty mouth and practiced fingers. I was the only one who could normally get me off that fast.

He pulled his fingers out of me with a devious look on his face. Then, he came to his feet, his dexterous fingers already unbuckling his suit pants. He hefted my ass onto the kitchen counter and thrust into me, riding out the last waves of my climax.

"Fuck," I gasped.

"God, your pussy is so fucking tight and so fucking wet."

He slammed into me, hard and fast. His cock lengthening, even as he fucked me. I reached back for anything to hold on to, grasping the upper cabinets and having a sudden fear that I'd rip them from their mounting. His grip was just as harsh on my hips as he rode me. The passion so strong that neither of us could have waited even a second longer. Let alone until the end of our evening.

"Close," I said, unable to believe that he could milk another one out of me so quickly. And yet...

"Come for me," he said.

Then, he gripped the back of my neck and wrenched me forward. Our lips collided and tongues clashed. There was no finesse in the embrace, just power and need. A drive to get us both there a second quicker than we would have otherwise.

My nails dug into his suit shirt. He growled into my mouth. Our movements picked up. And then there was nothing but euphoria. I hit my second release like an avalanche, picking up speed and force. It triggered his a second later, and I felt him hot and wet inside of me.

He leaned his forehead against mine. Our breaths mingled in the space as we both panted.

"Wow," I breathed.

"Happy birthday," he teased, pressing another kiss to my lips.

He slid out of me, and I dropped to my feet, dizzy with the aftereffects.

"Do you still want to go to dinner?"

He smiled. "Obviously."

I didn't know how I'd make it through without wanting to jump his bones again.

We both spent a few minutes cleaning ourselves up, and then he was opening the front door and escorting me to his car. Our fingers entwined between the seats as he drove us to the restaurant.

But when we pulled up to Flips—a local bar that served bar food and was known for hot dogs, of all things—I was side-eyeing the fuck out of him.

"Flips?"

"Yep."

"Not La Sirena or West Table or Funky Door?"

He laughed. "If you had preferences, you should have said them."

"But I thought you said we had a reservation," I said, confused.

Flips did *not* need a reservation.

"I didn't exactly say that," he said as he parked out front.

Now, I was really giving him a look. He *hadn't* said that, had he? He'd just said that we had somewhere to be. What the hell did that mean? I'd been too deep in the throes of passion to question it.

Whitt stepped out of the car and jogged around to the passenger side to open my door. He helped me out, all while my quizzical look remained.

"You told me to have fun. Could you do the same?" he asked with a shit-eating grin.

"I'm just saying gourmet hot dogs are not my idea of fun, sir."

"Noted."

He was smirking as he led me toward the bar in our fancy attire. I felt *way* overdressed for the occasion, but so was he. We'd at least make a spectacle together.

He tugged the door open for me, and I entered the darkened interior. My eyes tried to adjust to the absolute black inside. What in the hell was going on?

Then, the lights flickered on, and the entire place erupted with a cheered, "Happy birthday!"

I gasped, my hand going to my chest as I took in the scene before me. All of our friends in their best attire, shouting and jumping up and down, arms in the air and smiles on their faces. A balloon arch with *Happy Birthday, Eve* in the center. Streamers, confetti, and noisemakers were everywhere. A few people even had on little triangular birthday hats.

"Happy birthday," Whitt said through the din.

I looked up at him, trying to suppress the tears coming to my eyes. "You did this?"

"With help from Nora, Blaire, and Piper," he said. "Trust me, I am not the mastermind of decorations."

"That would be me," Nora said, drawing me in for a hug. She slung a white *Birthday Girl* sash over my head and placed a little plastic birthday tiara into my hair. "Happy birthday, gorgeous."

Blaire and Piper were there next, hugging me and wishing me all the best. Piper gestured to the catering they'd had brought in for the event, including a two-tiered birthday cake with green flowers like a ribbon down its center. My name in emerald letters atop it.

"Y'all are amazing. I can't...I can't even believe this."

My throat hurt, and I was choked up. I could barely get the words out. They'd all done this for *me*. The girl who'd never had friends. The girl who had always been talked about and shunned. The girl who had wanted nothing more than for others to see her as the soft, loving, friendly person I really was and not just the hardened outer core I'd developed to prevent myself from getting hurt over and over again. I wanted this with all my heart, and it meant everything that they'd all done this for me.

I threw my arms around Whitt and pressed a kiss to his lips. The crowd catcalled us. It was the most public display I'd ever given since we'd gotten together. And I could do nothing but thank him over and over again for everything.

"Better than dinner?" he teased.

"Much better. Forgive me for doubting you," I said with a laugh as a drink was placed in my hand and music filled the space.

"Forgiven. It was all worth it to see that look on your face."

I laughed, still buzzing from the fact that this had happened at all. "How did I get so lucky?"

"You belong here, Eve."

The words I'd always wanted to hear. I'd thought he was too good to be true, but really, it had been *all* of this. And now, somehow, it was my reality.

I drew him in for a hug. "Thank you."

He kissed the top of my head. "Of course. I like to see you happy."

We were drawn into the party with all of our friends. Drinking, dancing, and laughing like I hadn't laughed in years. I was on the dance floor, arms overhead, grinding with Blaire when I felt my phone buzz in my purse at my hip.

I extracted myself from the group to check my phone and saw that Bailey was videocalling me. I hadn't heard from her all day. I'd been waiting for this call.

Whitt was at my side a second later. "Everything okay?"

"It's Bailey. Going to take this."

"Okay. Let's get you somewhere quiet."

He escorted me away from the loud music and to the

corridor that led to the restrooms. At least here, I could hear myself think.

"Should I go?" Whitt asked, gesturing back to the party.

I shook my head. "Stay." Then, I answered the phone and saw my sister's pretty face on the screen. "Hey, Bails."

"Ahhh, happy birthday!" Bailey cried. She went into a full rendition of the birthday song while I laughed at her ridiculousness.

"Thank you."

"How does it feel to be old?"

I stuck my tongue out at her. "I hate you."

"I know. I love you, too."

"It's nice to have a fully developed prefrontal cortex, unlike someone I know."

My sister rolled her eyes. "Overrated."

"Are you ready to start school?"

She grumbled. "Let's not. Where are you? Sounds like a party."

"Yeah. My friends threw me a surprise party." Whitt arched an eyebrow, and I added, "And my...date spearheaded the whole thing."

"Date?" Bailey gasped. "Like a boyfriend?"

"Sort of."

Whitt's eyebrows rose sharply at that.

"Let me see. Let me see!"

I laughed and gestured Whitt into the picture. "Bailey, this is Whitton Wright."

"Hello, Bailey," Whitt said. "Please call me Whitt. Everyone else does."

Bailey grinned. "Oh my God, hi. I've never met my sister's boyfriend before. This is awesome."

"Bails," I groaned.

"Right. Right. Sort of boyfriend. And a Wright. Isn't that the new company you're working for?"

"Sure is," I said. "He works there, too."

"Ahhh, office romance," Bailey said with a wink. "I get it."

I shook my head at her. "You're silly."

"You and your sister have that in common," Whitt said.

"We definitely do." Someone else spoke on the other line. Bailey turned her head and yelled back, "I'm on the phone with Bailey and her boyfriend. Jesus Christ, give me a minute." Bailey looked back apologetically.

Fury burned in my veins. That had to be my dad. Fuck him.

"I have to go. I don't want to keep you from your fancy party anyway. I'll see you next week?"

"I'll be there. Love you. Call me later if you need to talk."

Bailey waved me off, said good-bye to Whitt, and then ended the call.

"She's a riot," Whitt said.

"That's Bailey."

"And you're going to see her when we're in Midland?"

"Yeah." I glanced down at my feet and back up into his impossibly blue eyes. "Do you want to go with me?"

"As your sort of boyfriend or your actual boyfriend?" he teased with a grin.

I laughed and pushed him backward. "Do you want to go or not?" I asked, breathless from the feel of his solid body against mine.

"Of course I do. Anything for you."

And he meant it.

PART IV

CHERRY BLOSSOMS

21

WHITTON

"Is this going to be like that barbecue place?" I asked skeptically.

Eve laughed and shrugged. "I mean, sort of. It's Midland. What did you expect?"

"With you, I'm never quite sure."

Her grin was triumphant. "I like to be unpredictable."

And unpredictable she was. In the best way.

We'd spent yesterday on site with the Kings, finalizing the plans for their new development. Wright Construction would be breaking ground in the next couple of weeks. We'd agreed to dinner with the Kings later tonight, but the rest of the day was ours.

Which was how we'd ended up at some barn-style restaurant with the word *Boose* in bright red neon letters across the front.

"Boose?" I asked.

"The story is that it used to be called Caboose when it was downtown. The first two letters burned out, and no one ever fixed them. Then, when it burned down in the '90s, they built the new place and dropped Caboose and just became Boose. Everyone called it Boose anyway."

My gaze shot to hers. "You made that up."

"Did not!" she insisted. "It's just Boose."

"And we're meeting your sister here?"

"Yeah. Bails said she'd be a few minutes late."

"Oh, so it runs in the family?" I joked.

She shoved me as we made our way toward the restaurant. "Jerk."

"Can't help it if it's true."

"I haven't been late for anything lately that you didn't make me late for."

"I don't apologize for fucking you first on your birthday." My hand slid from her waist to her ass and squeezed. "I was in control of the clock anyway."

She flushed. "You just made everyone else wait, you mean?"

"Are you complaining?"

"Not in the least." She winked. "I wasn't complaining last night or this morning either." Then, she slapped my ass and wrenched open the door to Boose.

I could do nothing but laugh at her. The weekend was already shaping up to be incredible. Starting with the hotel where, somehow, we'd gotten the same guy at the front desk. He even remembered that we'd had to share a room and offered an extra complimentary room since the rodeo wasn't in town this weekend. We'd declined, and he'd blushed.

Then, we'd promptly had sex on every surface of the place. As incredible as the sex was, I still felt like I had to hold back with her. Like we were so close to me being able to release entirely, but there was something between us. A gap that I couldn't bridge. I was hoping that meeting Bailey would be another piece of the puzzle that was Eve Houston.

I stepped through the door behind Eve and immediately stopped in my tracks. One thing I'd learned about both Lubbock and Midland was that the outside never matched the inside. Fancy restaurants could be hidden in strip malls, and apparently, dance halls with polished hardwood floors were hidden in run-down barns.

"Don't know how to line dance, do you, sir?" Eve asked, her eyes glittering.

I just shot her a look. Of course I'd never line danced before. Did they even have line dancing in Seattle?

Boose was styled like an old-school saloon with a long wooden bar down one side, complete with red-cushioned stools and a large, open dance floor. The other side of the room was full of booths, where the restaurant served lunch and dinner. A sign overhead read, *Boose: burgers, beer, and bops.*

Eve tugged my sleeve as we headed toward a woman with her hair in a white bun, standing before an antique wooden stand. "Hi, Ellen. Lunch for three, please. We're waiting on one more."

"Well, Eve, is that you?" The woman pulled out three menus and rolled-up silverware.

"Yes, ma'am." A hint of an accent came into her voice as soon as she spoke to this one.

"Love to see my local girls."

She gestured for us to follow her, and we headed into the sea of booths.

"You still playing soccer? You always were a spitfire."

"Yes, ma'am."

I glanced at her in question, and Eve just grinned.

"Ellen's daddy opened Boose years ago. She knows everything about everyone."

"Sure do," Ellen agreed. "And you're still in the big city?"

"Yep. Lubbock."

"Big city," I said under my breath.

She laughed. "Anywhere outside of Midland is the city."

Ellen stopped before an open booth, setting down the menus and silverware. "You tell your gram I said hi. I haven't seen her around for backgammon in a while."

Eve looked like she'd been punched in the stomach. All the air rushed out of her lungs at once. She swallowed hard. That beautiful, playful smile gone from her face.

"Uh, Gram passed, Ellen," Eve whispered, her words thick with emotion. "Last year."

"Oh, that's right." Ellen frowned and touched Eve's arm. "I'm so sorry. My mind is a steel trap most of the time, but it likes to forget the things I hate to remember. She was a special woman."

"She was," Eve agreed.

Ellen gave me a warm smile, patted Eve's arm, and then headed back to her booth. That couldn't have been easy to hear. Not with the way she'd mentioned her grandma to me. But Eve was already sliding into the booth, and it looked like the last thing she wanted was any sympathy.

I took the seat opposite her. "Eve."

"I'm fine," she said quickly, holding her menu up between us, like a physical barrier to her pain.

"You sure?"

"I don't blame Ellen." She tugged the menu down and met my gaze. "I don't want to remember that she's gone either." She reached across the table, placing her hand on top of mine. "Just don't bring it up to Bailey. She's more fragile than I am."

I saw all the makings of an oldest sibling in that moment. Saw myself reflected in her gaze. How much I protected West and Harley from our dad and always put on a brave face about it. I was the mediator. I was the one who kept the ship running. As far as I knew, I was the only one who still had contact with him. Even if I hadn't heard from him all summer. It had been a blissful break. One that I hoped continued.

We ordered waters and a mozzarella stick appetizer while we waited for her sister to show up. It was about twenty minutes later when Eve perked up. I turned in my seat and found a tall platinum blonde bouncing into the room in short shorts and cowboy boots. Eve waved her hand, and Bailey saw it and waved back. She tapped Ellen's stand twice and spoke to her briefly before dashing across the room.

Eve came to her feet, and Bailey fell into her embrace.

"Evie!"

"Bails!"

The girls held tight and turned in a quick circle. From this angle, it was clear that Bailey was a few inches taller than Eve, who was already taller than average. She was solidly built with sunbaked skin and heavily lined eyes.

Bailey pulled free and turned to face me. "Oh my God, you must be the boyfriend."

"Bails," Eve said again, this time with indignation.

"What? I'm meeting him. He must be important."

"Nice to meet you, Bailey."

I came to my feet and held my hand out. She took it in hers and shook, shooting a look at Eve with waggled eyebrows.

"Strong grip."

Eve's eyes went to the ceiling. "Lord. Sit your ass down."

Bailey laughed and then slid into the seat next to Eve, across from me. "So, tell me *everything*. Eve has never brought a guy home. Are y'all, like, getting married?"

Eve's forehead hit the table.

I just laughed. "We're dating."

"Ohhh, so it's like that," Bailey said. "I've *dated* a few guys, too."

"You're seventeen," Eve grumbled. "Please stop using *dated* as a euphemism."

Bailey shrugged. "Is she always this much of a downer for you, too?"

"She's wonderful."

Bailey fluttered her eyelashes at her sister. "He's a keeper, sis."

"I like him," Eve admitted.

My heart skittered over those words. They shouldn't have drawn such a reaction, but as much time as we'd spent together, neither of us had ever admitted to feelings. Hearing them from her, even as much as her liking me, was a revelation.

"When does school start?" I asked Bailey. "Eve said you're starting your senior year."

Her face soured at those words. "Yeah. I mean, I spent half the summer retaking Trig so they'd let me take AP Calculus. I haven't exactly had a break. But it's fine. I didn't want to be in the house anyway."

Eve bit her lip. "And you have everything you need to start on Monday?"

"Sure."

It didn't exactly sound convincing. Eve must have heard it, too, because she opened her mouth to ask more, but Bailey bulldozed over her.

"I just want to get back on the volleyball team."

"Which is why you cared enough to retake Trig," Eve said.

"Whatever works, right?" Bailey smiled up at me. "I couldn't play last year because I was on academic probation."

"She's going to turn it around this year though, right?"

Bailey rolled her eyes at her sister. "Of course. Have to get into college so I can play volleyball."

"Do you know where you want to go?" I asked.

"Nebraska," she said automatically. "Though wherever will recruit me to play all four years."

The waiter came back now that Bailey was here. We put in our order and chatted about her future plans while we ate. Bailey nibbled on a salad, Eve had a chicken sandwich, and I got the burger, which everyone had insisted was incredible, hence its placement on the sign. And it was every bit as good as described.

Bailey entertained us the whole meal. She could talk a mile a minute about anything that interested her. Like any teenager, she could shut down just as quickly when bored with a subject. Which appeared to be a long list of things— school, her grades, last year, work, the house, her dad. I'd thought Harley was a handful. Bailey gave her a run for her money.

"So, Nebraska is the dream?" I asked in surprise. I wasn't sure I'd heard anyone say they wanted to move to Nebraska.

"If they can fill a football stadium for volleyball, I want to go there," she told me confidently.

The waiter appeared then with the check, and I paid the whole thing before either woman could offer. Bailey shot Eve a look. I recognized it as the twin look that West and I shared. Though I didn't know Bailey well enough to read it,

I got the impression that I must have been doing something right.

We lingered over drinks as the crowd ebbed and flowed around us. Bailey kept trying to convince me to get out onto the dance floor and show off my line dancing moves.

"Come on," Bailey said, jumping to her feet and grabbing my arm. "I'll show you how it's done. Eve would never."

"You're right. I would never, and I'll bet you good money Whitt won't do it either."

"Yeah, you couldn't pay me to get out there."

Bailey sighed. "Come on, y'all. It's fun."

"You go then."

"Not without you. Come on, Evie."

Eve shook her head with a laugh, and then suddenly, the expression was gone from her face.

"What?" Bailey asked. She whipped around, and her expression froze, too. "Fuck."

I glanced over in confusion at their reaction. All I saw was a tall man in a cowboy hat, smiling at Ellen, and what looked like ranch buddies. I didn't know how else to describe the men who had sauntered inside.

"Dad," Bailey groaned.

Oh...shit.

22

___

EVE

The world narrowed to the moment when Dad saw the pair of us together. He was with his golfing buddies. Guys he'd known my whole life. They'd ride horses, barbecue, and attend church together with their wives and children. Dad had paraded us before them for too long. Long enough for me to know each and every one of them was a creeper.

"Sit down, Bails," I snapped.

The last thing I needed was for them to look at her ass nearly hanging out of her shorts. I didn't give a fuck what she wore, but I didn't want forty-year-old men to ogle the teenager.

Bailey didn't argue for once. She plopped her butt back in the seat and went strangely silent. Whitt's gaze shifted back to me. I'd told him the bare minimum about Dad, and I'd hoped he'd never meet the man. Because I knew exactly what was coming.

"Well, well, well," he said with a boisterous laugh, "look at my two beautiful girls." He left his posse behind and strode toward our booth.

If I could have gotten us out of there before this, then I would have. But there was no out with him, only through.

"Hello," I said crisply.

"Dad," Bailey said.

His smile was wide and fake as a snake. Ready to coil and strike at the right second. "This is a nice surprise."

Neither of us said anything. Then, he caught sight of Whitt, who had been unnaturally still. As if he sensed our discomfort, like a predator at our back. I knew the moment my dad clocked him for exactly who he was.

"This must be the boyfriend," he said.

Whitt, to his credit, came to his feet—a full head taller than my dad—and held his hand out. "Hello. Mr. Houston, I presume?"

"That'd be me," he said, shaking his hand, "but you can call me Rick."

"Whitton Wright."

"Wright." He pointed a trigger finger at Whitt. "Like Wright Construction, right? We see your signs all over town."

"Correct."

"Hope you're treating my girls to lunch because you know they can't afford it." He laughed, aiming a finger at us, as if it were a joke.

Whitt gave him an appraising look and didn't deem it fit to respond to that.

"Dad, what are you doing here?" I interjected, wanting nothing more than to put Bailey behind me like a physical shield.

"Here with the boys." He gestured to the table of his friends. "You remember Ron, Dirk, Mullen—"

He was going to list them all if I didn't intervene, so I quickly said, "Yes, I remember."

"Why wasn't I invited to your little lunch?"

Somehow, he managed to make it sound both our fault and condescending. Instead of the fact that none of us would have ever wanted him at our lunch.

"We're only here for a day. Thought I'd introduce Bailey and Whitt."

"Interesting," he said. "But not to your old man?"

"It's fine, Daddy," Bailey said with a laugh. "They're not serious enough for parental introductions. Don't blow it out of proportion."

I held back my wince. That wasn't exactly true. If I had a parent I gave a shit about, maybe I would have introduced them to Whitt. If Gram were still here...

"Ah, so just one in a line of many," my dad said with a laugh. He clapped Whitt on the shoulder. "Good luck with this one. She's a fireball."

"That's why I like her," he said, his jaw twitching.

Whitt wasn't feeding into Dad's ego the way that he wanted. I could see it now. He was going to go from obnoxious to so much worse any second. How could I extract us from this? I couldn't let him be his normal self. Not in front of Whitt.

"We were just leaving anyway." I scooted Bailey forward. She hurried out of the booth. "So, we're going to get back to work."

He narrowed his eyes. "Oh, so you are working again? I thought you must have quit since I didn't get the full payment this month."

I froze at those words, momentarily forgetting that Whitt was standing right there. "What do you mean? I sent the whole thing."

"I didn't receive it, Evie Jo," he said. "You might want to recheck your accounts."

Whitt tilted his head. I could see the questions in his blue eyes. I hadn't told him about the money. I never planned to tell anyone about the money. Not ever. That was private. My dad was spouting this bullshit because Whitt was there. He'd found a new way to humiliate me and taken the hit.

"It's all there," I snapped. "I can provide receipts."

"And you," he said, turning on Bailey.

Oh no.

"Leave it, Dad," I snarled.

"She's grounded."

"I am not!" Bailey said. "I have volleyball tryouts next week. We already talked about it. I have to be in the gym all weekend."

"Yet I found you here, eating greasy food instead of practicing."

"I can't practice at all hours..."

"You're telling me. I thought all you wanted to do was be in the gym."

She pursed her lips.

"Plus, you got a C in your math class this summer. I don't see why that would mean you would get to be out of the house with your sister."

"You got a C?" I asked.

"Yeah, but..."

"Bailey," I groaned.

Somehow, the man still got under my skin. He knew exactly what buttons to press, and it was too late to realize I'd fallen for one of his traps.

"Between the two of you, I'm over it!" Bailey said. "I'm doing the best I can. I don't need you on my ass," she said to Dad and whirled on me, "and I don't need you to act like my mom. You're not my mom."

"I know, Bails, but..."

"Sorry about all of this," my dad said to Whitt with his church smile. "Raising girls, you know?"

Whitt stared him down until my dad looked away. "Why don't we get Bailey home?"

"I don't need anyone's help," she said. "I'm going to the gym anyway."

Then, she pushed past our dad and headed out of Boose. My dad smiled at both of us, tipped his cowboy hat in our direction, and then headed to his friends. As if saying, *My work here is done.* The fucking tornado that he was.

I wanted to scream.

I wanted to rage.

I wanted to go back to ten minutes ago, before he showed up and detonated our afternoon.

Whitt put a gentle hand on the small of my back. "Come on. Let's get out of here."

I let him guide me out of the place. Bailey was in her run-down Civic, already pulling away by the time we made it outside. I sighed heavily. I should have known that she wasn't talking about school for a reason. That she'd gotten a C in Trig when the girl could do math in her head in her *sleep*.

"Well, that's my dad."

"Yeah. What a riot he is."

"Tell me about it." I chewed on my lip. "I'm sure you want to know about the money."

He shrugged. "Eve, you never have to tell me anything you're not ready to talk about. He was trying to get a rise out of you, and he succeeded. I know people like that. My dad is...similar. He's perhaps a bit slyer and more refined in his approach, but he's just as duplicitous. The best thing to do is to never give them the reaction they want."

"I know," I said, throwing my arms up. "I know that, and still, he drives me fucking mad. And Bailey...she was supposed to buckle down. She made it easy to drive the stake home."

"That has nothing to do with you, Eve. You're doing your best by her."

"It never feels like enough. And I just...hate him for making everything more difficult." Tears came to my eyes, and I swiped them away. Frustration written into every inch of my face.

"You know what? No."

"No?" I asked with a sniffle.

"No. We're not ending today like this. He doesn't get to win."

"He already did."

"No," I repeated. "Let's do something else. Something you loved to do when you were here."

"Nothing. I wanted to leave."

He grasped my hands. "There had to be something."

"I don't know."

"Yes, you do. Something to erase this."

"I could just do you," I teased.

He tilted his head down to look at me. "Eve."

"Fine," I said, an idea blooming in my mind. "Are you sure?"

"Anything."

"Just remember you said so."

He just laughed and kissed me.

23

EVE

"This wasn't what I had in mind," Whitt said with regret in his voice.

"You said anything."

An enormous arched sign with the name Rivers Ranch in all capital letters announced our destination. Whitt sighed heavily as he turned off the two-lane back road and onto the private property. His tires crunched over the gravel before he pulled into the only available spot in front of a horse fence. I hadn't considered that it was Labor Day weekend and they'd be busy. Hopefully, they'd have two horses free for us.

"Horses?" he asked skeptically.

"Yeah. The ranch has been around forever. I went to school with the girl who used to run it with her dad." I hopped out of the car, taking in the smell of grass and manure. "I don't know if she's still here. I heard her dad died a few years ago. Not sure who is running it now, to be honest."

"Well, great," Whitt said as he stepped out of the car.

The wind blew through the dark strands of his hair. I

was glad that I'd told him to wear something casual for Boose. I'd never seen him in jeans before today, and it was a good thing he was in them if we were going to ride.

"So, have you ever been on a horse?"

He shot me a look. "No."

"Oh, this should be fun," I said with a laugh. I linked our arms together. "Come on. I'll go easy on you."

"Why do I doubt that?"

"Because you know me."

His eyes were heated when he said, "I'm trying."

My cheeks turned rosy at the assessment. The scary thing was that Whitt did know me. He'd known how to handle my dad. He'd known how to banter with my sister. He'd seen when I needed an escape from what I'd gone through. He didn't push for answers I wasn't ready to give, and, God, he'd been so patient with me. While I found myself falling and falling and falling.

The front door creaked open to a one-story ranch with a white wraparound porch. A woman stepped out in bootcut jeans and a white tank top. She was sun-kissed with honey-blonde hair, shot through with natural highlights. Her lips were the shape of a bow about to be plucked and eyes so light blue that you could have drowned in a puddle. A dash of freckles layered across her nose and cheeks. She waved a hand, callous from use.

"Hey, y'all. Can I help you?"

"Arden Rivers," I said with a shake of my head. "What are you doing here?"

Her eyes widened in recognition. "Eve, is that you?" She hopped down the last remaining steps, a wide smile coming to her lips. "That is you!"

We embraced tightly.

I hadn't seen her in eight years. She'd married her high

school sweetheart and moved away. She was one of the few girls who hadn't been threatened by me. We hadn't had a lot of classes together, but I used to come ride horses with Gram a lot. Well, I'd ride horses with Arden while Gram gossiped with Arden's mom.

"I didn't know you were back in town," I told her.

"It's a recent thing." She sucked air in through her teeth and then added, "Divorce."

My jaw dropped. "Really?"

She shrugged. "Yeah, it's new." Then, she changed the topic of conversation. "And you? Are you back in Midland? I thought you were in Lubbock."

"I am. Just here on business." I gestured to Whitt. "This is my..." I glanced up at him and back at Arden. "Well, my date, Whitton Wright."

"Pleasure to meet you," he said, taking her hand.

Arden smiled up at him. "Nice to meet you."

"He's never been on a horse. Please tell me you have something that won't break him."

"Well, we're all booked up," she said regretfully. "But hell, why not? You can ride Bunny."

"Bunny?" Whitt asked.

I was laughing the entire way around back and into Arden's private stables. Whitt's face at the name was delightful.

Arden had a handful of horses that were used by friends and family. Some of them were because they weren't fit for the public. Either personal favorites, rodeo horses—ropers and barrel racers—or because, like Bunny, they were now past their prime but too beloved to do anything but let them live out their lives in the pasture.

"Meet Bunny," Arden said, gesturing to the aging caramel-brown horse. "She's not exactly what I'd describe as *sweet*, but she can't really canter anymore. She's an old lady, and you have to treat her nice like one. Got it?"

Whitt nodded. "Got it. Hello, Bunny."

He held his hand out to her. Bunny sniffed his hand, bobbed her head twice, as if expecting a treat, then dismissed him entirely when she found the hand empty.

"She works best with treats."

"Don't we all?" I muttered.

"Eve, would you rather have Bramble or Trouble?" Arden gestured to two horses. One dappled mare and proud and the other midnight black with white down the gelding's nose.

"Trouble," Whitt said with a laugh.

"Oh, but Bramble is so pretty," I said.

Arden shrugged. "Don't let her deceive you. She's equally a piece of work."

"Trouble it is," I agreed. "He looks like he wants to get out of here."

"Doesn't he always?" Arden said.

She went about saddling Bunny and Trouble while walking Whitt through the basic mechanics of riding. She had both horses in hand when she turned around and looked him up and down.

"Do you want boots?" she asked.

"Boots?"

I cackled. "Cowboy boots, Whitt."

"We have some in basically every size. Most people don't want to get their shoes dirty, and it's easier to have them on hand," she explained. "You're what, an eleven?"

"And a half," he said, dismay in his voice.

"Yeah. Grab some off that rack over there. Top shelf."

He sighed. "I'm only doing this for you."

"I know," I said with a satisfied grin.

Then, he headed over to the rack to find his size.

"You got yourself a guy who's never been on a horse or in boots," Arden said with a laugh. "Never thought I'd see the day."

"Plenty of guys like that since high school."

"What are y'alls plans after this? We could grab dinner and catch up. I heard about your gram."

"Yeah. It sucks. And your dad."

"Yeah."

We both sat in our grief for a second. It was nice to be around someone who knew what it felt like. Who knew that it didn't need an apology. Just silence.

"I'd love to do dinner, but we're working with the Kings on their new construction project. Malcolm invited us out to dinner to celebrate."

Arden wrinkled her nose. "Oil money."

"You could come with," I offered.

"The only thing my daddy liked less than the big city was the oil industry."

"You live in Midland," I said with a laugh. "You can't escape it."

"They've been sniffing around, trying to buy up our land for fracking. And it'll happen over my dead body, Eve. I don't think we'd mingle well."

She was probably right. Arden had never been one to hide her opinions. Much like me. I couldn't imagine her spending more than a few minutes in Malcolm's presence without denigrating their family business.

"Next time," I promised.

"Well?" Whitt said.

I turned to look at him, and my heart stopped. Arden wasn't wrong. I had an affinity for men in boots. When you grew up in Midland, Texas, around a bunch of cowboys, boots and hats ran in your blood. And made your blood pump. My reputation hadn't entirely been unearned.

"Well, hello there," I purred.

He shook his head at me. "I look ridiculous."

"Boots look good on you."

Arden nodded. "They're a fan favorite."

"If you insist," he said. "Just don't tell West or Harley. I'll never live this down."

I pulled out my phone and snapped a picture. "For my personal collection."

"Lord save us."

Arden laughed at the pair of us and then helped us onto the horses. It came back to me in an instant even though I hadn't been on a horse in ages. Whitt took to it like he did everything else—with ease. It was a little unfair that he was that good at riding, considering it was his first time.

"Looks like y'all got it," Arden said. "Have fun!"

I took the lead as we headed out onto a trail. "Do you have to be good at everything?"

"It's just about control," he assured me. Our eyes met. "I'm good at control."

My cheeks flushed. Of that I was well aware.

We ambled lazily through the brush and ducked into a thicket of trees. There wasn't a whole lot of tree coverage here in oil country, but the Rivers had owned this plot for generations. They'd cultivated the land around them, and like magic the earth opened up around them.

After a half hour, I gestured for Whitt to come off the trail and under a copse of trees. He didn't direct Bunny so much as the old girl followed Trouble without him having to make a movement. As easy as Whitt was on the horse, Bunny was even easier to deal with.

I hopped off of Trouble, and Whitt dismounted next to

me. He pulled out treats for the horses that Arden had given him before we left. She'd told us that Bunny might not move past halfway if we didn't bribe her. So, bribing her was now Whitt's favorite game.

I tied off the horses to a low-hanging branch and laid out a blanket. I sank back into the soft grass. Whitt dropped down next to me once Bunny was sort of satisfied. Trouble eyed her reproachfully, as if asking for extra snacks was beneath her.

"Well, this is going better than I thought," he said.

"You're a natural. I'm going to get you boots and take you riding when we get home."

He winced. "Maybe not that good." He wrapped an arm around my waist and tugged me in tight against him. "But I like trying new things with you. Living in the moment."

"And you had to remind me to do it. I must be rubbing off on you."

He kissed the top of my head. "You are in all the best ways." He ducked his head to meet my gaze. "You know that, right? That you're the best thing that's ever happened to me."

My breath caught at the admission. "What?"

"Maybe I'm moving too fast, but it's been two months, Eve, and I'm more smitten than I was when we started. I don't want to scare you."

"I'm...I'm not scared."

And it wasn't a lie.

"No? Then, I can tell you that I want this. I want you. I want all of this with you. I'll go at whatever pace you need me to go at, but this is it for me. You're it."

I wanted to accept that. Why couldn't I just accept the truth?

"But you don't even know me."

"I know that you've been unfairly treated by every person around you. That you have the biggest heart and loyalty to the people who matter in your life. That you'd do anything for your sister. That you are entirely selfless when it comes to your own wants and needs. You put everyone and everything before your own desires and close yourself off to keep your heart safe and secure." He tipped my chin up until I looked into his eyes. "I don't have to know every single thing about you to know and want *you*."

My throat closed at those words. At the reality of them. He saw me. Really saw me. I wasn't sure anyone else ever had. I'd kept myself behind bars so that I wouldn't be hurt, so that no one else would have to deal with everything I was dealing with. I didn't want to be a burden, and I wanted more for my sister than the hand she had been dealt.

And most of all...I wanted him.

I wanted him like I had never let myself want anything.

The cool girl who had never let herself get attached dissolved.

Suddenly, I was the little girl who had wanted so desperately to be loved that she offered the world ammunition to use against her. The girl who'd wrapped herself in body armor instead of glass. The girl whose soft heart still yearned for connection before she discovered it was impossible.

"Yes," I said even though there wasn't a question.

"Yes?"

"I want this," I told him. "I want you. I want to be the kind of person who can accept what you're offering."

"I'm not going anywhere, Eve."

My fingers trailed through his dark hair. "Good. I like you right here."

"But I want more, too. I can't deny that I want all of you."

He rubbed his nose against mine. "I want to be more than your date...more than a sort of boyfriend."

My heart trembled with fear. The armor turning to glass and shattering at the admission. I was done pretending that I didn't want that, too.

"You are," I told him, drawing his lips to mine. "Whatever words you want to use. You're mine, and I'm yours." The words came out breathier than I'd intended.

My emotions mingled with desire. We were alone on the trail, far from the rest of the world, with only the horses for company.

We reached for each other at the same time. As if we were of one mind. So synchronized in that moment that we didn't even need words.

My pants were shucked off to the side. Whitt's jeans came unbuttoned. His cock already hard and ready for me. I took him in my hand, and he hissed softly at the pressure. He pumped himself once, jerking for more friction before settling himself between my legs.

Our eyes met, and a sizzle passed between us that I'd never felt before. We hovered in that space. Longing— something that had always been ephemeral and transient in my life—now took up permanent residence in my heart. An ache for this man that tattooed itself across my skin. As ingrained in me as the cherry blossoms on my hip, the peonies on my shoulder, and Gram's writing on my bicep.

"Whitt," I whispered.

He pressed his lips to mine, quick and decisive. "Mine."

"All yours."

Then, we fit together. It had felt better than each time before. As if Whitt were a mind reader, running his hands down my body, knowing exactly where to touch and kiss and what speed to help me reach that pinnacle. But this time, it was as if he'd reached inside of me, and instead of him reading my mind, we shared a connection, a link. Every touch, every thrust, every kiss was an awakening.

Even as we sped up, it happened as one. Not rough or desperate, as we had screwed so many times before. But steady and loving. Every movement like he'd been made specifically for me.

As we came together, our cries drowned out in the hot Midland afternoon, I relinquished my last hold on control. I hadn't been waiting for a moment to show someone the real me. I'd been waiting for Whitt, the person who'd discovered it for himself.

24

WHITTON

Eve was my girlfriend.

Mine.

All mine.

On Monday morning, I was still on a high from the weekend away while I drove West and Harley to Ransom Canyon for the annual Wright barbecue at Jensen's lake house. Eve would be there later in the day after she finished the showing she had with a couple who had come into Lubbock for the weekend to look for houses for when they moved here at the end of the year. She hadn't been happy about not driving in with me. Frankly, I wasn't either, but I understood her work mentality. She rarely took a break and giving up a whole weekend to Midland had been a lot for her.

For my girlfriend.

Another smile hit my lips, undeterred.

"So, like, are you going to talk about it?" Harley asked from the backseat.

"Talk about what?" I asked.

West snorted next to me. "The stupid look on your face."

"I don't have a stupid look on my face." I dropped my smile at the comment. Ass.

"Yes, you do," Harley said. "Like you're in love or something."

Well, wasn't I? Holding Eve in my arms under the trees in Midland had been the closest I'd ever gotten to feeling like that. The feel of her heated skin under my touch. The taste of her sweet lips. The face she made as we came together. And better than all of that had been the words she used. The fact that she'd finally relented to what we'd both been feeling.

"Oh my God, you're in love!" Harley said when I didn't say anything.

"Adorable," West teased.

I punched him. "Shut up."

West laughed as he rubbed his arm. "Careful. I need these to play keys. I'm heading back to LA soon."

"Don't remind us," Harley grumbled. "I just got back, and you're leaving."

"He won't stop talking about it. I don't know how we could forget," I muttered.

"Can't help it that I'm famous now."

Harley groaned, and I punched him again. It was so nice to have siblings.

"Anyway, back to the important matter at hand," Harley said. "I see you changing the subject."

"I didn't. West did."

"What's going on with you and Eve?"

"We're dating."

"Yeah. You were dating before."

"She's my girlfriend," I added, the stupid smile returning to my lips.

"Yay!" Harley cried.

Even West grinned at that. "Congrats, man! She makes you smile. So, I like her."

"She's a badass," Harley added. "I approve."

"So glad I have your approval."

I pulled onto the main road that led into Ransom Canyon. West Texas was shaped like the surface of a golf ball with lots of flat spots and little divots all over. It was why it flooded every time it rained and why we had these beautiful canyons just outside of town. Ransom Canyon was the closest to Lubbock with beautiful houses around a large lake. Jensen's was on the far side of the lake, and we had to drive over a man-made dam. The house came complete with a dock with a boat and a few Jet Skis. Already, a bunch of cars lined the narrow road and covered the drive for the party.

I parked down the street and grabbed the cooler out of the back. Jensen had said we didn't have to bring anything, but I felt weird showing up to a party empty-handed. We were almost there when my phone rang in my pocket.

I tugged it out and saw *Dad* across the screen. I sighed. He'd called while I was in Midland, too, but I hadn't answered. Eve's family was enough to deal with. I hadn't wanted to add my own troubles to the mix. But now, I should probably figure out what the hell he wanted.

"I'm going to take this," I said, holding up the phone.

They saw who it was, and both groaned.

"Don't do it," Harley said.

"Yeah. Just come enjoy the party," West said. "He can wait."

"He called Friday, too. I should probably take it."

West sighed. "Fine. But be quick."

He jerked the cooler out of my hand and nodded his head at Harley. She dragged her thumb across her throat, as if to tell me what to do to the man we all called Dad. I shook my head, and she doubled down by pretending to tie a noose around her neck and sticking her tongue out.

I pressed the green button to answer. "Hello?"

"Hey, Whitton. Good to hear your voice."

"Yeah. You, too."

"What's going on over there?"

"I'm at Jensen's for his Labor Day party."

"Ah, Jensen. Yeah, you'll have to tell him I said hello."

I had no intention of doing that. Like most of my family, Jensen was hardly a fan of my father. It probably had something to do with him trying to undermine Morgan's ascension to CEO. Or maybe having a second family. Or maybe just his existence. There was a long list of misdeeds to choose from.

Still, I was the intermediary. I was the one who kept the peace.

"What's going on? Do you have plans?"

"Oh, just here and there," he said. Which meant no. "I do have business in Austin next weekend though."

Oh no.

"I thought that I could pop up to see you while I'm there."

"Just me?" I asked even though I knew the answer.

"Well, all of you," he said.

All of us. Jordan, Julian, me, West, and Harley. His two families, all happily together...without him.

"I don't know if that's such a good idea."

As far as I knew, Jordan and Julian were still no contact. Harley didn't see him, even when she went home. West had seen him in LA when he signed with Cosmere, but I didn't know what their current relationship was like. And me? Where did I factor in all of this? I didn't know. I couldn't put two and two together when it came to him. I'd told the others to give him a chance, and I wasn't sure I even wanted to.

"Come on. It'd be great. We can do dinner or go golfing. Whatever y'all want to do." He cleared his throat. "I'd appreciate it if you ask everyone for me."

I looked to the blue sky. Summer clinging on stubbornly while fall waited in the wings. It would have been nice to enjoy it.

"You want me to ask everyone for you?"

"Well, no one else took my call," he said sullenly.

I sighed. "Dad..."

"I know. I fucked up. You all want to punish me forever for it, but I'm still your father. I want to be a part of your lives. I regret a lot, but having all of you, raising all of you...never."

Raising us. I couldn't even comment on that. How could you raise people when you spent, at most, half of your time with both families? And Jordan and Julian had always gotten more of him than we ever had.

But I said none of that. It wouldn't matter to him.

Maybe Harley had been right, and I should have ignored him.

"I'll talk to them," I said like the faithful soldier I was.

"Thank you, Whitt. I appreciate it. I love you. Have fun at your party."

I said my good-byes and then hung up. Well, this was going to suck.

I stepped into Jensen's lake house. It was immaculate. Big windows on all exterior walls with a panoramic view of the lake. A huge open floor plan, currently covered in children running loose and parents with only half an eye on them. I clocked Colton on the patio outside with his arms crossed, ignoring the entire world for his phone. Poor kid.

I shook hands with Jensen, agreeing that I'd be at his next mayoral event—a silent auction in a few weeks that led up to the election. Then, I went about rounding up my various siblings. For once, I was glad that Eve wasn't here yet.

Once I had them all in a room off of the main area, where purses were piled up in corners, I closed the door and said, "Dad wants to come into town."

"What?" Jordan asked.

"No," Julian said at once.

Harley crossed her arms and shook her head.

West pursed his lips. "Why?"

"Look, he said that he has business in Austin next weekend and that he wants to see us."

"Why are you even still answering his calls?" Julian asked.

"I agree with Julian. I know that our relationship with him was different from yours, but honestly, isn't it worse?"

"I don't want to agree with Whitt," West informed them, "but he did seem changed the last time I saw him. I think it's gotten to him."

"Isn't that what he deserves?" Harley snarled. "He did this to *us*. We didn't do anything to him. Fuck him."

Julian pointed at Harley. "Seconded."

"What she said," Jordan said.

"He tried to see me when I was in Seattle, even after I told him no," Harley said. "Even talking to him is a bad idea. That's how he worms his way in. No contact is the way to go."

"He probably invented the Austin trip," Jordan added. "You know how he is."

"Definitely. I'd bet there's no business involved. He's just trying to find a way in," Harley said.

"That doesn't say something? That he wants to know us?" Whitt said.

"He just feels guilty," Jordan said with a sigh. "I wish it were more. Fuck, I wanted to believe him so many times, Whitt. So many times. Julian and I gave him a million and a half chances. I don't have any more to give."

"Tell him no," Julian agreed.

"West?"

West shrugged. "We can't make them. Dad told me he was going to be in LA when I got back, but I still haven't decided how much contact I want. He *does* have a tendency to weasel his way back in if we give him half a chance."

I didn't even know why I was defending the man. Why I was acting like I wanted them to give him a chance. I'd just always been that person. Maybe today was the day to let it go.

"Yeah. All right. I'll tell him," I finally relented.

My siblings nodded, clapping me on the back and thanking me for being the one to deal with him. It was never easy. Today wasn't going to be easy either.

I stepped out of the house, leaving my siblings to enjoy the rest of the party. I had to call Dad back. This was going to be fun.

"Hey there, handsome!"

I looked up and found Eve striding down the drive toward me.

My smile reignited. "Hey! I thought you weren't coming until later."

"Couple canceled. They decided they'd rather spend

time at the lake with friends than look at houses. Can't blame them. I'd rather spend the time with my boyfriend."

She vaulted into my arms, and I swung her around, planting kisses all over her face while she laughed. Then, I got a real kiss, long and languid. She melted into me, and I let the rest of the day slip away.

"I missed you."

"Of course you did. I'm awesome." She winked at me. "What are you doing out here?"

I ran a hand down my face. "My dad."

"What's going on?"

I explained the situation with my dad to her. She listened patiently while I detailed all the many reactions from my siblings...and the guilt I still felt about it all.

"He doesn't even deserve it," I blurted out. "I don't know why I feel this way."

"Look, I'm not exactly the best person to give parental advice. My mom disappeared, and my dad is an asshole, but I still deal with him because Bailey is there. Every time you talk about your dad, you make it seem like you owe him something for giving you half of your DNA. But he has done nothing but disappoint you time and time again. Have you considered that your siblings are right?"

"So many times. Yet I'm still the one talking to him. The one making excuses for him. I don't know how to let it go."

"Why do you think that is?"

"I don't know."

"Do you think you're the most like him?"

"Normally, I would say Jordan," I said with a shrug. "But even he's over it."

"But Jordan had him all the time. You were given scraps. It's like you're still begging for them."

I winced at the words. At the truth of them. No one had ever cut me bare so easily.

"I'm sorry," she said immediately. "Was that too blunt? I sometimes do that...I didn't mean to..."

"It's okay," I told her, calming her own fears easily. "You're right. Of course you're right. You see me as well as I see you after all. I want my dad's approval. I want him to want me the way he wanted his other life. I don't know how not to want that."

"You were innocent in this. He should have never made you feel like that."

"Yeah. Parents, huh?"

"Fucking tell me about it."

I sighed. "Yeah. I guess I should call him."

"Do it later," she said, threading our fingers together. "You don't have to run to him right away. Do it on your terms. He can wait. He made you wait long enough."

I smiled down at this force of nature I called my girlfriend. Why hadn't I been able to say that? He'd made me wait long enough. It was as simple as that.

"Plus, I have on a white bikini," she said with a grin. "Want to see it?"

I choked out a, "Yes," and she laughed, stripping out of her T-shirt and pulling me toward the party.

Tomorrow. I could think about it all tomorrow. Be more like my siblings.

Because right now, I wanted to be present with my girlfriend.

25

EVE

I blinked into the soft morning light, momentarily forgetting where I was. I jolted upright in the giant king-size bed, my heart racing a mile a minute. Then, the previous day washed over me.

Right.

I'd stayed the night with Whitt.

Whitt, who was not currently in the bed. I looked around his immaculately clean and perfectly decorated room and didn't see a trace of the man. As my eyes adjusted to the space, I realized that I could hear the shower running.

I released a breath with relief. I didn't know what I'd thought he'd do. It wasn't like he was going to run out on me, sleeping in his bed, but it was the first time that I'd stayed here despite our many adventures between the sheets. I'd always thought it was too intimate...too relation-shippy to stay the night. I hadn't snuck out or anything, but I'd still left before the morning.

Now, I sank back into his luxurious sheets and stretched out on the big bed. My bed back at the house was a double.

Why hadn't I stayed here before? Ten out of ten for quality of the sheets, pillows, and mattress. A girl could get used to this.

I rolled over and grabbed my phone. I jolted at the time. Christ, it was early. I still had a few hours before my meeting with Jordan later. I was pretty sure that Whitt didn't have to be in the office for at least an hour.

I tossed the sheets off of my legs and padded into the bathroom in nothing but the red lacy thong I'd had on the night before. Whitt's shower was enormous with just a thin pane of glass, revealing the muscular, naked torso through the fogged window.

I dropped my panties on the tiled floor and drew the door open. "Mind if I join?"

He grinned as I stepped into the shower with him.

"I'd mind if you didn't," he said, pulling me under the hot spray.

I laughed as water cascaded over me. "I wasn't going to get my hair wet! Do you know how long it takes to dry?"

"I have seen you with a blow-dryer before, yes, but I wouldn't get to do this."

His hands came up into the now-wet tresses, massaging my scalp. I groaned as he brought goose bumps to my skin. My body hummed to life at the feel of his fingers working their magic. I hadn't even realized that there was tension in my body until he dissolved it.

"That feels amazing," I muttered.

"Do you need fancy shampoo and conditioner?" he asked.

I nodded. "I'm a girl after all. I like nice hair products. You don't get tresses like this without quality care."

"Then, you should leave some here."

My eyes fluttered open. "Really?"

"Yeah. Whatever you need, I want you to have it here."

My heart constricted. That felt like a huge step. Only this weekend, we'd agreed to date, and now, he basically wanted to give me a drawer. And I wasn't upset about it. Just surprised that he wanted that level of commitment. He'd been saying it since the beginning, and still, I'd doubted him.

"I'll do that."

His smile was magnetic as he drew me against his slick body and pressed our lips together. That wasn't the only thing pressed into my skin. His cock was long and hard against my stomach. I reached between us and wrapped my hand around the head.

"Fuck," he growled.

"We've barely touched, and you're already hard for me," I teased.

He walked me backward until my ass was against the glass of the shower wall. "I was hard as soon as I saw your hot, naked body." His hands moved to my hips. "I wanted to bury myself inside of you the instant I saw you through the glass."

"Yes."

He grinned at the raspy gasp in my voice, the breathy desire. "You want that, too, do you?"

"Oh, yes."

He lifted one wrist and the other until they were above my head. "Don't move them."

My breasts hung heavy from the position. My nipples peaked.

He ran his thumb over my wrist. "What's this?"

"Crescent moons," I told him. They were two crescents, side by side—one filled in and one open.

"Why'd you get them?"

I shrugged helplessly. He smirked, and his hands leisurely moved down my arms and to my shoulders.

He traced my peonies. "What does this one mean?"

"My favorite flower," I told him.

"And this one?"

One hand gripped my thigh, right over my dream catcher.

"I used to have bad dreams, but not anymore."

"Hmm." His hand rose to my hip, where a semicircle of cherry blossoms bloomed in soft pink. "And this one?"

"Gram always called me her cherry blossom," I admitted.

He arched an eyebrow as his fingers traced the line of my Gram's handwriting on my bicep. "You don't seem much like a cherry blossom."

"She said that when she was a girl, she went to a cherry blossom festival, and the flowers were the most striking thing she had ever seen, but they were feisty, temperamental things. A single storm or cold weather would drop them off the trees after a mere day."

He laughed. "Feisty, temperamental little thing. I can see that."

"I only bloom under perfect conditions."

His look was full of mischief when his hand slipped between my thighs. "Think I can make you bloom?"

Was that even a question? All I'd done was open like a cherry blossom in his presence. And the the look on his face said he knew it.

Whitt lifted my hips up, leveraging me against the glass window. Our bodies aligned, his cock pressing against my opening. He slowly lowered me onto him, and I squirmed the entire way down.

"Oh," I gasped when I was fully seated on his cock.

My hand dropped unintentionally, and he reached up and grasped both wrists in one hand and slammed them back against the glass. My eyes widened in surprise, but he tightened his grip on my hip that braced me against the window. Then, he began to move.

He thrust his hips up, sliding in and out of me with such force that I saw stars. I could do nothing but hold on as he speared me wide open. With my hands above my head, I had no sense of control. Whitt owned my body, and I wanted him to. It wasn't until I came hard on his cock that he finally emptied himself as well.

He gently released my wrists as he pulled out of me. I slid down to my feet on wobbly knees. He lifted me back up and put me back under the spray, using his soap to clean the mess we'd just made. Then, he turned off the shower, wrapped me in a big, fluffy towel, and sat me down on the edge of the enormous bathtub.

"You looked like you were going to faint," he said as he pushed a glass of water into my hand.

I took it gratefully. I hadn't realized how much I needed it. "I guess...I just gave up all control." My head was still buzzing. I couldn't believe the words leaving my mouth. "I liked it."

His eyes were molten at the words. As if I'd struck at the heart of who he was. Did he want me to give up all control? Because if it was like what had just happened in the shower, then maybe I'd be up for that.

"If I didn't have to get to work, I'd drag you to bed right now."

"I think I'd let you," I teased.

His hand went back through his hair. "Fuck."

"You can't be late," I wagered.

He shook his head. "I can't."

I drained the rest of the water and came to my feet. I pressed a kiss to his lips. "You wouldn't be you if you were late. I'll see you after I finish work later."

"All right." He dragged me in for another kiss. "Good luck at your meeting."

"You too."

I kissed him and then headed home, delirious from Whitt on every dimension.

Wright Construction's lush lobby was full of morning traffic. Since I started contracting with the company, I'd been here many times, including a few occasions just to see Whitt.

But I wasn't here for him today.

Today, I had my own meeting with Jordan about my job, which was now unfortunately over. I'd contracted for the project, and now, the project was wrapped. While I'd had an incredible weekend with Whitt, reality was creeping back in.

I had one more payment for working at Wright Construction. I'd sold one house this month. I still had to pay my dad for next month. While Whitt might not have asked about the money, that didn't mean it wasn't still on my mind. I'd double-checked that the deposit for this month had gone through, which it had.

But when I'd looked, I'd seen the dwindling funds in my account. What was I going to do after today? The couple I'd thought would buy this weekend was second-guessing buying instead of renting. I had exactly three leads, and I was pretty sure they were dead ends. It just wasn't buying season. I had no idea how I was going to make ends meet.

I clenched my hands into fists and then released them.

I'd figure it out.

I always did.

Right now, I had to survive my final meeting with Jordan.

After navigating the lobby, I took the elevator up to the top floor. My heels clicked against the floor, and I stopped before Jordan's office door.

"You must be Eve," his assistant said, reaching for a phone.

"That's me."

"Just let me tell Mr. Wright that you're here."

I wondered how confusing that was in this office. How many Mr. Wrights worked here? At least Morgan probably got Ms. Wright, like the badass she was.

"He'll see you now," the assistant said. He gestured to the door. "Go on inside."

"Thank you."

I took a deep breath and then walked inside. No matter that Jordan and I had been drinking beer lakeside together yesterday, today, he was my boss.

"Eve," Jordan said, looking up from his desk. "Come in. Have a seat."

I straightened out my pencil skirt and dropped into a seat in front of him.

"I hope you don't mind, but I went ahead and direct-deposited the last payment into your account. I thought it'd be easier than a paper check. It should clear this afternoon."

"Oh," I said slowly. I'd thought I was here to pick up that check. What did he want to have this meeting for if not to hand over my money?

"You're probably wondering why I called you here today."

"I was actually."

Jordan leaned forward, opening his hands palm up in welcome. "I want to offer you a job."

I blinked. "Come again?"

"Our previous commercial agent left for a spot in Dallas with her wife, who just got into medical residency. We have a spot that I'm supposed to put on the market this afternoon. According to Morgan, I was supposed to do it two weeks ago, and she asked why I was dragging my feet."

"Why...are you dragging your feet?" I asked, as if I couldn't quite comprehend the words coming out of his mouth.

"Because I want you to take the position," he said simply. "You did excellent work in Midland. Malcolm King is a hard man to impress, and he said he liked you. In fact, he said, in the future, I should send you down for their needs, which leaves me in a position where I need you."

I opened my mouth and closed it. Was he for real?

Jordan paused, judging my reaction. "It's a competitive salary, but I'm open for negotiations if you want more."

He pushed a sheet of paper toward me. When I saw the figure printed on the paper, I thought I might pass out. I hadn't seen money like this...ever.

My eyes flicked up to his. "You can go higher than this?"

He grinned. "If you want the job, I bet I can get another ten grand out of Morgan."

I just barely managed to keep my jaw from dropping. "Wow."

"So...do you want it?"

"Jordan, yes," I said, my hand shaking as I set the paper back on the desk. "This is incredible! Thank you so much for thinking of me."

K.A. LINDE

"Oh good! You had me worried for a minute when you went silent."

I laughed. "You're never worried."

"You forget I'm married to Annie. That woman keeps me on my toes."

"At least someone does."

"Fair." He stood and held his hand out. "Welcome to the team."

I shook his hand. "Happy to be here."

Jordan filled me in on all the details while I listened in utter shock. I had a mountain of paperwork to fill out, and I'd start as soon as it was all filed. He even offered to show me my office, which had been vacated by the previous owner two weeks earlier.

I walked around the space like I was in a dream. It wasn't the corner office that Whitt or Jordan had. In fact, it was an interior space. So, there wasn't even a window. But there was a door and a desk, and all of it belonged to me.

Before I knew what I was doing, I was back up the stairs and striding, uninvited, into Whitt's office. "Did you know?"

"Know what?" he asked with a smirk that said he damn well had.

"And you kept it from me!"

He laughed. "Did you accept the offer?"

"Of course I did! With an increase in the salary!"

"Congratulations!" He rose to his feet and swung me into his arms. "I'm so proud of you."

"Did you do this?"

"No, you did. You earned it."

"I can't believe it," I whispered. "Maybe I should have negotiated more."

He just chuckled. "I'm sure Jordan was fair. He usually is in my estimation."

"He was."

I shook my head. Just this morning, I'd been hanging on by a thread, and now, I had a nearly six-figure salary in my future.

"We'll have to celebrate at the silent auction on Friday," Whitt said. "Let me get you a new pair of fancy shoes."

"You don't have to do that."

"Who said I had to do anything?" He pressed a kiss to my forehead. "I want to."

A knock on the door broke us apart, and Colton Wright strode inside with a coffee in hand.

"I went to Monomyth," he said before glancing between us with a sly smile. "Did I interrupt?"

Whitt snatched the coffee out of his hand. "You did not. We were just discussing your dad's silent auction on Friday. Are you going?"

"That's for old people," he said with complete seriousness.

Whitt and I exchanged a look. *Youths.*

"And anyway," Colton said, taking a sip of his own coffee, "Dad's flying me home on Sunday so I can start school on Monday. I'll be out of here for good." He added under his breath, "Thank fuck."

"Well, the soccer team will miss you," I told him.

He grinned. "Yeah, fair. You didn't suck."

"I guess I'll take that as a compliment."

"He's fifteen and completely self-absorbed," Whitt said, pushing Colton in the back of the head. "He doesn't do compliments. Now, go and get to work."

"Roger that, boss."

"You're going to miss him when he's gone next week," I observed.

"Yeah," he said with a sigh. "Guess we'll just have to go to New York and harass him."

I laughed and kissed him again. "Sounds like a plan."

"Unfortunately, I have to get back to work as well. Come by my house later?"

"Yes, sir," I chirped.

He smoldered at the word. "See you soon."

"Not soon enough."

And then I skipped out of the office, a bounce in my step that hadn't been there in so very long.

26

EVE

I stared down at the black box on my bed.

"Girl," Blaire said, crashing down onto the bed beside the box.

"Even I know that's fancy," Piper said.

"My brother doesn't play." Harley looked down at her black-and-gold manicure and then back at the box. "Are you going to open it?"

My fingers traced the red Louboutin logo. The heels that Arnold had purchased for me had been my go-to for the last year. They were starting to show wear, and if I was honest, wearing them made me feel a little gross now that I was in a happy relationship. Maybe it was time to retire my fancy shoes that had been given to me by my abusive, asshole, married ex.

I lifted the lid from the box, and inside were a pair of matte-black heels with the traditional red-lacquered bottoms. I pulled one out to a chorus of oohs and aahs. My old shoes had nothing on these.

When I slipped it onto my foot, I felt just like Cinderella.

"Damn," Harley said. "I need a pair. Think Whitt will buy me some?"

The girls laughed, and Harley grinned. She might be younger than the rest of us, but she liked being part of the group as much as I did. I was glad that I'd invited her to get ready for the auction with us. Even though she'd said that she had homework to work on instead. She'd still donned a Wednesday Addams-esk black chiffon dress and shown up with thick makeup for the occasion, ready to dance the night away.

"Man has good taste," Blaire said.

"Hollin would never," Piper said with a snort. "I'm trying to imagine the hulking, tatted cowboy ordering designer heels."

Blaire cackled. "Never. And Campbell would absolutely get me some, but he'd probably hand it off to his publicist."

"Sounds right," Piper agreed.

Harley shrugged. "I'm going to be the girl who buys her own damn shoes."

"Fair," Piper and Blaire said in unison. There was appreciation in their eyes.

Harley was a force, and I looked forward to seeing her take over the world.

"Okay, okay. Finish getting ready so we can go!" Piper said, dragging Blaire toward the door. "The boys should be here soon."

I pulled on the splurge black dress that I'd gotten for the occasion. It had tiny spaghetti straps and a scooped neckline with a soft shimmer to the shiny material. The dress just hit the floor in my new heels. I'd styled my hair in long waves down to the middle of my back and donned my signature red lipstick.

The look on Whitt's face when I opened the door was worth all the effort.

"Do you like?" I did a twirl.

"Like?" he asked, mesmerized. "Love. You look incredible."

"Thank you. And the shoes." I stuck one tanned leg out toward him. "They fit perfectly."

He slid his hands around my waist and pulled me in close. "I'm going to fuck you in them later."

I squirmed against him. "You'd better."

"Guaranteed." He pressed a kiss to my shoulder and then tugged me out the door.

I groaned, wanting nothing more than to take him up on that offer before *and* after the event tonight. Whitt laughed at my protest and helped me into the car, smacking my ass before I took my seat.

Jensen had rented out a ballroom at a downtown hotel, conveniently located only a block from Wright Construction. Whitt pulled his Lexus into valet, and I was assisted out of the car. Whitt held out his arm and escorted me inside.

"I have another surprise." Whitt removed something out of his pocket and held up the key card.

"You got us a room?" I asked with a laugh. "I live five minutes from here."

"But neither of us has to drive home if we drink."

"Safety first."

He squeezed my hip and winked at me. "Something like that."

Whitt handed off our tickets to the man at the door, and we stepped inside. The ballroom had a sky-high ceiling with a second-story balcony that wrapped around the room. Chandeliers dotted the room, emitting a soft glow upon the festivities. A dozen round tables were decorated with fresh flowers for the dinner portion of the event. And along the back wall was a row of auction items to bid on.

"I heard that Morgan is offering a trip on the private jet," Whitt told me as we found our seats.

"Jesus, how much is that going to go for?"

"Who knows? A small fortune."

I still couldn't believe that people could afford anything like that. Let alone that the Wrights had a private jet on standby for them. That Jensen would be using it on Sunday to take Colton back to New York City.

"What else do you think they have?"

"I know that Jordan said they were going to do a limited vintage wine, named after the recipient, from the vineyard."

"That's cool."

"We can go look if you want."

"Drinks first," I insisted.

I wasn't buying anything. I'd need a drink and some food to mingle with people who could.

We ran into Jordan, Julian, Annie, and Jennifer at the bar. We grabbed drinks and stepped away from the congestion of free booze.

"Did you ever hear from Dad?" Jordan asked.

Whitt shrugged. "I told him we weren't interested, but he said he was going to come up anyway, just in case."

Annie wrinkled her nose. "Typical."

Jennifer put her hand on Julian's arm. "Your dad is coming into town? You didn't tell me."

"I only knew he wanted to," Julian said. "Maybe we should all plan a trip out of town." He gestured to the first auction item. "We could all get away to Vegas for the weekend if we win this item."

"A stay at the Bellagio for two nights," Annie said with a glint in her eye. "I do like to gamble."

"You're *terrible* at gambling," Jordan said with a laugh.

"You're not supposed to be good at it!" Annie insisted as she scribbled Jordan's name on the paper.

He sighed heavily. "You're paying for that."

"No, I'm not," she said as she walked to the next item.

"Get married, they said. It'll be great, they said," Jordan said under his breath.

Annie looked back at him, and he simped for her. The softie. He'd definitely pay for that Vegas trip if he won.

"What are you wanting to win?" Julian asked Whitt as Jordan and Annie walked off to say hi to her best friend and the youngest Wright cousin, Sutton, and her husband, David.

"Whatever Eve wants."

They all turned to look at me.

"Oh, I don't need anything."

"What about this?" Jennifer asked. "You like the gym, right?"

I looked down at what she'd suggested and found a year membership to the nicest gym in town, plus personal training. My eyes rounded. That would be insane. I'd hit all my personal bests if I had a year of personal training. I'd used all of my personal training special that I'd gotten when I first signed up at my gym, and there was only so much YouTube videos could train a person on.

"This looks amazing," I said in awe.

The starting bid was already over a thousand dollars though. Even if I had that handy, I wouldn't be spending it on something I could normally pay monthly. That was a pipe dream.

Whitt scooted me out of the way and wrote his name on the paper.

"What are you doing?" I demanded.

"I could use a personal trainer."

He smirked at me, as if asking me to call him a liar. Well, I wouldn't back down.

"That'd better not be for me."

Jennifer put her hand on mine with a shake of her head. "That's a lost cause. You'll learn. These Wright boys don't listen."

I wanted to argue anyway. I definitely intended to scribble his name out, but then Whitt took my hand and pulled me along.

"You're a menace," I grumbled.

"What? It goes to a good cause. I was intending to buy something either way. Why can't it be for you?"

"You already bought me these shoes," I said, pointing at my feet.

"And then?" He laughed at my irritated expression and continued walking.

There were some other extravagant auction items, like season tickets to the Broadway series at The Buddy Holly Performing Arts Center with a meet and greet with the cast of *Lion King* after the show, Louis Vuitton luggage, and a helicopter ride around the Grand Canyon. It was interspersed with some more normal auction items—a spa package, seats at a Texas Tech home football game, and gift certificates for local restaurants.

We were nearly to the end when I saw a business logo on the top of a page that I hadn't been expecting—Sinclair Realty. My stomach felt stuck in my throat as I saw that Arnold Sinclair had donated a weekend at his ski chalet at the bougie resort, Holliday Ski, in New Mexico, plus mountain passes and ski rental. The chalet that I had absolutely spent a weekend in last year before shit hit the fan with Arnold.

Fuck.

Did that mean he was here? Surely, he wouldn't offer something this extra and not be here to let everyone know he'd done it.

"We should go," I said without thinking.

"Go?" Whitt asked in confusion.

And then I saw it.

Not Arnold.

Charlotte.

And she'd seen me a mile off. Now, our eyes met in the six feet that separated us.

I'd never met the woman. Arnold's wife. She was gorgeous. A petite woman with straight blonde hair and blue eyes. She was thin and toned, like the Pure Barre moms I saw come into the gym sometimes. She had some wrinkles. Enough to say that she'd lived a good life, smiled a lot. She should have been treasured, a woman like that.

When we'd met, I'd had no idea he was still married. He insisted that they were separated and the divorce was in the works. To be honest, I didn't ask too many questions. That was stupid of me. I wasn't entirely innocent in all of it, but I'd ended it as soon as I'd discovered that he was a fucking liar. I never told his wife.

But someone had.

Because her eyes were red-rimmed and sad. Like she might burst into tears at any moment.

I wondered what she thought of me.

I knew what she thought of me.

I wished that I could tell her I wasn't who she thought I

was. That I regretted dismantling her life. That I thought she deserved better.

But I didn't get to say any of that before Arnold stepped into my line of sight, breaking my eye contact with Charlotte Sinclair.

"What are you *doing* here?" Arnold hissed. He reached out and grasped my wrist—hard. "You need to *go*. You don't belong in a place like this."

I tried to jerk my arm out of his grasp. "Let me go."

"I'll let you go once you go back to where you belong."

Whitt was still at my side. "Ah, Arnold Sinclair. I've heard a lot about you." He stepped forward menacingly. "I would recommend you release my girlfriend."

Arnold dragged his eyes away from me and took in who Whitt was. He quickly dropped my wrist. "Girlfriend," he said, as if the word was anathema to my existence.

"Indeed," Whitt said.

But Arnold was already looking away from him, back to me. Assessing me. Judging me. The way I'd seen him judge a million other people when we had our illicit affair. I knew what he was thinking before he said it. Knew what he saw with me in a slinky cocktail dress and designer shoes, on the arm of a Wright. But there was no way to prevent it. Not now.

"So, you're with a Wright now? From a Sinclair to a Wright. Classic Eve."

"Shut up," I snarled.

Then, he laughed in my face. "The same gold-digging slut you always were."

I saw black at the words. Even though it wasn't the first time I'd heard them. Even though they were the furthest from the truth. If I was such a gold digger, then why was I so goddamn poor? Fuck.

For a second, I thought Whitt was going to clock him. His blue eyes hardened in fury. He pushed forward into Arnold's orbit. The rest of the party seemed to turn as one to take in the action.

"I would suggest you take back your words and apologize to the lady or else we are going to have a problem," Whitt said.

"Lady," Arnold said on a laugh.

"I don't think you understand where you are, Mr. Sinclair," Whitt said in a voice I'd never heard from him before. It was lethal, unyielding, and more than a little terrifying. "Perhaps I should have introduced myself. I'm Whitton Wright. You're currently at an event for Jensen Wright to become the mayor of Lubbock. All of his friends and family are here. That includes Eve. Your family has a shoddy history at best with our family. Does Sinclair Realty want to get on the wrong side of Wright Construction? Do you want to be on the wrong side of the Wrights?"

Arnold straightened his suit. "Are you threatening me?"

"Of course not," Whitt said. "Just reminding you of reality because the minute you denigrated my girlfriend, you crossed a line that I sincerely doubt you want to see come to fruition."

"How dare you!"

I pushed past Whitt, my blood pressure spiking at all of it. "He means, get the fuck out of here," I snapped. "And don't show your lying, cheating face again."

"Security," Whitt called. He snapped his fingers, and two men appeared as if they'd done this a million times. As if Whitt had personally thrown people out of an establishment.

"You can't do this."

"But I can," Jensen said smoothly. "He gave you a chance, Arnold."

"Jensen, you don't even know what happened!"

"I trust Whitt implicitly," Jensen said.

"You're going to lose my campaign donation!"

Jensen smiled, ever the politician. "I think I can do without it."

Then, the security guards intervened and escorted Arnold out of the room.

27

WHITTON

E ve was shaking.

"Hey," I whispered, shielding her from the prying eyes and ears of the crowd. "Let's get you some fresh air."

"I'm fine," she lied.

"Eve, come on. It's me."

She looked up at me with her otherworldly green eyes. She thought that she could hide her pain from me. But I'd spent the last couple of months learning every single expression on her face. I'd memorized her joy and fear and pain. Mapped out the way her lips twitched when I did something she hadn't expected. The wrinkle of her nose at my taste in music. And the haunting look that came into her eye when discussing her sister. I could see it all right now.

"I'm fine," she repeated.

"Well, I'm not."

Her eyes widened. "You're not?"

I shook my head. "I can't stay in here another second, knowing he hurt you."

She softened. She couldn't let her guard down after

what happened, but she could do it for me. "Okay," she whispered.

I wrapped an arm around her waist, and we exited the ballroom. The noise dissipated as we stepped out into the cool evening air. I drew her into the alcove that led to the outdoor pool area, which was currently empty. She sighed and sank onto a cushioned pool chair.

"He made a fool of me," she said into her hands.

"He made a fool of himself and no one else."

She laughed disdainfully. "He called me a gold-digging slut in front of everyone."

"Something that no one else believes."

She shrugged. "You don't know that."

"The people who matter don't think that. We know you."

"And everyone else?"

"Since when do you care what everyone else thinks?"

She looked away from me. The reflection of the pool highlighting her features. "I don't."

The words were warbled, as if she didn't quite believe them herself.

I took the seat across from her. "Hey, look at me."

"Is that how you see me?" she asked, jutting out her leg toward me. "I got the shoes, right?"

Anger pulsed through me. This wasn't Eve. This wasn't the strong woman I'd spent the last months with. This was the shell of a person Arnold Sinclair had left behind after he obliterated her life.

"You know what I see when I look at Arnold?" I asked, changing the subject from her spiral.

Her gaze finally slid to mine. "What?"

"My dad."

"What do you mean?"

"Arnold Sinclair, having his cake and eating it, too, and then being pissed off when he gets his ass handed to him for it. I didn't think I could hate my dad any more for what he had done to my family, but I never considered what exactly it must have been like for my mom."

Eve shuddered. "Oh."

"He treated you like you were precious, and then the second you had thoughts and opinions of your own, the second it affected his life, he thought he could treat you like scum. That you would just let him."

"I didn't."

"I know. It was beautiful to watch. I wish my mom had half of your audacity."

She ran a hand back through her long hair. "It's hard to walk away. It was hard for me, and I didn't expect to get married and have kids. Your mom was probably just doing the best that she could. She loved him. She loved her kids. Don't blame her."

"That's just it. I blame him. I've always blamed him. None of this is her fault. None of this is your fault."

Eve straightened. As if they clicked in her brain. She came to her feet and paced toward the pool and back. Her hands were clenched into fists and her back ramrod straight.

"Guys like him, they always come out on top. Why does the world benefit them?"

"The world was built for them. Unfortunately, it's working as planned."

She gnashed her teeth together. "I'm so tired of all this hypocritical bullshit. Women are constantly ridiculed for our bodies and sex lives and clothing. If we have sex, then we're a slut, but if men have sex, then they're kings. Women shouldn't show too much skin or else we're sluts. If we don't show any skin, then we're prudes. And no matter what, our actions are used against us to prove that we were just asking for it.

"We can't go out alone. We can't drink. We can't party. We can't just live our lives without it being used against us. Women have to work twice as hard for half the pay. We have children, run a household, work, and still measure up short. We can't have hobbies or else we're basic. We can't like 'male' hobbies without an interrogation. *Oh, I'm sorry, Chad, I don't want to name the entire offensive line of the Dallas Cowboys. Can you name a single Taylor Swift song that isn't played on the radio?*"

She huffed angrily, dropping her hands to her sides. "I want to be free from all of this. I want to be able to go out for a nice evening with my boyfriend without having to endure toxic male behavior. Is that too much to ask?"

"No," I said softly.

"No," she agreed.

She turned back to me. The fire was back in her eyes. "He doesn't get to ruin my evening."

"It's okay to be upset."

"I'm upset that he upset me," she said. "He doesn't get to have that power over me. Not ever again. He's the one who fucked up. Not me."

"I meant what I said to him about making an enemy of the Wrights. So, hopefully, he's suffering after tonight."

"Guys like him never do." She shook her head. "You know what? I don't want the night to end like this. When we were in Midland, you didn't let my dad ruin my day. I'm not letting Arnold ruin it either."

There she was.

I smiled. "Do you want to go back inside?"

"No."

"No?"

"I can't go back into that room. Not yet. Not when I'm like this."

"Okay. We can stay out here."

She slid her body against mine. "I want you to fuck me in these heels."

My body heated at those words. Oh, how I wanted to do that, but I didn't want to disregard her feelings either. I couldn't just throw her over my shoulder and forget everything else.

"Are you sure?"

"You have a hotel room," she said, reaching into my pocket and producing the key. "Take me upstairs and make me forget."

I snatched the key card out of her hand. "I have a better idea."

Her eyes widened in confusion, but I took her hand and snuck out through the pool garden gate. The benefit of this hotel was that it was next door to Wright Construction. When we had visitors at headquarters, we put them up at the place so that they could walk right over. Like we were currently.

"What are we doing?" she asked as we came up to the side entrance.

Only a few people had access to the building late at night. I'd been given a key with my promotion and used it to let us inside.

"Whitt," she breathed as we traversed the dark corridors, illuminated by soft red light.

I put my finger to my lips even though it was unnecessary.

No one was here.

Empty building. Empty floor. Empty office.

I dragged her into the latter, and she made a noise of delight at the view of the Tech campus, all lit up from my windows.

"And what are we doing all the way up here?"

My hands came down to her hips, wrapping around her waist and drawing her against me. I pressed a kiss onto her shoulder. "I've been dreaming about fucking you on my desk for far too long."

She shivered at the words. "How long?"

"March."

She coughed out a laugh, turning in my arms. "You didn't even have this desk in March."

"A guy has to have goals." I walked her backward until her ass hit the edge of my desk. "And I envisioned you right here."

Eve leaned her elbows back on the desk with a mischievous glint in her eye. "How do you want me?"

"Every way."

"Tell me," she breathed.

"Bent over the desk, ass in the air, my hand in your hair, cock in your cunt."

I trailed a finger down the front of her dress, cupping her pussy through the material.

Her pupils dilated. "Yes."

"Against the glass, bare ass for the world to see."

"Please," she panted as I shifted her dress out of the way and slid my hand into her panties.

"Flat on your back, legs spread wide, my hand on your throat."

I pushed her the rest of the way down, my hand closing gently around her throat. I waited there. Not moving, except my thumb stroking her clit. I wanted to let go, to give her all of me exactly as I was. But I needed to make sure she was okay with it first. How wet she was told me everything I needed to know about the effect my words had on her body, but I needed to hear it from her mouth.

Eve shivered under my touch.

"If you want it," I said.

"I want it," she said, her voice heady and rough. "I want it all."

"And this?" I asked as my grip tightened on her throat.

Her hand came over mine, and she squeezed. "Put your back into it."

I grinned. "That's my girl."

I removed my hand from her panties to take my cock out from my suit pants. I stroked it up and down with her eyes on me, her legs spread, as I'd always envisioned. I pushed her panties aside, aligned our bodies, and crashed into her waiting pussy.

Her body rocked up the desk at my entry, but my hand held her pinned to the surface. And then I was fucking her. No graceful, gentle coddling. Nothing like what we'd experienced together under the trees after horseback riding in Midland. This was primal passion, delivered with brutal force and heady control.

Our bodies slapping together into the quiet, empty building was an orchestral crescendo to her orgasm. Her beautiful pants and whimpers and needy gasps—I loved every single one of them.

I had to force myself not to let go as she rode her high down on my cock. Her hand unknowingly clawing my hand that was still pinning her to the desk. Her eyes rolled into the back of her head. Her body writhing under me.

I wanted to finish off inside of her, but I needed another orgasm from her, and I was determined to get it.

She was still mewling like a kitten as I pulled out,

grasped her hips, and flipped her over. I dragged her backward until her ass was level with my cock and plunged back inside of her.

"Oh," she cried out. Her hand reached backward for me as I sank in to the hilt. "Please."

"Grip the top of the desk."

Her eyes flicked back to mine, but she slowly grasped the desk. One of my hands tangled in the dark oil-stained threads of her hair, tugging her chin upward and her head back. A grunt of approval came from her lips, and I lost it.

The beast uncoiled in my chest and released. I pumped into her, hitting her as deep as I could on each stroke. Her back arched, her ass high in the air, giving me the best view of my life—my cock sinking in and out of her sweet cunt.

"Fuck," I growled as I felt her second orgasm hit long and hard.

I couldn't hold on to my own for the life of me. Not like this, with her under my control and at my complete mercy. I slammed into her one more time and came hard and fast. Only when I was empty did I pull back and watch my cum slide out of her.

I didn't know what came over me, but I slicked my finger through our mingled wetness and stroked it upward until it was poised over the pucker of her ass. She gasped but didn't stop me. I pushed my wet finger down knuckle by knucle and watched as her body trembled.

"Fuck, baby," I ground out. "Look at how perfect you are."

"You...you're going to make me come again."

She pressed her ass back toward me, pushing my finger deeper into her. I added a second finger on her next push.

"My filthy girl."

"Yours," she agreed.

I withdrew my fingers to a whimpered protest and replaced it with my still-wet cock. Not inside, just stroking up and down between her ass cheeks. All those juices creating a slippery surface for me to press sweet friction against her hole.

"Whitt," she gasped.

"Tell me what you want."

"You."

I pressed the tip of my cock against her ass, and she moaned as I breached the tight ring. I nearly saw red at the feel of her. I wasn't going to last long a second time with her begging for it. And, oh, how I wanted her to beg.

I pulled back and then went a little bit farther in, stretching her. "This?"

She responded by pushing backward against me.

"You're going to need to relax. I don't want to hurt you."

Her chest rose and fell a few times on the desk before she settled entirely, and I heard her whisper, "Do it."

At her command, I could do nothing else. I pushed forward, slipping into the tight, muscled entrance and claiming it as my own as well. She cried out, tensing as I settled nearly all the way in. Then, a second later, she relaxed, shoving her ass harder against me, and I bottomed out.

"Oh fuck," I groaned. My hands tightened on her hips. "You feel fucking amazing, baby."

"Can't...can't..." she muttered incoherently. She was a delirious mess on the desk. Her hair wild and her chest heaving.

I reached under our bodies and found her clit. Then, I stroked it to the tempo as I worked her ass. She squirmed to try to get away from the sensations assaulting her body. But I leaned my body down upon hers, pinning her to the desk.

There was nowhere for her to go as I fucked her body and took what she'd offered. What she'd demanded.

"Fuck, fuck, fuck," she muttered, and I felt her body shiver and contract as an orgasm hit her for a third time.

I continued strumming her clit as she rode it out. I felt every throb against my cock, and then just as she finished, I roared my approval, emptying a second time. My entire body constricting to that single solitary moment as the control I'd held for so long shattered.

She was mine.

Mine.

And I didn't want any of it any other way.

PART V

CRESCENT MOONS

QUESTIONS

28

EVE

I woke to the feel of a hard body pressed to my back and an arm holding my hip down. I yawned and rolled over to find Whitt fast asleep on the pillow next to me. After our festivities at the office, we'd skipped out on the rest of the party and come up to his hotel room. We'd enjoyed the jetted tub and had enough sex that I was going to be feeling it for days.

There was nothing I wanted to do less than get out of this bed.

I pressed a kiss to his lips. "Morning."

"Mmm," he murmured in his sleep.

"When is checkout?"

"Eleven," he said, dragging me in closer.

"It's already nine thirty."

"Still an hour and a half." His eyes fluttered open, and he found my lips again. "We can do a lot in that time."

I chuckled. "It's like you read my mind."

I pushed him onto his back, hiked my leg up over his hip, and straddled him. His hands came to my thighs,

K.A. LINDE

digging into the muscle. I rocked back and forth on him and could already feel him stirring from the attention.

"You going to ride me?"

His eyes lingered on my mostly naked body. From my perky breasts to my bare stomach and lower, where my thong covered next to nothing. His fingers dug in harder.

"I get to be in control for once?" I teased.

His eyes flared. "You're on top. You're in charge."

"Yes, sir."

He grinned at the nickname and then flipped me over. My body slammed back into the mattress, his body covering mine. "On second thought," he murmured against the shell of my ear.

"Control freak." I ran my nose along his jaw.

"All my favorite pet names. What are you going to call me next?"

"Dom," I said, running a hand down his chest.

His eyes flickered wide for a second. "What does that make you? My defiant, feisty little thing?"

I grinned. "I accept defiant, feisty little thing, thank you."

We were both startled from our foreplay banter by an obnoxiously loud buzzing sound.

"Alarm?" he asked.

I shook my head. "Shouldn't be. I don't go to the gym this early."

We both waited for it to stop, and just as I relaxed, it started up again. Something settled into the pit of my stomach. There was only one phone number I let through my Do Not Disturb mode.

"Do you need to get that?" Whitt asked.

"Yes," I said regretfully. "I think it's Bailey."

Whitt rolled back onto his side of the bed as I scrambled

248

out of the comforts of the comforter. I dug through my purse and pulled out my phone. As I'd expected, Bailey's name was on the screen.

"Hello? Bails? Everything okay?"

"It's me, Eve."

"Dad." I shuddered.

Whitt's head popped up in alarm at the name. I turned away from him. I didn't want to know what was coming next. I didn't want him to see my reaction to whatever my dad was about to say.

"Why do you have Bailey's phone?"

"Is she with you?"

"Bailey? No, she's not with me. Why would she be with me?"

"Because she's gone and she left her phone behind."

"Gone?" I asked, my distress mounting. "What do you mean gone?"

"I don't know, Evie," he snapped. I could practically feel him pacing on the other side. "She went to the gym yesterday to practice for volleyball and hasn't come home."

My insides froze over.

"Yesterday?" I asked, my voice like ice. "You mean, she's been gone a whole day, and you're just now contacting me?" He didn't say anything right away, and that was when I realized, "You had no idea she was gone last night."

"I had a church function, and we stayed out late. I didn't know she wasn't home until this morning."

Fury tore through me. "I cannot believe you did this. You're supposed to be watching her."

"Don't yell at me, Evie Jo," he ground out.

"Have you contacted anyone else? Anyone from the volleyball team?"

"I'm not an idiot." I would disagree with that statement. "No one has seen her. She never showed up to practice."

I put my hand to my head and breathed in through my nose and out through my mouth. I knew what had happened. I knew it without him even having to say it. We both did. That was why he'd called me.

"I'll be right there."

Then, I hung up and reached for my clothes. Whitt had thrown clothes on while I was talking and was standing in the hotel room with concern on his perfect face. I wanted to explain, but how did I even begin?

"I need you to take me home."

He nodded. "All right. Everything okay? What happened with Bailey?"

"I don't know," I lied.

But he must have seen it on my face because his lips pursed in disapproval. "You can talk to me, Eve."

I turned away from his reproachful eyes. He had no idea what he was asking. No idea at all.

"Is it your dad?" he asked. "Did he do something shitty again?"

"No, it's not my dad."

"Then, what happened? He sounded like the same prick as normal."

I clenched my hands into fists. I hadn't ever wanted to tell him. I'd been keeping everything bottled up for so long, but I could feel it all trying to escape me now.

"It's not my dad. It's never been my dad."

His hand came to my shoulder. "What do you mean?"

I looked up at him then. "He's a jerk, but he's not the problem."

"I don't understand. I met the man. He's assuredly a problem."

"Yes, but...not *the* problem."

"Explain."

I took a deep breath and released it. Then, I met his confused blue eyes and uttered the words I'd been avoiding for the last year. "Bailey is the problem."

He still looked confused. Of course he was. Why wouldn't he be?

He'd met Bailey. My wild, whimsical sister who loved volleyball and joked about dating boys. The one who smiled easily and rolled her eyes about school because it had always been a piece of cake. He'd seen the girl that I'd wanted him to see.

Not the girl that she was.

"A year ago, Gram died," I said, starting the story from the beginning. "Bailey and I were both devastated, but I was on my own. I was here in Lubbock, living my own life. I fell in with Arnold as a coping method. She was stuck with Dad in an old house with a man she hated and nothing but free fall under her feet. And when she fell, they caught her."

"Who?" he asked, his brow furrowed.

"The drugs."

His eyes widened as the pieces fell together.

"She'd always been smart and driven and focused. She'd been an athlete with friends and good grades and a future. But those things didn't provide her an escape from her reality." I sighed. "A little weed was fine. Then, weed with Luke turned into coke with Michael. Until Michael couldn't give her what she wanted and introduced her to Xavier." I felt sick even saying his name. My eyes were haunted as the memories hit me fresh. "I learned all of this after the fact. I didn't know she was falling until she fell. Until she overdosed and had to have her stomach pumped. Until a judge said rehab or jail."

Whitt blinked, and I turned away before he could see the tears in my eyes.

"Dad would have let her go to jail," I continued. "And maybe that was the one thing he was right about, but I couldn't let it happen. I loved her so much, and on some level, I understood the appeal. I, too, was using someone to not have to think about the world around me. To not have to feel the pain of loss and resentment.

"So, Dad and I made a deal. I'd send her to rehab. I'd pay for her stay. And when she was done, she'd come to live with him to finish her senior year instead of him releasing her to the state. That's where the money went. I've been helping take care of her ever since."

Whitt nearly choked on those last words. "Eve, that's terrible."

"Yeah."

"You're wrong, you know? Your dad still is the problem."

I shrugged. "Yeah, he's an asshole. He was supposed to watch her." I blew out heavily. "But I can't place all the blame on him. She chose this, and now, she's missing. And I don't know if she's in the gutter somewhere or..." I couldn't say the words. I couldn't even think it.

"We'll find her," Whitt said.

I froze at those words.

"No," I said slowly. "No, *I'll* find her."

I took a step backward. He didn't understand. There was no *we* in this situation. I was responsible for Bailey, and I was going to have to be the one to go down there and find her.

"I have to do this alone."

"Eve, you don't have to do this alone. I can help." He ran a hand back through his hair and I saw him step into planning mode, where he existed best. "It's been more than twenty-four hours. You need to file a missing persons report and..."

I took another step back in horror. "No. Do you know what they'll do if they find her?"

"Would you rather not find her?"

"I'd rather get down there and exhaust all options before I get the police involved. They're not going to help her. They're going to just make everything worse. *I* can handle this."

"I know you can, but... "

"You don't understand."

"Then, make me understand," he said, stepping toward me.

"I'm all she has. I have to find her." I grabbed my purse and stuffed the phone back into it. "I don't have time to argue with you about this."

"We're not arguing, and I'm happy to drive you."

"I said, no," I snapped before I could stop myself.

I knew he wanted to help. I could see he was just offering because he cared, and yet all of my defenses went up at his words. Whitt needed to be in control. It was a joke between us in our sex life. I enjoyed it in that context, but he didn't get to insert himself into a situation in which he didn't belong.

"Eve."

"No," I repeated. "I don't care if that makes me stubborn or whatever you want to say, but she's my sister. This is my problem. I just need some...space."

He took a sharp breath at the word *space*. I hadn't meant it that way, but it was true, wasn't it? I needed space.

"I have to go to Midland. I have to find Bailey. Every second that we stand here, arguing, is another second I am not on my way to her."

Whitt set his jaw and nodded. "Okay. Then, let's go." He grabbed his car keys and wallet off of the table and wrenched the door open for me. "After you."

I took a deep breath and exited the hotel room. I hated the hardness in his voice, but there was nothing else I could do. I couldn't deal with Whitt's feelings right now.

Once I found Bailey, I'd be able to think clearly again.

Not before then.

29

WHITTON

I watched her drive away with a stone in my stomach. I couldn't shake the feeling that space meant *space*. No matter how she'd meant it.

Space.

She wanted space.

I closed my eyes and dropped my head onto the steering wheel. I'd driven her home. I told her to call me when she found out what had happened with Bailey. And then I'd let her go.

What else was I supposed to do?

She had made it perfectly clear that she didn't want my help. No matter how much I wanted to give it to her. I wouldn't be the kind of guy who forced himself into a situation.

This wasn't about me. It was about Bailey. Her sister had to be her first priority. If it were my sister, I'd do anything I could to make sure she was safe, damn the consequences. And with Bailey's history, I could hardly blame Eve for being worried.

It wasn't like she'd said we were breaking up or anything.

No. Space wasn't break. Wasn't break *up*.

But that didn't mean that I couldn't see what she was doing by using the word with me. I'd memorized Eve's expressions. Yesterday, I'd used them to save her from dealing with the party after Arnold's humiliation. Today, she wouldn't let me save her from anything.

Instead, she'd closed herself off. Gone was the vibrant girl that I'd fallen for over the last couple of months. The one who made me laugh and want to spend every moment with her. In her place was the girl who I'd first met. The one I'd wanted to crack open and see what made her tick. Except, now, she was using that hardened shell to push me away. In fear for her sister perhaps, but it didn't feel good either way.

"She'll call," I muttered as I pulled out of her house.

It was my mantra throughout the day.

She'll call.

As I put my running shoes on and clocked six miles.

She'll call.

As I showered away my run.

She'll call.

As I watched a replay of the final game in the Seattle Kraken season.

She'll call.

As I sat at my desk in my home office and tried to get ahead of work.

She'll call, I thought, even when she hadn't called.

"Fuck," I growled, pushing away from my desk.

She wasn't going to call.

I was trying to feel better about all of this, and no matter what I did to distract myself, I wasn't okay. After the night we'd had, I'd thought we were stronger than ever. I'd thought that she'd want my help with something like this. That I could be here for her. But that wasn't what she wanted.

It wasn't about the phone call.

I was certain that she was busy and freaked out and dealing with all this stress. That was the problem. That she had to deal with it alone. I knew that she *could*, but that didn't mean she had to.

Yet I couldn't barge down there and insist that I could help. That would be a dick move. I just had to sit here and hope that she knew I was waiting for her.

It was bad enough that my phone kept dinging with texts from my dad, telling me he'd be in town tomorrow and asking when we could meet up. As if I didn't have better things to do. I ignored his latest text and dialed my brother's phone number instead.

He answered a few rings later. "Yo."

I shook my head. "Let's go get a drink."

After a pregnant pause, West asked, "What happened?"

"Can I tell you about it over a beer?"

West sighed. "Should I come over or—"

"Sure. Bring some beer with you."

"Okayyy," he said. "I'm going to pick up Harley on the way."

"She can't drink."

West snorted. "She's in college. She absolutely *can* drink."

"Fine. I don't even care."

"Christ, what happened?" West asked, as if my dismissal of Harley's alcohol consumption made it worse.

"I'll tell you when you get here."

Then, I hung up and went in my fridge in search of a beer to get started.

West and Harley appeared a half hour later. They'd gone to the grocery store and picked up beer and some kind of seltzer for Harley. I didn't bother asking. Just took a Stella out of West's hand and popped it open. Harley and West exchanged the look that I was normally my go-to.

"I'm fine," I muttered.

"Were you fired?" West asked.

I nearly choked on my beer. "No."

"Did Eve break up with you?" Harley asked.

I tipped my bottle at her. "Not exactly."

West's eyes widened. "That doesn't make sense. You two were all perfect together."

"What did you do?" Harley demanded. "I like Eve."

"I like Eve, too," I snapped back. Then sighed. "I might love her in fact."

Harley popped a seltzer and sank cross-legged onto the couch. "Wow."

West similarly sat down at that declaration. His lips forming an O.

The word I hadn't been able to say to her last night but had been thinking for weeks. The words that stuck to the roof of my mouth every time I opened them. As if, at any moment, she'd read them in my eyes when I stared down at her in adoration. I hadn't wanted to scare her away. We hadn't been officially together for that long. Not that it mattered. I'd felt it long enough to know it was true. The *might* in my statement was the only lie I'd told.

I absolutely loved Eve Houston.

And watching her drive away without me had driven a stake through my still-beating heart.

I lifted my beer to them. "So, yeah."

"What happened?" West asked.

I explained as much as I could. I didn't want to divulge Eve's secrets, especially since she had spent so much time trying to hide what had happened with Bailey. But I gave my siblings enough details to understand that she was gone.

"But she's coming back," Harley said. She looked to West. "She's coming back, right?"

"I don't know," I said with a shrug.

West crossed his arms. "You know what the problem is?"

"What?"

"You're completely out of control."

I narrowed my eyes. "What does that mean?"

"Come on. Don't bullshit us. We know the real Whitton Wright. You're the five-year-plan guy. You have to be in control of everything and everyone around you. And now, everything that fit into place is all disrupted, and you can't do anything about it."

I clenched my jaw. "And?"

"And you need to stop."

"Stop what?"

"Trying to control the situation." West set his beer down. "Eve hasn't called or texted. She left for home without you. There's *nothing* you can do about it, man."

"But I want to be there for her."

"You're just going to have to deal until *she* wants you there," West said.

Harley nodded, downing more of her drink. "It's not going to be fun, but she'll appreciate that you're waiting for her when she returns."

I sighed heavily, dropped my phone and beer onto the coffee table, and put my head in my hands. "Fuck."

Harley patted my back. "It'll be okay."

West plucked the beer off the table and took a sip. "In the meantime, we can still drink."

"Yeah," I grumbled. "Thanks for coming over."

"Anything for your melodrama," Harley said.

I jerked my head up at her, but she was already laughing.

"Siblings are the best," I muttered sarcastically.

Harley and West laughed at me, but they did the best by me that they could. Harley turned on some rom-com that we both groaned about. West ordered pizza. It tasted like ash in my mouth, but at least it helped me forget, even for a short period, that I still hadn't heard from Eve.

I got up to get another slice of pizza when Harley called from the living room, "Oh, your phone is ringing!"

I rushed back into the room. "Eve?"

Harley shook her head, and I frowned, snatching the phone off the coffee table. Colton's name showed on the screen. What the fuck?

"Colt?"

"Hey, boss," he said, the sounds of a raging party in the background. "I think I messed up."

30

EVE

No one knew where Bailey was.

I'd reached out to every person in her phone who might know where she was. Her volleyball coach said that she'd never shown up for tryouts. The girls on her team claimed that she'd gone off and gotten "weird again." Trevor, the last person she'd contacted in her phone, said he hadn't heard from her, but she owed him two hundred dollars.

Not promising.

I'd driven around every place I could think that she might frequent.

The high school claimed she hadn't been at her last class on Friday. I didn't inform them that the dentist note was definitely forged. The gym she went to said they hadn't seen her in weeks. Ellen at Boose said the last time she'd seen her was when I was in town.

And each and every single place I'd tried, progressively getting more desperate, had the same story.

"She isn't here."

"We haven't seen her."

"Not in weeks."

I sank into the front seat of my 4Runner and slammed my hands on the steering wheel. It was nearing evening, and I'd been in the car all day with no luck. I couldn't call it quits. There had to be somewhere that I hadn't looked. I couldn't get the police involved...not yet.

My phone buzzed, and a text came in from my dad.

Any luck?

I blew out a breath. The best I could say for the man was that he'd gone out of his way to look for Bailey, too. I'd covered one half of town, and he'd driven to the other. He'd grumbled about it since he wanted to get the police involved. I'd vetoed that immediately, but I didn't know how much longer I could hold out. If Bailey was back to her ways —and everything indicated that she was—then we were going to need all the help we could get. The longer she was gone, the harder it would be to find her.

Not yet. You?

Nothing. We're going to have to call it.

I closed my eyes and clenched the phone in my fist. No. I wasn't ready to give up.

This was Dad's fault. She was his responsibility. That had been the entire point of making her stay with him through her senior year. I'd wanted custody, and he'd insisted that we shouldn't uproot her life any more than it had been due to rehab. But he should have been checking his accounts better. The fact that Bailey had been siphoning money without him even realizing or checking to see what was going on was bullshit. And he'd accused me of not giving him enough money when, in fact, Bailey had stolen it.

This was my fault. I should have been paying more attention. Instead, I had been so into my own life that I neglected what was right in front of me. If the money was missing, then there was a reason. I didn't want to believe that the reason was Bailey. But I should have been more diligent. Not wrapped up in my own shit.

And the truth of it all, this was Bailey's fault.

She'd chosen to steal from Dad.

She'd chosen to lie to us.

She'd chosen to disappear.

I loved her, but right now, I had never hated her more.

Let me check a few more places.

Eve, it's a waste of time. We're not going to find her.

I threw my phone to the side, ignoring the string of texts he'd sent. I didn't care what he thought. That negativity was never going to help anything.

I was parked trying to plot my next move when the phone rang. Not mine, Bailey's.

I lunged for it and saw Trevor's name.

"Hello?"

"Hey, this Eve?"

"Yeah. Yes. Have you heard from Bailey?"

"Sorta. She texted me from a new number and invited me to some party."

I blew out a breath of relief and horror, all mingled in one. "What party?"

"Some house party in the country. I didn't know if I should call you. You were pressed earlier."

"Yes. Thank you so much for calling. Can you send me the address?"

"Uh..." He paused, as if searching his messages for the address, then added, "You going to get me my two hundred dollars back?"

"Of course," I said through gritted teeth. "Not a problem. As soon as I find Bailey."

"Bet."

He sent the address in a text to Bailey's phone. I thanked him profusely and then hightailed it out of the parking lot I'd been camped out in.

As Trevor had described, the house was in the *country*. Even for Midland, which was known for its sparse housing and backwoods locales, this was the middle of nowhere. The house was two stories tall, surrounded by oil rigs on all sides. And it was hopping.

I could hear the music from the street. Bright lights were bouncing around inside like a rave. And I had to park in a field nearby because there were so many cars. We were far enough away from civilization that the cops wouldn't bother with it. No neighbors to issue noise complaints.

This was going to suck.

And there was nothing to be done for it.

I tied my hair up into a ponytail, threw both of the phones into my purse, and headed down the street toward the house. I didn't look like a teenager, but I was still young enough not to look like a typical adult. I was glad that I'd changed into something casual for the drive—jean shorts and a tank top with white tennis shoes.

When I stepped into the house, I was assaulted by the smell of beer, weed, and vomit. I refrained from gagging, feeling a contact high imminent. There had to be over a hundred people inside. More than half with red Solo cups in hand, dancing to the music, and the rest in various stages of undress, hooking up. I had no fucking clue how I'd find Bailey in this.

Still, it was my mission. Thanks to Trevor, I actually had something to go off of. It was my only lead.

I gazed around the living room but didn't see any sign of Bailey. All the people I asked said they didn't know her. Great.

Likewise, she wasn't in the dining room or the office space. A bunch of drunk bros tried to cajole me into doing a keg stand in the kitchen. A girl looked like she was drowning under an upside-down margarita.

"Hey, have any of you seen Bailey?" I asked one of the guys by the keg.

"Bailey?" guy number one asked. His eyes were blood-shot, and he was drunk.

"Yes, Bailey Houston. Have you seen her?"

"Haven't seen her," guy number two said.

"Bet she's upstairs with Xavier," guy number three said.

Xavier.

I felt sick to my stomach. Of course she'd gotten involved with that bastard again. She'd refused to rat him out to the cops, and even when I provided evidence that he'd been dealing, somehow, he had gotten out of it. Something to do with his daddy working for the force. I hated him with every fiber of my being.

"Said he was going to rail her on the balcony," guy number four said.

"Oh yeah," guy number one said.

They all high-fived like they weren't disgusting degenerates.

"Thanks," I said before muttering, "I guess," under my breath.

If Bailey was with Xavier again, we were fucked. Xavier dealt to half the town. So much for the tens of thousands of dollars I'd spent on her rehab.

I found the stairs at the front of the house and climbed them. The first few doors I opened were full of random hookups. One even had a full-on orgy. I didn't want to ask questions. I just shut each door and moved on.

"Bailey?" I called into the house.

Literally how many bedrooms could it have?

On the fifth, I found the one that the guys must have been talking about. It was the only one with a balcony. But instead of Xavier *railing* my seventeen-year-old sister, she was huddled in the corner of the balcony. Her head lolled against the balcony door. Cocaine was cut into lines on the glass table in front of her. A rolled dollar bill sat next to it. Pills were in a mess of little bottles. A few had opened and spilled out onto the table. A discarded bong was on the wood floor. No Xavier in sight.

"Bailey!" I gasped, sprinting to her side. I lifted her up and forced her to look at me. "Bailey. Bails, are you okay? Can you hear me?"

She laughed. Her pupils were blasted out, as wide as saucers. "Evie!"

"Bailey, we need to get you out of here."

"No, Evie, stay!" She tugged on my arm. All the strength

from her athletic training evaporated in the wake of the drugs. "Stay! We're having such a good time."

I recoiled from that assessment. She wasn't in her right mind. She needed help.

"Sorry, kiddo, it's time to go home."

"No! I'm not going home. I'm never going home again. I hate him. I hate him. I hate him." She slurred the last word and tugged out of my arms. "I'm going to stay here, where it's quiet."

Quiet. Yes, a rager was so quiet.

I knew she meant in her mind. It was one of the things she'd confessed to me after rehab with all her many hours of therapy. The problem when Gram had died was that her grief was so severe that she couldn't quiet the anxiety in her mind, that loud voice that yelled at her constantly day and night. Medicine helped to an extent. If she had stayed the course, I was sure antidepressants and anxiety pills could have done the trick, but too late. She'd found something that worked a lot faster.

"You don't have to go back with him, but you can't stay here either."

"What the hell are you doing?" Xavier asked from the bedroom. He was in a grungy white tank top and distressed jeans. He'd grown a curly mullet since I'd last seen him, and it did him no favors.

"We're leaving."

"Fuck no, you're not."

"Try to stop us," I snarled.

He tipped his chin at her. "She owes me two thousand dollars."

I nearly screamed. "What the fuck did she take for two thousand dollars?"

He shrugged. "She was going to work it off with me. I don't mind if you want to help."

Then, he winked, and I considered punching him in the face.

This was the first moment that I'd wished Whitt were here. That guy would have never fucking said that to me with him at my side.

"I'm going to pretend you didn't say that," I said, tugging Bailey to her feet.

"Look, baby—"

"I already called the cops," I lied. His eyes narrowed. "I know who your daddy is, but even you can't escape what's all over this house."

"You wouldn't do that while she's here."

"You sure?"

But he wasn't. I could see it on his stoned face.

"Fuck," he ground out. Then, he turned and walked out.

"You called the cops?" Bailey asked, fear suddenly registering.

"Yeah. We have to get out of here."

I didn't give her a chance to respond. I grabbed her wrist and pulled her out of the bedroom, down the stairs, and out of the house. Xavier's fancy sports car zipped away just as I got her to the car. He hadn't even told anyone else that the cops were coming. What an asshole.

I forced Bailey into the car. My anger mounting every second that she fought me along the way. I wanted to kick and scream and rage at her. But I was just so relieved that she wasn't dead. All I could do was buckle her seat belt and drive away.

There would be time for my anger.

Time for her to account for what she'd done.

But right now, she was safe.

31

WHITTON

Harley was the only one sober enough to drive since she'd given up her seltzer hours earlier. She held her hand out. "Keys."

I blinked at her. "You're not driving my car."

"I didn't drive here. West picked me up."

"West, give her the keys."

West grinned as he admired his new red BMW M2. It was the fancy car he'd always wanted when he was broke as shit. "It's a stick shift."

"I can drive a stick shift," Harley said with a wicked grin on her lips.

West snorted. "Oh, we've seen exactly what you do with a stick shift. You almost ruined Mom's transmission."

"Hey! That wasn't my fault."

"Whose fault was it then?" West asked. "No way are you destroying my brand-new car."

I cursed under my breath. The world was conspiring against me. "Why would you buy a stick shift anyway?"

West shrugged and pointed at the shiny sports car. "She handles better."

"Fine." Harley waggled her fingers. "Keys, please."

I closed my hand over the keys, reluctance in every fiber of my being. Then, West's words came back to me. Control. I had to be in control. I'd always known that. But what had it gotten me anyway? Eve was gone, and no amount of control could keep her here.

I was in free fall. Might as well jump.

I slapped the keys into her hand. "Please be careful."

"Oh, I will." She skipped around to the driver's side.

Dismay settled over me as I yanked open the passenger door. Today, I was going to have to break all of my rules.

Harley took turns too fast and drove over the speed limit and played the music too loud. I vetoed her crappy music choices. That was the one thing where I put my foot down. She just laughed at me and sped up. The demon.

Luckily, the drive into Ransom Canyon was only twenty minutes from Lubbock, so I didn't have to endure it for too long. Any lingering buzz I'd had evaporated from fear of her crashing my car the whole way. And fear about what I was going to find once I reached Jensen's lake house.

The best I could say was that the place was still standing when we arrived.

West whistled from the backseat and leaned forward. "When you said he threw a party, I didn't expect this from a fifteen-year-old."

Neither had I.

I'd never really been the rebellious type. I'd left that up to my twin. But even he wouldn't have known where to begin to throw this wild of a house party at the ripe old age of fifteen. Music blasting, teenagers jumping into the lake, people screaming on the lawn, every light on in the place, and I could count at least three kegs on the deck. Not to mention the large outdoor window was smashed to pieces. Great.

"How have they not had the cops called on them already?" Harley asked as she found an open parking spot.

"Off season?" West guessed.

Ransom Canyon was full of people Memorial Day to Labor Day weekends, but only locals were here in the off season. Still, I would think someone would have already called about the noise.

"We'll see," I said as I got out of the car.

I'd put on a suit, and I'd made West put one on despite his protests.

We looked more intimidating as a pair, and I wasn't particularly looking forward to breaking this up. Because if this didn't get shut down by me, it was certainly going to get shut down by the cops.

I took a deep breath and then strode toward the house. Teenagers looked at me with fear on their faces. A few grabbed at each other and darted out of the house. They were the smart ones.

Colton appeared then. Miraculously, he wasn't drunk. He'd been smart enough to call me. But now, he looked worried. I was certain he was second-guessing his decision.

"Hey, boss," he said.

I continued toward the front door.

Colton trailed me. "What are you going to do?"

"What I have to."

I stormed through the living room and stopped the music. Jensen's rather impressive full house stereo system was silent all at once. Everyone looked around in confusion as the bass beat to their party disappeared.

"All right, party's over. Head on home!" I called into the crowd.

A groan came from all assembled.

"Come on, man. We're having a good time," some guy yelled.

"It's either you leave when I ask or you leave when the cops do."

The guy flipped me off, put his arm around a girl, and headed out of the party.

Colton crossed his arms over his chest and sighed. "Fuck."

I looked down at him and just said, "Hmm."

West came to stand at my side. We looked like a set pair. Though he didn't quite look like he fit into my suit. We were the same height, but West never wore clothes like this, and thus they wore him and not the other way around.

"Should we just be letting them leave?" West asked.

"Happens all the time," Harley said. "They'll have a plan to get home."

Colton frowned. "This is bullshit."

That was when Colton's "friends" from earlier that summer appeared. Monk, Chet, and I hadn't gotten the third kid's name.

"Colton, what the fuck?" Monk asked.

"Yeah. Did you call someone to break this up?" Chet asked.

I glared at the pair. "I have a friend who lives over here," I lied. "They let me know what was going on. Colton will get his due. And if you three didn't get enough when Jensen found you stealing tequila from his campaign event, then I can hold you here and contact your parents as well if you'd like."

Colton looked at me, both relieved and terrified. I hadn't

ratted him out to his friends. Calling me had earned him that courtesy, but he could hardly get away with this. He had to know that.

"Fuck that," Monk said.

Chet nodded. "Good luck, Colt, but we're out of here."

I wanted to hold them. To force them to have to deal with the consequences of their actions, but I wasn't actually going to call the cops to get that accomplished.

Already, the kids had mostly cleared out. And however many there had been in attendance, they'd wrecked Jensen's beautiful lake house.

"Well," I said once the last few stragglers were gone and we could look at the worst of the house, "you're fucked."

Not only was the back window shattered, but there was also so much trash. Red cups, beer cans, water bottles, plates of discarded pizza, and used paper towels were scattered everywhere. The floor was tacky with spilled beer. There was vomit in the bushes. Someone had taken all the cushions off of the furniture to use outside around the deck. The furniture was stained, and one of the toilets was overflowing. All that was missing was spray paint. Ironic since that was what Colton had gotten busted the first time.

Colton sank onto the only chair still at the dining room table. "Yeah."

"Bad business, coz," Harley said. She wrinkled her nose as she toed a soggy blob on the floor.

West nodded out back. "I'm going to take stock of the deck. Harley?"

"Yep." She scurried off after West.

I waited until they were gone and then met Colton's fearful gaze.

"Should I bother asking what you were thinking?"

Colton opened his mouth and then closed it. "Look, it

started out fine. Monk and Chet wanted to throw me a going-away party."

"Uh-huh," I said. "You thought anything to do with those two was a good idea?"

"I thought it'd just be a couple of guys. So, I offered the lake house."

"And stole your dad's key?"

He shrugged. "I know the key code to the back door. I didn't have to steal anything."

"Your dad gave you that key code? He told you that you could use it whenever you liked?"

Colton said nothing. Because of course Jensen hadn't.

"Then what?"

"They invited the entire high school. But I didn't know, I swear!" Colton insisted. "They showed up with kegs and shit. I'd only planned to have a few guys over. I mean, we were going to drink, but it wasn't going to be anything like this."

I believed him. He wouldn't have called me if he'd thought he could get away with this kind of party. Monk and Chet had used him. They'd taken an opportunity to have a wild party at Jensen's fancy house, and Colton hadn't seen through them. I didn't know what about those private school losers Colton couldn't get his head around. He had more street smarts than this.

"You know what you have to do, right?"

Colton looked around in dismay. "Clean it all up."

"Well, yes, but you're going to have to tell your dad."

"Wait, I called you so I didn't have to tell him," he said, suddenly frantic.

"You know that's not how this works."

"But you showed up!"

"Of course I did. I wouldn't leave you to deal with this

alone, and I understand not wanting your dad here for it in front of everyone. But look at this place, Colt. Really look at it. How are you going to fix the window without him knowing?"

Colton put his head in his hands. His voice was strained when he said, "He's going to keep me here."

"He might," I acknowledged.

"I can't stay."

"You knew that was a possibility if you did this."

"Yeah, but..."

I waited. He'd known. He'd risked it anyway. I'd help him, but I wouldn't hide this from Jensen. I respected him too much for that.

"Can't *you* just tell him?" Colton asked.

I laughed. "You want *me* to face off with Jensen? Not a chance."

Colton scowled. "Great."

I clapped a hand on his shoulder. "He'll appreciate all of this more if you take responsibility for what you did. You did the right thing in the end. That's what matters."

"He won't think so," he said softly.

West and Harley came back inside then.

"All clear," West said. "Where should we start with cleanup?"

"Leave it," I said. "Colton is going to come back up here to deal with it later. Aren't you?"

"Yeah, boss. I'll take care of it." Colton straightened. He pushed his shoulders back, and I saw a hint of the man he was going to be. "First, I have to talk to my dad."

Jensen answered after I rang the Ring doorbell a few times. He was bleary-eyed as he yanked the door open and looked at me. Then, he became immediately wide awake at Colton's appearance.

"What happened? Are you okay?" Jensen asked.

"I'm fine, Dad," Colton said.

He glanced up at me. "Why are you dropping him off at home?" Then down at Colton. "Why aren't you in your room?"

Colton took a breath and then released it. "Monk and Chet wanted to throw me a going-away party. So, they picked me up, and we went to the lake house."

"What?" Jensen snarled.

"I swear we were just going to hang out. But they invited all of their friends." Colton straightened. "I called Whitt when things got out of hand."

Jensen looked up at me and then to his son. "But you didn't call me."

"I thought you'd freak the fuck out."

"Is there a reason that I shouldn't?"

"Look, I fucked up," Colton said. "I knew it when I called Whitt, and I hoped that he'd get me out of it. But I realize now, that was the second way I fucked up. I shouldn't have thrown that party."

"No, you shouldn't have," Jensen said. "Though I appreciate you admitting to that."

"Yes, sir," Colton said.

"Get inside. We'll discuss what we do from here," Jensen said. He shook his head as Colton scurried past him and into the safety of the house. He clenched his hand into a fist and then released it, sticking his hand out to me. I put mine in his.

"Thank you for going to get him."

"Anytime."

"I don't know how you got him to admit that he was wrong," Jensen said. "We only butt heads day and night."

"He knew he was in the wrong as soon as he called me. Not sure it was anything that I did."

Jensen sighed. "Either way, thank you."

"Are you going to let him go back to New York?" I asked even though it was none of my business.

Jensen's eyes flicked back to the direction Colton had disappeared. "I don't know. What would you do?"

I laughed. "No idea. I was a rule follower in high school."

"Yeah. So was I. How trashed is the lake house?"

"Ah," I said on a wince. "I'd make him clean up as much as he can before you go look at it."

"That bad?"

I nodded.

"All right. Well, thanks, Whitt. I know you didn't have to do any of this."

I waved him off and then headed back to the car. Before the door closed, I turned back. "He's a good kid, you know?"

Jensen nodded. "I know. Somewhere down deep."

I didn't prod any more. Colton would stay, or he would go. He'd earned it either way. I was glad I'd been able to help. Like I wished that I could do with Eve right now.

32

EVE

Bailey was throwing up in the bathroom of our dad's double-wide.

"It's just a hangover!" she insisted as she leaned her cheek against her porcelain throne.

A hangover.

Right.

Like I hadn't seen her incapacitated last night. As if there hadn't been an entire table of illegal drugs in front of her. As if I hadn't dragged her ass out of that party against her wishes. She would have happily stayed with that idiot Xavier.

"You're not fooling me."

Her response was to wretch into the toilet.

I cringed and took another step back. I was glad Dad wasn't here to witness it. He was off at church, pretending like nothing had happened. It was better for everyone that he was out of the picture.

He'd raged last night when I finally brought Bailey home, high as a kite. It was one of the few times that I agreed with him.

Every single thing he said to her about her irresponsibility had been true. Even if it wasn't helpful. But it only made Bailey worse. Oil and water mixing. And watching the exchange made me wonder how I'd ever thought this would work.

When he'd stormed out of the trailer this morning in his Sunday best, neither of us had stopped him. Bailey hated him, and I didn't think much more highly of him.

Bailey finally stopped throwing up and flushed the toilet. She was pale, and her pupils were swallowing her irises. "Ugh, feel awful."

"I bet."

"I wasn't trying to fool you," she said as she stood between what had originally been our two rooms.

"Really?" I asked, raising my brows. "So, you left your phone on accident?"

"Yes."

"And the burner phone I found on you? The one you used to text Trevor?"

She bit her bottom lip. "It's a friend's. I borrowed it since I'd forgotten mine."

"Uh-huh. And Xavier?"

"I didn't know he'd be there!"

I snorted. Likely story. By my estimation, it had been his party. Not that that line of reasoning would get through to her. *Reason* wasn't her strong suit.

"And the drugs I saw you sitting in front of?"

"I wasn't using."

My eyes rolled so far into the back of my head that I saw into the other room. "Right."

"I wasn't."

"So, you'd pass a drug test."

She fidgeted then. For the first time, her demeanor

cracked. We both knew she'd fail with flying colors. The way she had failed her junior year of high school.

"Just let it go, Evie," she said instead of answering.

She pushed past me into her room, but I wasn't done. I followed her.

"I can't *just let it go*. Xavier told me you owe him two thousand dollars."

Bailey whirled on me. "I don't owe him shit."

"He said that you were going to work it off with sex!"

She scoffed, "Like I'm a prostitute."

"I don't know what you'd do for your next fix. I didn't know before, and with a relapse, I certainly don't know now."

"I haven't relapsed!"

"Bailey, just stop! I was there. I saw you high as fuck, sitting on a balcony in front of enough drugs to OD. *Again*. Xavier offered for me to help pay off your debt, too. Do you know that?"

She winced at that. "He did?"

"YES! He did!" I shook my head in frustration. "Do you not see what's happening? Do you not care?" I revealed my wrist tattoo of the two crescent moons, one full and one empty. I grasped her wrist and turned it over, revealing a matching set. "Does this mean nothing to you?"

"I'm not using again." She yanked her wrist out of my grip and looked down at it. "I maybe had a little weed. That's it."

I closed my eyes in frustration. Same old, same old. A string of lines, couched in a tiny molecule of truth. But never the *whole* truth.

The tattoos were supposed to help that. We'd gotten them after Bailey left rehab. They were a dedication to staying clean. We were only ever half unless we were together and whole. A reminder that she'd clearly forgotten.

It was then that I realized she'd never get it. Not alone. Not without me here.

She hated Dad with good reason. I didn't blame her for that. It'd been a mistake to expect him to care about her like I did. He never had. And I couldn't let her continue down this path because I knew if she did, she'd end up dead.

A tear came to my eye, and I brushed it off my cheek. I knew what I had to do.

"I'll move back," I told her.

"What?" she asked, hope blooming in her eyes.

"I'll move back. You can live with me."

"That'd be great!"

At her excited face, I couldn't seem to contain my own despair. I wanted this for Bailey, but at what cost? The cost of everything I'd fought for in the last year. The life that I'd gained while she crumbled.

My new perfect job.

Gone.

My friends at the house.

Gone.

Whitt.

Gone.

And then the tears came, hard and fast.

"Eve, don't cry. It'll be okay."

Bailey was comforting *me*. As if she had any idea what torment was going on in my mind. I couldn't hold it back. Not anymore. My shell had cracked. And from the crack came a torrential downpour.

"I'll have to call Wright Construction. They offered me my dream job, and I can't work it remote." I hiccuped. "I haven't been on the job that long. They can...they can find someone new."

Bailey frowned. "What dream job?"

"Piper and Blaire will have to fill my spot in the house. They probably know someone who needs a room. They take in people like stray cats." I sniffled, scrubbing at my eyes. "It was nice to have friends though."

"Friends," Bailey whispered.

I nodded. "Yeah. I was on their soccer team. We were probably going to win the whole thing this season."

"Eve..."

But I kept going. I couldn't stop. Like a runaway train.

"And Whitt..."

Oh God, I couldn't even say it. I had to say it.

"Well...I'll have to break up with him."

"What?" Bailey gasped. "Why? You could...you could do long-distance."

I laughed. It was a raw, hoarse thing. "You don't know Whitt. You met him once," I said with another hysterical sniffle. "But you don't know him. He's...all control. And I walked away yesterday, saying I needed space to find you. *Space* nearly shattered his poor, precious heart. Moving away?" I shook my head. "He couldn't take it, and he doesn't deserve it. He deserves someone who will be there for him a hundred and ten percent, and how can I do that for him when I have to be here for you?"

And that was it, wasn't it?

I had to be here.

Whitt had to be there.

It couldn't work.

I sank onto the floor of my sister's bedroom, resting my back against the wall. I dropped my head between my knees and cried. Not pretty crying. Just great, heaving sobs. Tears streaming down my face. My pain coming so quick and so fast that I couldn't suck in enough air. In a matter of seconds, I was hyperventilating.

Bailey stood, paralyzed before me, fear in her expression. She'd never seen me like this. When she'd overdosed, I'd cried while she was in the hospital. She'd never witnessed it. I'd only shown her the strong, brave woman that I needed to be to get her clean. Now, I couldn't hold back.

"If it looks too good to be true, it usually is. And Whitt and Wright Construction and this friend group—all of it—was too good to be true. I probably...probably"—I hiccuped—"never deserved it anyway."

Bailey sank onto the floor next to me. Her face was hollow, and tears came to her eyes, too. "You deserve it, Eve. You do."

"It doesn't feel like it," I said, clutching my chest. "Like my life was just getting so good. And now, that's over."

"I don't want it to be over for you."

"Yeah, well, I can't leave you here with him, and I can't bring you with me."

Bailey opened her mouth and closed it. She looked down at the crescent moons on her wrist. Then the matching set on mine. And then she sighed, sniffled, and nodded. "I was high."

"No shit," I said with a tear-filled laugh. "I was there."

"It's just so hard."

"Yeah, well, life is hard."

"I wanted it to be easier," she whispered.

"By doing drugs again?"

She shrugged. "Maybe."

"That's stupid."

"Yeah. I was working so hard to get back to myself. And I

still got that C in my summer class. Then, the volleyball coach said she didn't think I should try out without talking to all the girls about it since I'd screwed up so bad last year. I couldn't bring myself to do it. None of them understood what I'd gone through. The last thing I wanted to do was go before them and grovel." She clenched her hands into fists and then released it. "Then, my anxiety spiraled again. I couldn't handle it. I panicked. And then Trevor had some weed. We were making out, and I just thought a little wouldn't hurt. It wouldn't lead to anything else."

"Until it did," I said.

"Until it did."

"I don't want this for you," I told her. "I want you happy and healthy and living your best life."

"I want that for you, too. I love you, Eve. I just don't know how to be who you want me to be."

That sentence stretched between us.

Who I wanted her to be.

Not who *she* wanted to be. We were still at a point where the drugs were easier than dealing with her problems. She hadn't figured out how to do that, and she needed help to get there. And I was the only one who could give it to her.

I took her hand, linking our fingers together. Our crescent moons slid together to make one moon.

"I got you," I said, another tear rolling down my cheek. "No matter what."

"Don't give up your life for me. I'm not worth it."

"Oh, Bails, you're worth it. We'll figure it out."

Bailey laid her head against my shoulder. "Thanks, sis."

I stroked her hair off of her face. "I love you."

"I love you, too."

33

WHITTON

S till no text from Eve the next morning.

I sent her a message, asking if she'd found Bailey and if everything was all right, but it was left on Delivered. Either she wasn't looking at her phone or she was ignoring me. I was going to go with the former. She was probably too busy.

I was making my morning coffee when there was a knock on my door. For a second, I was certain that it was Eve, and she would walk through the door, and all would be well.

I yanked the door open and froze in place.

"Dad?"

"Hey, Whitt," he said with an unassuming smile.

I stared at him in disbelief. I'd gotten the texts that he was coming into town. He'd messaged, asking to see us all. Despite the fact that I'd already said that no one else wanted to see him, he'd still shown up on my doorstep.

"What are you doing here?"

"Didn't you get my message last night? I decided to stop by to see you." He grinned broadly. "How's Jordan and

Julian?" When I said nothing, he quickly added, "And West and Harley?"

I blinked. This couldn't be happening. I didn't have time or energy for this.

"But what are you doing here?"

He tilted his head in confusion. "What do you mean? I wanted to see you."

"I told you that no one wanted to see you."

"Sure. That doesn't include you though." He clapped me on the shoulder. "We've always had a good relationship."

I took a step back, forcing him to drop his hand. "Have we?"

"Of course."

"Why do you think that is?"

"Because you're the sensible one," he said with a laugh.

My dad had no idea what he was talking about. He thought he was legitimately paying me a compliment. Because I was the pushover that wanted his company so desperately, wanted his attention and affection so bad that I'd do anything to have him in my life. Despite the fact that he'd only ever given me scraps my entire life. He might have put me on the right trajectory, but that didn't make him a good dad.

Eve had been right. I'd given him a million chances, and I was still at the bottom of the barrel.

"I'm starting to think I'm the only one without sense."

He frowned. "What does that mean?"

"Jordan and Julian don't want to see you. Harley is completely no contact. West is only talking to you because I begged him to when Cosmere went big. And he's so *go with the flow* that I don't think he even cares as long as he can continue to play the keys. But me...I wanted this relationship."

"Well, here I am," he said, opening his arms.

"But I don't anymore."

His face fell. "What do you mean?"

"I don't want a relationship with you anymore. You don't care about anything but yourself. You want us all to forgive you for something that is unforgivable. Let alone the fact that you haven't done anything to earn our forgiveness. You just want to feel better about the shitty person that you are."

His jaw dropped open. For a split second, I watched his genial mask slip and the cruel businessman appear. The narcissist that I knew he was. "All I want is to make things right with all of you."

"On your terms," I interrupted.

"I'd do it on your terms, if you gave them to me."

"Our terms are to leave us alone and let us figure it out."

"Those aren't terms," he said, bristling. "That's not having any of you in my life."

"Whose fault is that?"

He pursed his lips. "So, you're just going to punish me forever?"

"No. We're not punishing you. We're setting a boundary. We're saying that what you're doing right now isn't acceptable."

"That's the same thing." He waved his hand. "A boundary is just another punishment."

I forced out a harsh laugh. "Only someone who needs a boundary sees it as punishment."

My dad sputtered at that assessment and launched into a gaslighting critique of my judgment. But at this point, I was too frustrated by my weekend to deal with him. He'd never learn. That was something he'd proven time and time again. He did things for his benefit and his benefit alone. If we fit into his schemes, then he included us, but never what we wanted or needed. I was tired of being a pawn in his endless game. I was ready to take myself off the board.

"Go home," I said, cutting him off. "Make yourself the victim all over again. We're in the wrong. Always. *Always.* Whatever you have to tell yourself. But it's not my problem anymore. Just go home."

Then, I closed the door in his face. He banged his fist on the door twice. I leaned back against it and waited for him to leave. I knew I'd have a bunch of texts and calls, railing against me for asserting myself. I had a pit in my stomach at the thought of it all. And before it could happen, I blocked his number.

A weight lifted from my shoulders the second it was done. Owen Wright was out of my life. He wouldn't get another way back in. He'd try—I knew that much—but it wasn't like he was suddenly going to go to therapy and become self-aware. So, it wasn't my fucking problem.

I waited until he retreated to his rental car and drove away before moving from my position. It was finally over. I never would have gotten there before Eve. I wanted to call her and tell her what had happened so bad. I even pulled my phone out to do it, but at the same time, I didn't want to cross *her* boundary. She needed space. She'd let me know when she was ready to talk.

Instead, I found a text from Colton waiting for me. It was a picture of him sweeping at the lake house. He was flipping the bird at me.

Despite everything, I laughed. What a little shit.

How'd it go?

Yeah, I'd expected that. Jensen had been relieved that I'd gotten him home safe. That didn't mean there weren't consequences to Colton's actions. Consequences he likely deserved after the shit he kept pulling.

Need any help?

dad said no help

I can deal with Jensen.

good luck with that boss

Maybe it was overstepping my bounds, but I felt responsible for Colton after everything he went through. He'd wriggled his way into my life, and I didn't want him to suffer alone. Plus, I couldn't sit around here all day after what happened with my dad and wait to hear from Eve. Some physical labor might help.

So, I changed into jeans and a T-shirt and headed back out to Ransom Canyon for the second time in so many days.

The house looked worse in the light of day. A half-dozen large black trash bags were already full to bursting on the front porch. I hadn't even noticed the outside when we drove up last night, but the lawn was littered with trash— beer cans, plates, toilet paper. Glass glittered from the deck surface. Another window had a hole in it the size of a baseball. Had someone put their fist through it?

I parked my Lexus next to Jensen's pickup out front. I was nearly to the door when Jensen came outside.

"Did he call you?" Jensen asked.

"Text."

"I told him he had to do this alone. Sorry you drove all the way out here."

"Oh yeah, he told me."

"Then, what are you doing here?" Jensen pushed the door closed behind him, shielding his fifteen-year-old son from our conversation.

I shrugged. "You know, I really don't know. Except that I feel responsible for the kid and I want to help."

Jensen looked skeptical. "He should do all the manual labor alone."

"Probably. I could stand by and make fun of him while he works, if you prefer."

Jensen cracked a smile, the first break in his veneer. "I'd pay you to do that."

I snorted. "I'd do it for free, man."

He stepped off of the front porch, as if giving up guarding his youth from getting out of his consequence. We walked back to the cars, and he leaned against his truck, tilting his head back. "Have kids, they said. It'll be fun, they said."

"Could be worse."

Jensen's head popped up. "How?"

My mind went to Bailey. The vivacious youth that Eve thought the world of. The one who had overdosed last year and was missing this year. There were many more worse off than Colton Wright being a rebellious dickhead.

But I didn't say any of that.

"You love him and want what's best for him. So, no matter what he does, he has you to fall back on."

"Yeah," Jensen agreed. "I wish he wouldn't use me quite so literally as a cushion."

"He'll learn. We all did."

"When I was his age, my mom was dead, and my dad

was a raging alcoholic. I was raising my five younger siblings and holding the entire family together by the skin of my teeth. I had Colton too young and took over the company too young." Jensen shook his head. "He has no fucking clue how good he has it."

I nodded and clapped him on the back. "The consequence of trying to give your kid better than you had it."

Jensen chuckled. "I suppose so."

"My dad is a dick, too," I told him. "If it makes you feel any better."

Jensen clenched his jaw. "Well aware that Owen is a singular brand of asshole. I don't know how he raised so many respectable children."

"Breaking the cycle," I told him. "Also...it probably helps that he didn't raise any of us. We can thank our moms for that."

Jensen sighed. "Is that where I went wrong? I left Colton with Vanessa."

"Maybe," I said honestly.

He nodded, accepting his fate. "Well, that won't be the case any longer."

"Keeping him here?"

"At least for the school year."

I nodded. "How'd he take it?"

Jensen's laugh cut like a razor. "Go ask him."

"I'll do that." I clapped him on the shoulder again. "You're doing the best you can."

"Thanks."

I left Jensen to mourn the decision he'd had to make with his son. I was sure it wasn't going to be easy to have a sulky teenager in the house with his two young kids. But I had a feeling it was going to be the best thing that ever happened to Colton. Whether or not either of them knew it yet.

I headed inside to find that the living room and kitchen had been cleaned of trash. It still needed a thorough scrubbing, sweep, and mop, but it was a start.

"Hey," I said, finding Colton on his phone at the open window that led to the back deck.

He stuffed his phone back into his pocket. "Hey, boss. I wasn't on my phone."

"I didn't see anything."

He breathed out. "Bet."

"Heard you're going to be here this year."

Colton's face went dark with rage. "Sure am."

"Look on the bright side."

"What fucking bright side?" he snarled.

"You get to keep playing on the Tacos."

Colton shrugged. "I guess."

"And you can continue to be my intern. I bet we can even pay you."

He huffed and said nothing.

"Well, either way, you have two options. I can either help you put some of this away or make fun of you while I watch you do it."

"Dick," he muttered under his breath. But a ghost of a smile came to his lips.

"Make fun of you it is," I said, pulling myself up onto the kitchen island and gesturing to some food on the floor. "You missed a spot."

Colton shook his head at me. "Come on, boss. Help a bro out."

So, I slid back off of the island and helped him. With the two of us working together, we made much faster headway on the disaster that was the gorgeous lake house. Halfway through the day, Jensen brought us pizza, and a window company came out to look at what needed to be done. We ate pizza on the deck and watched them work.

"Not much left," I said, finishing off a third slice.

Colton had seemingly devoured an entire pizza in a matter of seconds. Lord help Jensen with the bottomless stomach of a teenage boy. "Just upstairs."

"That's all you. I'm not touching whatever is growing in that toilet."

Colton wrinkled his nose. "Yeah. Fuck people."

I laughed. "You threw the party."

He rolled his eyes and returned to work. I stood to follow him but stopped when my phone started ringing.

My eyes nearly bugged out of my skull when I saw Eve's number pop up. "Eve, hey."

"Hey," she said.

"Did you find Bailey? Is she okay?"

"Yes. I found her. She's here with me now."

"Thank God," I breathed. Relief flooded my chest. "I was worried."

"Sorry that I didn't call before. It's been...a wild twenty-four hours."

"It's fine. You said you needed to deal with it. I wanted you to do that."

"Thanks. You said you wanted to help before I left. Do you still want to do that?"

I tilted my head in surprise. "Of course I do."

"Any chance you have access to a truck?"

I thought about Jensen's pickup sitting out front. "Probably."

"Could you bring it to Midland?"

"When?" I asked.

She sighed. "Right now?"

As if I'd deny her anything.

"I'll be there in two hours."

She laughed at our old argument about the drive time. "It only takes an hour and a half to get here."

"Ah, but I'm in Ransom Canyon."

"What are you doing there?"

"It's a long story. I'll tell you when I get there."

"All right." She was silent for a moment before saying, "Thank you, Whitt."

"Anything for you."

34

EVE

"It's not much stuff," Bailey said.

We stood over the boxes that contained the entire contents of Bailey's life. She was right. It really wasn't much. But considering I'd figured out how to move everything in my place in two large suitcases, a few garbage bags of clothes, and a mattress strapped to the top of my 4Runner, this felt almost luxurious.

"It's perfect."

"He's never going to let me take the furniture," she whispered.

"He's not going to have a choice."

She looked so young and vulnerable in that moment. A waif of a girl who had let herself float into corruption and was finally seeing the light. It wasn't going to always be easy, but this was the first time she'd admitted to her own folly.

And a plan had formed.

"If you say so."

I put a trash bag around the bottom of the last of her clothes and tied it off at the top. "We should get this into my 4Runner. Have as much packed before Whitt gets here."

"Any word?"

"He said he'd just made the turnoff."

"I can't believe he's coming."

My stomach twisted. Neither could I. Not after how I'd acted. I had so much to say to him when he got here and no time to say it all. Maybe I could just kiss him and hope that was enough.

I winced. It wouldn't be enough. Not for him.

"It'll be fine," Bailey said to me again.

I'd told her what had happened with Whitt, and she'd insisted that the boy was still smitten with me. That my reaction had been reasonable. Even though it didn't feel like it had.

"He's driving all the way here," she reminded me.

I shrugged. "Maybe he's doing it as, like, a last-ditch favor."

"Now who is the pessimist?"

I grinned at her. After having it out on Bailey's bedroom floor, we'd both come to the conclusion that this wasn't tenable. And when we'd concocted a new plan, I'd called her a pessimist for suggesting it wasn't going to work.

It had to work.

Hopefully, I'd get to keep Whitt at the end of it all.

Ten minutes later, a pickup truck idled in the front of the trailer. Watching Whitt hop out of it did something to my insides that I couldn't explain. The same feeling I'd gotten when I saw him in a hat and boots and on a horse. Honestly the same feeling I got every time I saw his face and he broke into a smile at the sight of me.

He didn't this time.

There was a wariness to him that I hadn't seen in months. I hated that I'd put it there.

"Hey," I said as he approached.

"Hey."

I bit my lip. There was so much that I wanted to say. To thank him for helping us out. For driving out here in a borrowed truck to put Bailey's stuff and drive it back to Lubbock. To not think my plan was ridiculous and go along with it.

But none of that came out of my mouth. I just stared at him in fear that I'd ruined the best thing that had ever happened to me.

"I'm sorry," I finally got out. "I'm really so sorry. I shouldn't have left like that. I was so scared about Bailey and what was coming. I'm not the kind of person that can take help. I had to do it on my own. Everything on my own. And I know that makes me stubborn, but it's how I operate. It wasn't until I met you that I even knew that I could rely on someone else. I understand if you think I screwed us all up." I swallowed, watching his big blue eyes for a reaction. "I understand if this was too much for you, if I'm too much for you." My lips trembled. "But I don't want any space between us. I want this...with you."

"Eve."

"Yeah?"

"Shut up," he said.

Then, his hand was in my hair, and he kissed me.

I fell off the high dive and splashed into depthless water. My head disappearing beneath the waves, my lungs filling with liquid, my ears ringing, my eyes burning, my insides turning to dust. I was drowning. And he was pulling me under.

All of my fear evaporated as I descended with him and

let the tide take us.

My arms came up around his neck, and he tugged me even tighter against his chest. Our bodies remembering the ease with which we moved together. Our lips pressed tight together. Our tongues a delicate dance.

It wasn't until he kissed me so thoroughly that I was certain I'd never come back up for air that he broke away.

"Oh," I whispered.

"You don't have to apologize to me."

"But..."

"You don't have to," he repeated.

"I know, but..."

"I was being a control freak. You needed to deal with this. I'm glad that you called and brought me in when you had the space for it."

"Yeah, but..."

"Eve, don't," he said again, claiming my lips. "I'm here for you. I'm here for Bailey. I don't need an apology when you have nothing to apologize for."

"Okay. I don't apologize, but I wish that I'd handled it better. That I hadn't cut you out."

"It's okay." He laced our fingers together. "I'm here now."

A throat cleared behind us. "If y'all are done making out, can we get back to work?"

I found Bailey standing at the door with her fingers in the loops of her jean shorts. "All right. All right."

"What do you need from me?"

"We need to load up all of her furniture and probably help with some of the heavier boxes." I showed off my bicep. "I'm a beast, and I can squat your body weight, but I wouldn't mind some extra muscle."

"Got it."

Whitt followed Bailey into her room. She was joking

with him like they were long-lost friends. His smile was easy, and hers was bright.

My stomach, however, felt like it had been yanked back on a yo-yo. So much fear rolled into this one meeting, and it had been for nothing. Maybe we'd both needed this time to figure out how important the relationship was to us.

"You coming?" Bailey asked when she saw me holding back.

"Yeah."

I hurried after them to get the truck loaded. With Whitt's help, it went much faster. I worked out in the gym several times a week, and still, I was nowhere as strong as him. It was entirely unfair.

We'd finished with almost all the furniture when another car pulled up beside the trailer.

"Shit," I said, dashing up the stairs and back inside. "Whitt! Bailey! Dad's here."

"Fuck," Bailey snapped. "Why is he back so early?"

Whitt's brow furrowed. "Wait, does he not know?"

Bailey sighed. "I told you we needed to talk to Dad before moving everything."

"I thought it'd be better to beg for forgiveness than ask for permission."

"Great," Whitt said, looking between us in consternation. "What are you going to do?"

Whatever I had to.

"Evie Jo! Bailey Lou!" Dad called as he stepped into the house. "What the fuck is going on? Why is there a truck, loaded with stuff, at our place?"

I took a deep breath and then stepped up to the plate. "Because Bailey is leaving."

"The fuck she is."

"I'm taking her back to Lubbock with me."

His face was turning red. "You can't do that. She's my kid. I choose what happens to her."

"Look at how well that's worked out so far," I snarled at him. "She is back on drugs. Last year, she overdosed under *your* watch."

"She's an addict! I was doing the best I could."

I actually laughed. "Your best isn't good enough. I should have taken her then and there, but I let you trap me. I paid for rehab. I paid for her to come home. I've paid for everything since."

"And you're going to keep paying!"

"No, I'm not," I told him, crossing my arms. "I'm done bankrolling your life. I wasn't in a position to take her before, but I am now. I have a good job. I have a house that I'm renting with some other girls. And I have receipts from the last year that prove I'm the one who's been taking care of her financially."

He scoffed. "You can't just take her away from me. No judge will approve of her going to a sister rather than to her father."

"Why do you even want her here? You clearly don't care about her."

"Hey!" he yelled. "I was out there, looking for her yesterday, just like you were."

Bailey laughed. "For what reason? You never see me. And when you do, it's only to remind me of what a failure I am. You don't care about me or Eve. You never have. Only Gram did."

"I took care of you after your mom skipped town."

"What do you want a medal?" Bailey snapped.

"That's your job," I added hotly. "You're a parent. Taking care of us is the bare minimum!"

"If you take her now, it's kidnapping," he warned.

This time, I couldn't stop from laughing. "Is that so? You'd have to take me to court to prove it."

"Then, I will," he snapped.

He could see the house of cards crumbling. Instead of seeing what was best for Bailey, he was doubling down. Typical.

"You want your church friends to find out about all of this?"

He winced. If I knew anything about him, he wanted to keep it away from his friends. He wanted to appear on the outside as the perfect father, the perfect man, but none of them really knew him. Worse, they were just as grimy as he was. The call was coming from inside the house.

"You'd need a lawyer!" he blustered. Clearly, he had no other response.

Whitt cleared his throat, stepping into view for the first time. "I actually have a lawyer."

My dad's eyes widened in alarm. "What are you doing here?"

"When my girlfriend calls, I come running," he said simply. "If my deadbeat dad taught me anything, it's to have a team of lawyers on standby. I didn't squander that advice at least. Wrights know how to go to bat."

"That's...that's..." he sputtered incoherently.

"You're neglectful, and I can prove it," I said, lifting my chin and refusing to back down. "I have a case, Dad. You know I do."

"You don't have your own house," he argued in his last-ditch effort. "No judge will approve her to live in a room with you. She has to have her own room."

I bit my lip. I hadn't known that. I didn't even know if it was true. I looked to Whitt with wide eyes. Because I did not have a place for her to live on her own. I was just going to move her into my room. I didn't care what else happened as long as I got her away from here.

Whitt met my gaze and frowned. As if he could read the terror on my face at the thought that Dad might be right.

"They can live with me then," Whitt said without missing a beat. "I have two extra bedrooms. One of those belongs to Bailey as long as she needs it."

My dad laughed in his face. "Evie Jo would die before moving in with a boyfriend. She's too independent for that."

Whitt shot me a look. A question in his eyes.

I still couldn't believe he'd even said it. Was he serious? Or was he just saying it to get at my dad?

The shocking thing was that despite my dad being right, I'd never considered moving in with a boyfriend. But I didn't feel that way about Whitt. That felt right. That felt like something I wanted to do.

"You're wrong," I told my dad. "We'll move in with Whitt."

He shook his head. "Wow. I see you've thought of everything." Finally, he sighed and met Bailey's gaze. "Is this really what you want?"

"Yes," she said desperately. "I want to be with Eve. Dad, just...let me go."

He nodded. "It's a bad idea, but if this is what you want and I can't change your mind, then fine. Go move to Lubbock." He met my gaze. "But you do it right, Evie Jo. You get her enrolled in school. You keep her clean. Okay?"

"I will," I told him, my heart threatening to beat out of my chest with shock.

It had worked.

It had really worked.

I almost didn't believe it when Dad stepped back out of the trailer and left us for the last time.

35

WHITTON

"You didn't have to do that," Eve said once her dad was well and truly gone.

I blinked at her in surprise. "Do what?"

"Offer to have us stay with you."

"Even if I didn't have to, I wanted to. I want you to live with me, Eve."

"We haven't been dating that long."

He smirked. "Somehow, there is no prerequisite for how long a couple has to be together before moving in together."

"Yeah, but it doesn't feel early?"

"Only if you don't want to. Otherwise, I will lie through my teeth for you and move Bailey into your room with Piper and Blaire."

Bailey cleared her throat behind us. "Uh, I do not want that if there's another option."

Eve laughed and shoved her. "Go finish packing!"

"Fine. Fine," Bailey said. She slunk off to her room.

"You really want this?" she asked shyly.

"Yes." I took her hands into mine and pressed a kiss to her knuckles. "I want you. I thought that was obvious. I've

303

been the one pushing for this from the start. It's you that I've had to convince. Are you convinced?"

She grinned. "I suppose I am."

I tugged her forward, capturing her lips in another searing kiss. I'd been fucked up, thinking I was going to lose her. And I was never going to take for granted having her in my arms. If I could throw her over my shoulder and take her to the nearest bed, I would, but we didn't have the time...or the privacy.

Instead, I reluctantly released her and helped move the rest of Bailey's stuff into the truck. Her 4Runner was packed to the brim.

Eve patted her car twice. "She'll get the job done."

"Let's hope she doesn't break down with all the extra weight."

She rolled her eyes. "Not going to happen. Where'd you get this truck anyway?"

"It happens to belong to Jensen Wright."

"What?" She laughed. "How the hell do you have Jensen's truck?"

"That is a long story. And has a lot to do with Colton accidentally throwing a rager, being forced to clean up the party alone."

Her eyes widened. "Does that mean he's not going back to New York?"

"Nope. He's staying in Lubbock for the year."

"Wow."

"So, he and Bailey will be at the same high school."

"Who is this?" Bailey asked. "A hot guy?"

"He's fifteen," Eve said.

Bailey sighed. "Fine. Can't help a girl out."

"Let's focus on academics, eh?" Eve said with an eye roll. "And maybe the volleyball team."

"No way will some rando volleyball team that doesn't know me let me try out when school has already started."

I shrugged. "I know someone who works at the school. We'll see what we can do."

Bailey looked hopeful for a second, and it warmed my heart that she could still hope.

Eve dragged me in for another kiss before we split up and made the trek back up to Lubbock. It was much closer to two hours with so much stuff in the vehicles. On the way, I texted my siblings to meet me at the house. I did not want to unload all of this alone. It'd take a fourth of the time to have them all there.

So, I was happy to find West's, Jordan's, and Julian's cars on the street when we pulled up to the house. I hopped out and clapped hands with West as he came out of the house. I was glad that I'd given him a key.

"You're lucky I'm not already in California," West said.

"He's leaving tomorrow," Harley whined. "I did not sign up for him ditching us all fall."

"How's Nora taking it?" I asked.

West grinned. "She decided to come with while she builds her celebrity wedding business."

"I'm glad for you, man."

"And what's happening here?" Jordan said, shaking hands with me.

"Unloading."

"Where do we start?" Julian asked next.

"The furniture is in Jensen's truck. The boxes and clothes are in Eve's SUV."

Eve headed over to the guys with Bailey trailing uncertainly behind them. "Hey, y'all. This is my sister, Bailey."

They all said hi and welcomed her to Lubbock. We'd all

moved here ourselves in the last couple of years. We knew what it was like to be a newcomer.

Harley slid her arm through Bailey's. "Come on. I'll show you which room you want."

I groaned and Harley just cackled. I'd forgotten they were only two years apart. As my sister dragged Bailey away, I hoped that a friendship would bloom. Bailey needed the support, and Harley was as strong as they came.

"So...what happened with Dad?" Jordan asked once they were gone and we moved to unload.

"What do you mean?"

"He's been texting us nonstop," Julian said as he hopped into the bed of the truck.

"Has he?"

"Hasn't he been messaging you?" West asked.

I blinked. The conversation with Dad had completely slipped my mind. This morning felt like a lifetime ago. "I blocked his number."

They all gaped at me, Eve included.

"Since when?" Jordan demanded.

"Since this morning, when he showed up, uninvited, to my house, and I told him I wasn't interested in seeing him again. That he only wanted to be a part of our lives to assuage his own guilt."

Jaws dropped. West's eyes rounded. Jordan and Julian shot each other looks. But Eve clapped.

"That's amazing!"

"It felt good," I admitted.

"And then you blocked his number," Julian said, as if in awe. "Why didn't we think of that?"

Jordan sighed. "It's complicated."

"Well, I decided that it wasn't. He doesn't deserve the relationships he wants from us now. I like the relationship I have here with all of y'all. The one we built rather than the one he demands."

They were all silent for a moment, surprised by my change of heart. The one that Eve and Bailey and Colton had solidified in me over the past couple of months. Family was what you made of it. And I was building a new one here.

"Well, good," West said at last. "Harley will be happy."

"I bet she will," I said with a laugh.

And then we all went back to unloading. Dad was forgotten in the physical exertion. It wasn't until Bailey's stuff was deposited into her room and my siblings left that Eve left Bailey to unpack and drew me into my bedroom.

"So, that's some big news about your dad. How do you feel about it?"

"How do you feel, having Bailey in Lubbock with you?"

"Amazing."

"That's how I feel, too," I told her. "I'm tired of reaching for scraps. I want what I have here with you and Bailey and Colton and my siblings. I don't want the fake relationship he's always offered."

"I'm proud of you."

I guffawed. "Look at how you stood up to your dad. I'm proud of you. You saved your sister."

"I hope she's happy here," she said, worrying her lip.

"It'll take time, but she'll figure it out."

"And you really think we can live here?" She glanced up at me with that same hope in her eyes. Then a mischievous glint. "I can stay in the other guest bedroom."

I snagged her around the waist, lifting her over my shoulder, like I'd imagined earlier. She shrieked as I tossed her back on the bed and growled, "Don't you dare."

She giggled, stretching her arms above her head. "I'll pay rent. I have a fancy new job now."

"If you like," I told her. I didn't care one way or another. My lips came to the sliver of skin that was exposed near her belly button.

"I'm not paying in sex," she teased.

I snorted. "I accept Venmo."

It was her time to laugh. "God, I can't believe this is real. When do I wake up from the fairy tale?"

I slid up her body, covering her with my own and pressing another kiss to her lips. "You're awake. This is real."

Her hand cupped my cheek. "I thought you were too good to be true."

I melted at her words. Affectionate and real. "I love you."

Her eyes rounded, and a small gasp escaped her lips.

"You don't have to say it back, but I've known for ages. I love everything about you. I wanted to tell you, but I was worried that it would drive you away. That you'd realize I was all in and it would scare you. But I don't know how much more all in I can be with you moving in. I love you. I love you so fucking much."

A tear came to her eye, and she smiled, soft and dreamy. "I love you, too, Whitton Wright."

Then, our lips touched, and the world was forgotten.

We'd come this far.

We had forever to go.

But at least we were going together.

Wright together.

EPILOGUE
EVE

Two Months Later

"The tallies are in!" a woman said enthusiastically into the microphone. "Your new mayor of Lubbock is... Jensen Wright!"

Jensen strode onto the stage in a black suit with a blue tie and crisp white button-up. He smiled his perfect politician smile and waved enthusiastically. He was forever a man of the people. Despite being the former CEO of Wright Construction, the new head of Wright Architecture, and a fucking billionaire to boot, he was just a normal guy. And now, the mayor, too.

So many people said that money and his name were buying this position for him. But anyone who had met him knew that he'd do a great job.

"Lubbock! Thank you so much! I stand before you now as your mayor, happy, humbled, and altogether honored to be the next mayor of this great city," Jensen said, beaming.

His wife, Emery, along with their two kids, Robin and

Logan, and of course, Colton stood off to the side, watching with pride on their faces. Even Colton's, to his credit.

"Think he's going to do something stupid?" I asked Whitt, who stood with his arm around my waist.

"Jensen? Nah, he's a professional."

I shot him a look, and he laughed. Then, he turned his phone toward me. On it was a picture of Colton flipping him off from backstage.

I snorted. "Typical."

"I told him to behave."

"Oh, I'm sure he'll listen," I said sarcastically.

"About as well as Bailey."

My eyes found my sister in the crowd in front of us. She was with a group of her volleyball girlfriends, chatting through the whole thing. Her eyes were bright, and her heart was full.

After we'd enrolled her at Lubbock High, Emery—who was a government teacher at the high school—had spoken with the volleyball coach on her behalf. And then Bailey got a tryout...and made it! After that, she'd found a group of girlfriends that I'd wished so desperately to have all through high school. People to rely on and have slumber parties with and do makeovers. She had that and more. I was so proud.

Bailey waved when she saw me watching. I waved back, but she was already turning around. I loved her, but she was still a teenager.

"No, he is definitely worse than Bailey," I told him.

"To be fair, he was raised by a breed of humans who eat their own."

I laughed and covered my mouth when the people in front of us looked back at us. Whitt smothered a smirk and apologized profusely.

Thankfully, Colton was also doing well even if he was a sullen mess about it. He'd remained on the Tacos and taken us to a rec title. Now, he was on the varsity team at the high school. I was terrified that he'd be running the entire place if he stayed more than this year. Only time would tell.

Jensen finished up his speech, and we stepped up to offer our congratulations.

I pushed Whitt toward the line. "I'm going to use the restroom first."

He frowned. "It won't take that long."

I laughed and gestured to the hundred people in front of him. "Yeah, right."

He rolled his eyes and then tugged me in for a kiss. "Get us drinks while you're at it."

"Done."

This whole song and dance was too much for me. I couldn't handle the political theatrics, as I still maintained that no politician was out for anyone but himself. Jensen Wright included.

So, I left my boyfriend to find a restroom. Miraculously, the line was short, and I made it in and out in a matter of minutes. I was heading back to the drink line, which I could already spot was *not* a short line on the other side of the room, when I saw Harley's latest platinum-blonde dye job. I'd recognize it anywhere with the bob and bangs she'd dramatically cut.

I opened my mouth to say hi, only to see Chase Sinclair grasp her by the back of her head and smash their mouths together. My eyes widened in alarm. Chase was...what? Ten years older than her? At least. And she'd assured me that Chase wasn't interested. Even though I could see with my own two eyes that he was *very much* interested.

I was frozen mid-step, uncertain whether to say something in her defense or walk away. I certainly couldn't tell Whitt.

But I didn't have to do anything.

Harley wrenched her head back away from him. I couldn't see her expression, but I didn't need to. The crack of her hand across his face was enough to know exactly what she was thinking.

Chase slowly turned back to look at her. There was fire in his eyes. Intense, demanding desire in every single inch of his demeanor. He was a caged lion who had picked the lock and was barely holding himself back.

"*You* were the one who said to wait," she snarled. "Fuck you."

Then, she pushed out of his embrace and dashed in the other direction. I wanted to run after her. To comfort her. But if it were me, I wouldn't want anyone to know that it had ever happened. I bit my lip and was just about to go after her when Chase decided for us both, jogging out of the hotel ballroom in her direction.

Good luck with that, buddy.

I went in search of drinks. I got us our usual and then found Whitt at the head of the line. He said his congratulations to Jensen, ruffled Colton's unruly hair, and then found me with a smile.

I passed him a bourbon and Coke, and we left the bustle of the election-night win to the rest of the Wrights. We stepped out onto the open-air balcony overlooking the lit-up Texas Tech campus. Whitt leaned against the railing and watched me with intense eyes.

"What?" I asked with a disarming laugh.

"Just can't believe this is my life."

"Compared to what?"

"Seattle," he said evenly with a shrug. "I dated, but

nothing ever went anywhere. I had a job, but no one respected me or cared about my ideas. I had friends, but I haven't spoken to a single one since I moved."

"I know what you mean. My life is completely different from just a year ago...let alone what it was like when I lived in Midland."

"And so much of it is because of you."

I leaned into his chest. "All of it is because of you."

He laughed, a rumble against me. "Your job and friends and Bailey and the soccer team are all because of you, love."

"Fine. Then, you make it all come together."

"I accept this."

He tipped my chin up to look into his eyes, and there was something deep and probing there.

"What?" I whispered breathlessly.

"I want to marry you."

I laughed as shock took root in my body. "You what?"

"I want to marry you," he repeated.

"Like today?" I joked.

He shook his head and took another sip of his bourbon. "No, not today. You're not ready."

"How do you know?"

"Because I know and love you, Eve Houston."

I huffed. My insides were squirming at the words. Oh, how I wanted it to be true. To see a forever future with him. And how scared I was to commit to anything, even when it felt perfect in every way.

"So, what do you say?"

"To marrying you?" I gasped.

"Yes. Someday."

I swallowed and then really thought about it. Wouldn't it be a dream? To have the man of my dreams and not to have to ever worry about the state of us again? Wasn't that what I wanted after all?

"I might say...yes," I offered.

He plucked the words out of thin air and put his hand into his pocket. "I'll tuck that away for later."

I laughed. "So, you're not going to do it?"

"What? Right now? I don't have a ring," he said, offended. As if he'd propose without a diamond.

"Well, I guess we can't do it without a ring then."

He slipped his hand into my hair and pulled me close again. "One day, I'm going to propose to you. You'll never see it coming, love. It'll be so romantic that you'll be weak in the knees and barely able to get words out."

My heart hammered in my chest. I wanted that. Fuck, I wanted it.

"But not tonight," he finished, pulling my lips to his. "Tonight, you're just mine. But one day, you'll be mine forever."

"Forever," I whispered throatily. "I like the sound of that."

"Good. I intend to keep that promise."

Forever was a promise worth keeping. One I planned to hold him to. But right now, I was happy with living in the moment with him. As long as we were doing it together.

The End

Thank you so much for reading WRIGHT TOGETHER! I loved writing Whitt & Eve's very sexy story. I could not keep these two off of each other, and I'm not upset about it

Ready for more Wrights? Try WRIGHT KIND OF TROUBLE featuring Harley Wright & Chase Sinclair in an enemy's little sister age gap!

"He didn't know I was ten years younger.
I didn't know he was a Sinclair.

He didn't care that I was a Wright.
I knew exactly what I wanted.

It's only after our mind-blowing night that it sinks in.

Our families hate each other. No one can know what we did.
Everyone—especially my two older brothers—will run him out of town if they find out.

And still...I want him."

FANTASY ROMANCE

ROYAL HOUSES

House of Dragons

House of Shadows

House of Curses

House of Gods

House of Embers

ASCENSION

The Affiliate

The Bound

The Consort

The Society

The Domina

BLOOD TYPE

Blood Type

Blood Match

Blood Cure

THE OAK AND HOLLY CYCLE

The Wren in the Holly Library

ACKNOWLEDGMENTS

Thank you to everyone who helped me write this book. This was my first book that I wrote after I had my son, and it was an effort in patience to get back to myself. I might have been slower, but dare I say, the words made me even more proud. I managed to write them this pretty even through sleep exhaustion and nursing and all the hard but beautiful baby things.

So thanks to Squish and his incredible dad who was a SAHD through all of this so that I could bring you these words!

The soundtrack to this book was: Taylor Swift's Hits Different and All the Girls You've Loved Before, Vampire by Olivia Rodrigo, Look at Us Now by Maren Morris and Marcus Mumford, and Kelly Clarkson's album chemistry.

ABOUT THE AUTHOR

K.A. Linde is the *USA Today* bestselling author of more than thirty novels. She has a Masters degree in political science from the University of Georgia, was the head campaign worker for the 2012 presidential campaign at the University of North Carolina at Chapel Hill, and served as the head coach of the Duke University dance team.

She loves reading fantasy novels, binge-watching Supernatural, traveling to far off destinations, baking insane desserts, and dancing in her spare time.

She currently lives in Lubbock, Texas, with her husband and two super-adorable puppies.

Visit her online:
www.kalinde.com

Or Facebook, Instagram & Tiktok:
@authorkalinde

For exclusive content, free books,
and giveaways every month.
www.kalinde.com/subscribe

Made in the USA
Las Vegas, NV
21 November 2023

81199286R00184